RALPH COMPTON

THE WOLVES OF SEVEN PINES

A Ralph Compton Western by
E. L. RIPLEY

BERKLEY
New York

BERKLEY
An imprint of Penguin Random House LLC
penguinrandomhouse.com

ISBN: 9780593102367

First Edition: May 2020

Printed in the United States of America
1   3   5   7   9   10   8   6   4   2

Cover art by Chris McGrath
Cover design by Steve Meditz
Book design by George Towne

"Shall we try again?" Silva asked, taking the pan, not bothering to hide the eagerness on his face. Panning wouldn't make him rich, but it was a novel diversion for a while.

Birds erupted from the trees, and the crack of a rifle shot was what had made them do it.

The bullet struck the pan, sending it spinning in the air, sand and water flying.

Silva was faster to act than Carpenter was, pulling him down to the stream and behind a boulder. Silva held his pistol above the water but didn't lean out to look. The shot had come from upriver, in the trees on the south side. The shooter had to be some distance off, or he wouldn't have missed.

The pan struck the water and Silva rose, firing rapidly as Carpenter made a run for it, splashing through the shallows and onto the bank. He snatched up what he could of their belongings on his way to shelter behind a thick tree.

Another shot came from the rifle, but Silva scrambled out of the river unscathed.

They plunged into the trees, making as fast as possible for better cover.

There was nothing as obvious as crashing footsteps to give away their pursuers, but all the birds had gone quiet, and a new sound rose up over the rushing of the river. They stumbled to a halt, gasping for breath and looking up in wonder.

The howling was such a powerful chorus that Carpenter wouldn't have thought there could have possibly been so many wolves in the world.

THE IMMORTAL COWBOY

This is respectfully dedicated to the "American Cowboy." His was the saga sparked by the turmoil that followed the Civil War, and the passing of more than a century has by no means diminished the flame.

———◦◦◦———

True, the old days and the old ways are but treasured memories, and the old trails have grown dim with the ravages of time, but the spirit of the cowboy lives on.

———◦◦◦———

In my travels—to Texas, Oklahoma, Kansas, Nebraska, Colorado, Wyoming, New Mexico, and Arizona—I always find something that reminds me of the Old West. While I am walking these plains and mountains for the first time, there is this feeling that a part of me is eternal, that I have known these old trails before. I believe it is the undying spirit of the frontier calling me, through the mind's eye, to step back into time. What is the appeal of the Old West of the American frontier?

———◦◦◦———

It has been epitomized by some as the dark and bloody period in American history. Its heroes—Crockett, Bowie, Hickok, Earp—have been reviled and criticized. Yet the Old West lives on, larger than life.

———◦◦◦———

It has become a symbol of freedom, when there was always another mountain to climb and another river to cross; when a dispute between two men was settled not with expensive lawyers, but with fists, knives, or guns. Barbaric? Maybe. But some things never change. When the cowboy rode into the pages of American history, he left behind a legacy that lives within the hearts of us all.

—*Ralph Compton*

PROLOGUE

May 1, 1862

WOODSMOKE AND WORSE were so thick in the air that it was almost enough to cover the pervasive odor of black powder that liked to find its way into everything. The bugs had fallen silent, and the distant harmonica as well. Sleep was everywhere, or it had been before that shot cracked the night wide open and left two hundred soldiers scrambling not for their rifles but for some notion of what was happening.

The same notion Bill was grabbing for with both hands like a drunken man about to step off a cliff.

Echoes of the shot were still making their rounds around the valley, trying to fill the space that the cicadas had left behind, and up went the bugle call, startling Bill from whatever hole his brain had tried to crawl into, and Byron cried out, arching his back and spitting blood on the ground at his feet.

There went another bugle somewhere, and shouting, with plenty of healthy swearing.

Men rushed past and raised voices filled the air as fully and suddenly as smoke would flood the battlefield upon the first salvo. Bill fell to his knees in the mud, seizing the other man and staring at the wound in his breast as though staring and assessing were the same thing, as though anything he had to offer might have done a lick of good. He was no physician, and he didn't need to be one to know that nothing could be done.

All the same, he tore the bandanna from his neck and wadded it up, pressing it to the wound, but the blood came like water from a geyser, only hotter.

And it was still coming, even though the light was already gone from Byron's eyes. The flood was canceled, but the rains hadn't yet gotten the telegram.

It didn't seem fair, but what was? A rabbit could come out of his den just to find his foot in a snare. Those eyes wouldn't be dead; they would be wide and wild, darting every way while the rest of the animal was as still as a stone. The mind racing, and the body going nowhere. Bill had seen it more than once: boys and grown men like statues in the middle of a battle, heedless of what was coming—and it was *always* coming. He knew what it was to be stuck in a moment; he'd just never expected it to happen to him. It had never seemed worth thinking about, so he hadn't bothered. Even if he had, it never would have crossed his mind that he might get caught in one and never leave.

PART ONE

— ◇ —

THE WOLVES AT HIS HEELS

CHAPTER ONE

I T WASN'T QUITE twenty years ago that someone had stolen Carpenter's saddle in broad daylight on a crowded street in Charlotte. That was only a memory. It had been nearly that many years since the war—so the war should've just been a memory too, but it was never that simple.

Lumps of hard resin marred the varnish, and the edges of the chessboard had all the signs of a dull saw and a shaky hand. The kindest word for this work was shoddy, and the piece was altogether out of place in an otherwise respectable lodge. The very chair Carpenter sat in was a work of art, some of the finest wickerwork he'd ever seen, and there were carvings on the hearth that wouldn't have been out of place in a church. The chessboard, though—it was a disaster.

Well, even bad work was good for something: you could always learn from it.

"Do you play?"

Carpenter looked up, setting his thoughts aside and finding his voice, which took a moment.

"Your pardon?" he said.

This man had already been here when Carpenter had walked up earlier in the day, gingerly leading Oceana by the reins. He'd been out on the porch in his shirtsleeves with his legs crossed and a book in his hand, but he hadn't been reading it.

He was well dressed in gray, and the cloth had a nice tartan pattern, but Carpenter couldn't tell the difference between a suit from overseas and one that was just meant to look that way. In any case, the fellow held a respectful distance, and that thick bear rug must've muffled his footsteps as he approached. Not that footsteps would've made any difference; Carpenter's senses weren't what they'd been, but they weren't gone entirely. He'd just been trying so hard to let his mind go anywhere but here, and for a moment, he'd succeeded.

The man indicated the board with his eyes, and Carpenter looked at the knight in his hand.

"Not well," he replied, putting it back. "Just admiring the craftsmanship."

"And how is it?"

It took an effort, but Carpenter found something like a smile. "It's got the right number of squares."

The man let out a little snort of laughter, but it wasn't much. A blind man would've been able to tell this fellow wasn't having much of a day himself.

"These, though," Carpenter added after a moment, shaking a finger at the pieces. "Someone worked hard on them." They'd all been whittled by hand. Not well, but they were all recognizable. The artisan had even taken the time to paint the eyes of all the knights red.

"It's a better job than I could do," remarked the man in gray.

"I'm the same." Carpenter leaned back in his arm-chair. "No talent for detail."

"Could I interest you in a game?"

Nothing could have interested him less, but playing couldn't be worse than just sitting there alone.

"Why not?" Carpenter gestured at the other chair.

The other man nodded politely and seated himself, adjusting the chain of his pocket watch and the gun at his hip, which was about the most foolish thing Carpenter had ever seen. It was polished so brightly that it would blind anyone in the sun, with enough inlaid gold and engravings for a dozen picture frames. He hoped he was imagining that sheen in the grips, and that they were just ivory and not real mother-of-pearl. There was more gaudiness in that gun than in entire shops of jewelry in Richmond.

But Richmond was a long way away. This was California.

Carpenter halfheartedly shoved a pawn forward two spaces. The man in gray moved one as well. Seven moves went by without a single word spoken, and that was merciful. He'd been afraid this man had been lonely, the type who needed to talk to pass the time. Maybe he wasn't as bad as his gun and his exaggerated grooming made him look. Who was he trying to impress here anyway?

There were only four other guests at the lodge: two businessmen traveling together, their driver, and a younger fellow dressed like a cowhand, who kept to himself.

And the dog, of course. It was a good-sized stag-hound curled up on the rug by the window, where the sun was warmest. Not a woman in sight, but this chess player wanted to be as pretty as he'd be going to a dance.

A brand-new wagon waited outside, and an older

stagecoach. The stagecoach belonged to those two others, so this fellow was the one with the wagon. He didn't just look educated; he sounded like it too, something in the way he made sure to say each piece of each word just the right way.

Carpenter moved his rook. He didn't care if the stranger had been educated in a school or in a barrel; it was none of his business. He was just glad to have something to do, though he wouldn't admit it.

The other fellow turned toward the dog, who had lifted her head to look at the door, which opened.

It was Dr. Ambrose, still a bit stooped, still fidgeting with his left hand. He didn't say anything; he just caught Carpenter's eye.

"Excuse me," Carpenter told the man in gray, who nodded.

Maybe it didn't look good to walk away from a game of chess that he was losing to a man at least twenty years his junior, but that didn't matter. It was warm and sunny outside, but cold in his belly as he trailed the doctor onto the porch, down the stairs, past the towering pines, and over to the stable. He'd left his hat in the lodge, and he squinted at the sun, which got lower every minute. He knew what that felt like.

Any other afternoon, the doctor's bright red nose and unruly mustache might've made him difficult to take seriously. As it was, Carpenter couldn't have smiled even if he had tripped and fallen headfirst into a gold mine.

They stopped outside the doors, but well within the smell of the stable.

Ambrose wasn't about to tell him anything he didn't already know, or hadn't seen in his eyes, but the doctor went on and opened his mouth anyway.

"It's like you thought," he said, looking Carpenter in the eye. "The colic. Bad."

Inside, out of the sun, Oceana lay on her side, flank rising and falling with all the power of a dying sparrow. Strange noises came from her nostrils, and her eyes were shut. Her legs trembled.

Carpenter stared down at her, and Ambrose stood at his side for a minute or two.

"I seen that bird gun in your things," the doctor said hesitantly. "Would you like a rifle, Mr. Carpenter?"

It was the last thing he wanted, but he nodded anyway. The doctor went to his own horse, and Carpenter stood there. Just the standing was difficult enough; doing anything more seemed unreasonable. His breaths were as deep and slow as hers were shallow and fast, but they were just as desperate.

Something cool touched his hand, and he took the rifle from the doctor without even looking at him.

Quietly, Ambrose led the other horses out into the sunlight. It was best if they weren't startled by what was coming. Carpenter wondered if it was the same for them as it was for people, if seeing one of their own die would stay with them. He hoped not; horses didn't get to drink whiskey, after all.

The hay was fresh, the feed in the bags was not, and something had died recently in this stable. The odors crowded in, and this must have been what it felt like to wear a corset on a hot day, only Carpenter didn't faint, because someone touched his arm.

It was the man in gray, and there was no longer any sunlight coming in through the crack in the barn door. Carpenter blinked and then wiped his eyes, looking around hurriedly. Oceana still lay at his feet, still breathing, though now the breaths were almost too shallow to see.

The sun was nearly down. Just like that, the time had gone. Vanished, like his saddle twenty years ago in Charlotte.

Dr. Ambrose was probably still standing out there with the other horses, waiting. Carpenter took a breath, and when he swallowed, it was like a strong man had rammed a handful of gravel down his throat.

He still had the doctor's rifle, but the man in gray put his hand out, offering to take it.

"No," Carpenter said, straightening. "No, I'll do it."

The stranger nodded, and then he took a step back and covered his ears.

CHAPTER TWO

T HERE WOULDN'T BE another horse.
    The couple who owned the lodge was sympathetic, but they couldn't sell their mare. It went without saying that the owners of the stage and the wagon couldn't very well part with their teams. There wasn't a horse to spare, nor was there anywhere to get one less than sixty miles away.

The last town Carpenter had passed through hadn't even had a name, much less the guarantee of a mount for sale, if he could even make it that far on foot. He didn't like to think of himself as an old man just yet, but he wasn't a young one, either, and he'd never felt it like he felt it now.

There might have been a chance of going aboard that stage, but they were headed the wrong way. Might as well go on to Antelope Valley; no sense going back. It would be a little farther, and a little harder, going uphill and all. Horse or no horse, it would be a tough trail. The difference was that with no horse, it would also be a long one.

Back in the lodge, the owner handed him a glass of something clear and strong, but Carpenter just sat in his chair. It would've been nice to just drink it, get his boots off, and let it all go until morning. Only if he was going to make it that far on foot, being sick from whiskey, or whatever this swill was, wouldn't help.

The staghound got up from her place in front of the fire and padded over, pushing her face at his thigh. Carpenter straightened and scratched the dog behind her ears, and she made agreeable chuffing noises, leaving the leg of his trousers covered in her dark hairs.

"What is that you're drinking?" the man in gray asked.

This time Carpenter didn't look up. And the other man didn't wait for an invitation; he just took his seat on the other side of the chessboard. The businessmen from Charleston were maintaining a distance that probably had nothing to do with manners. It wasn't lost on any of them that Carpenter had stood there for half an hour, frozen, before this man had entered the stable to nudge him into doing what he had to.

They all probably thought he wasn't right. That didn't particularly offend him. Dr. Ambrose had been thoughtful, or perhaps just wise, to wait him out. Or had he sent this young man in? It didn't matter.

The dog drew back, looking at Carpenter expectantly. He let out his breath and looked at the glass.

"I don't rightly know," he said at last, taking a sniff.

The man leaned forward, holding out a hand. Carpenter gave up the glass readily, and the man in gray took a brave drink. He wrinkled his nose, but stopped short of making a face.

"Interesting," he said, giving the glass back. Carpenter put it down. "No shame in taking a drink on a day like today."

"No shame in taking one any day," Carpenter replied, watching the staghound, who stared straight back at him, tongue out. He reached out and rubbed her head again.

The other man nodded, then glanced at the board. "Would you like to finish?"

"You've got me licked."

"You didn't see this?" He pointed, and Carpenter looked. There *was* an opening there.

"I didn't." Carpenter went ahead and knocked his king over.

"Neither did I. Can't call that a won battle, can you? One you win through sheer luck." The other man knocked his over as well. "I'm sorry about your mare."

"Thank you."

"I heard the doctor call you Carpenter. What do you do, Mr. Carpenter?"

"Besides walk?" At another time, the self-pity might not have come so easily. It wasn't just today, though. It wasn't just Oceana, and walking *would* be his primary occupation for the next few days.

"I've only seen you sit. My name is Rafael Silva. I know it's not a good day, Mr. Carpenter."

"It's almost over, though." He picked up the glass, held it up, and took just a sip. It was like drinking fire, but it wasn't the first time.

Silva took the glass from him and sipped as well, this time prepared for the distinctive flavor, if that was the word for it.

"I know you're stranded," he said, setting the glass down.

No sense denying it. Carpenter nodded. "Least of my troubles," he replied, gazing at the glass.

"I do have whiskey," Silva noted. He lowered his voice, glancing at the owner, who was in the kitchen. "What isn't clear to me is why *he* doesn't."

"I'm sure someone like me came along and drank it all."

"To be sure. Mr. Carpenter, if you're making west, you're welcome to ride with me." Silva put his hand out to his right, and the staghound automatically moved to position her head for easy scratching. "And Maria."

"I wouldn't do that to you, Mr. Silva. But thank you. You show a lot of kindness to a stranger."

He shrugged and scratched Maria fondly. The staghound flopped over, and he leaned to scratch her belly.

"It costs me nothing," he said. "Good night."

Carpenter said nothing in reply. He couldn't have, even if he'd wanted to. He watched Silva go, and there was a temptation not to move. To stay put in the armchair and let the firewater do all the work.

But he'd regret it tomorrow.

Resignedly, he dragged himself to his feet, and up the stairs, and to his room. It was hard to know exactly what the night would hold for him; the only safe bet was that he wouldn't much care for it. Getting his boots off was always a chore, but doubly so tonight. It didn't matter if it was age or self-pity that was slowing him down, because either one was sure to get worse before it got better.

A reasonable man might have expected to be visited by the memory of his faithful horse, but Carpenter had a feeling he wasn't that lucky. He settled down on his bed, a luxury not to be taken for granted with a long walk ahead of him. There had been a time when he'd felt something like fear when sleep came, but that was far behind him. The years had taken what had once been an ordeal and turned it into what could only be called business as usual.

He closed his eyes, and as though the years had never gone by, he saw the night of April 16, 1862.

There was no moon that night to shine on the eighty men on the march, though "march" wasn't the right word for what they were doing. Rumor of a couple detachments that got cut loose after the scrap at Allegheny had reached them just the day prior, and Bill didn't care for that. The news had come from irregular cavalrymen just passing by, not from a courier, not with a seal, not with any attached orders. It was a rumor that there *might* be a few bands of Yankees about, hoping to do some damage.

Evidently that unverified intelligence was sufficient grounds to stow the march and move quietly under cover, if this was what passed for quietly. Sure enough, strolling along was a good deal quieter than a rigid march, but it also put a stake through the heart of anything resembling discipline, and the chatter more than made up the difference in noise. This gaggle was about as stealthy as a sack of bricks falling down the stairs.

The captain didn't seem concerned, cantering along at the head of the formation. It wasn't lost on Bill what he was doing; he didn't believe for a minute that they were in danger from roaming Yankees, but the store was low, and hungry men would rather stroll than march, and here was an excuse that would *probably* hold under scrutiny.

Although there wouldn't be any scrutiny. McClellan was coming for Richmond with forty thousand men, and nothing else was likely to matter after that dust settled, if it ever did.

The captain wasn't wrong.

Stanford Yates ambled along at Bill's side, not showing any nerves to speak of, but at least he was keeping his mouth shut. It didn't matter if there were Yankees about; making this much noise on the move was bad business no matter where you were. It was a grievance he'd voiced to the captain more than once, but the captain was more interested in morale than tactics, and Bill drew the line at telling him that morale was small comfort to a man with a bullet in his head.

"There it is," Yates muttered, jerking his chin at the sky. Bill had seen it too: the slightest hint of the moon up there glancing out shyly from behind the clouds. It needed to come on out; it was a terrible road, and in the dark, the artillery was taking more abuse than it needed.

He heard a wheel crash into a hole, and the swearing that followed, and stopped in his tracks. Bill couldn't take any more.

"Go and get him," he said, clapping Yates on the shoulder and turning back, lifting his hand. "Hold on. Hold on," he said, raising his voice to be heard, but short of really calling out.

Yates jogged up to the captain, and in a moment the column began the awkward process of coming to a halt. Had they been marching, that would've taken place much more gracefully. It wasn't that Bill *wanted* to march, because he didn't. It was just that if you were going to do something, you might as well go about it as though you had some sense. That wasn't *so* unreasonable, was it?

Joe Fisher came up out of the dark. "What's the matter, Bill?"

"We lose an axle here, we won't just be late for

Johnston. We'll slow down our own reinforcements," Bill replied, pointing. It wasn't completely true, but he didn't fancy being the one trying to repair or fashion new wheels for these guns if the carts all broke from hustling along blind in the dark.

It was a nice hole, right there in the middle of the road. And this was about the center of the column, so close on forty men had obviously walked *around* this hole as their lamps showed it to them, and Dan Cantrell had just driven right into it. Was he asleep?

The cart and the gun were canted over at a bad angle.

"Wait, wait," Bill said, pulling a boy back. "Get out of there." The others were tying ropes, getting ready to haul the thing clear, and these young strategists wanted to get in the hole and push. If one of those lines broke with a man down there, Bill would be making a new wheel *and* a coffin. "Tie it on," he added. "Run on to the rear and get O'Doul and Fred." Along with Bill himself, they were the biggest, strongest men, but also the slowest walkers. "Are the horses all right?"

"I'm more worried about my guns," the captain said from the back of his own mare, trotting up. Bill might've told him that his guns wouldn't do him much good if he lacked the means to move them, but the captain hadn't meant anything by what he said. That was just his way, trying to lighten the mood.

This wasn't the time for that, though.

"Let me do it." Bill nudged a soldier aside and took his place to tie a knot that made sense, and stepped back.

"Hold them," the captain warned the man with the horses. One of the two mares was calm enough to stand still during a battle. The other would occasionally try to bolt if someone sneezed, and right now even the chirping crickets were enough to agitate her.

"Captain?"

"Go on, Bill. You're in charge." The captain smiled down at him. As always, Bill had to tell himself that the captain wasn't smiling because he didn't understand the gravity of the situation; he was smiling because he wanted people to be at ease.

Bill wasn't going to be at ease. Not tonight. He put his hand up, squinting in the weak light of their lamps at the gun, the cart, the hole, the lines, the knots, and the men ready to pull it out.

"Do it," he said, bringing his hand down and setting his jaw, but that did nothing to help his nausea. One way or another, that cart was coming out of the hole. But would it be in one piece?

The wood creaked and wailed, and everyone who wasn't a part of the effort was just gathered around to watch. Joe twisted his hat between his hands, and Yates trimmed a stray string from the cuff of his uniform with his whittling knife. What were they even doing out here? Marching in the dark because of Yankee spies? News that one more artillery company was on the move to reinforce General Johnston's offensive against the federals wasn't exactly an intelligence coup, was it? Why not march in daylight?

It didn't matter.

Groaning all the way, the cart inched up over the lip of the hole and came onto the surface of what passed for this road. The men pulled it another foot yet and let go of the lines to get their breath.

It appeared to be intact.

"I prefer a happy ending," the captain muttered, lighting a smoke as though this outcome had been a foregone conclusion. Isaiah was the one with the horses, and Bill put his hand out to stop him before he could even think of hitching them all up again.

"Take the powder off the cart," Bill told the men who were untying the ropes.

"I didn't order an inspection, Bill," the captain noted dryly.

"Captain, would you like to order an inspection?" Bill asked, turning on him.

"Do you think it best, Bill?"

"I do."

"Do what Bill says, boys. Go on and wipe it down. Wouldn't want him to singe his eyebrows."

They did it, using damp cloths to make sure most of the powder residue was gone. Bill was going to have to get down there under the cart with a lamp, and an explosion or a fire would halt this gun the same as a broken wheel would.

Byron came over to Bill, offering his lamp, which he took.

The wheel itself was sound, but it was harder to tell with the axle. Bill squinted and probed, but they'd have to take it apart to really test it. He couldn't *see* a problem with it.

"Oh, dear."

"What is it?"

"Byron, have a look at this."

Byron knelt, then crawled under the cart to join him. Bill, lying on his back, pointed.

"What do you make of that?" he asked, and a bit of grit from the underside of the cart fell in his eyes. He blinked rapidly, and all he could see of the men around the cart was the glow of their smokes.

"Could've been a rock," Byron replied, frowning. He leaned over and peered at the hole. "When it slipped."

"That," Bill said, chewing his lip. "Or someone took a hatchet to it."

Byron let his breath out slowly, and for a moment they stared at each other. "Could be," he admitted after a second.

"Captain," they said in unison. There was a theatrical sigh, and the sound of the captain's riding boots hitting the ground. A bit grumpily, he joined them.

"What is it?" he asked around his cigarette, which Byron took away from him and flung out from under the cart. There were still traces of powder all over it.

The captain scowled at him. "You're my brother, Byron. Not my pa."

Byron gave him a jab with his elbow. "I know. Pa would've used his belt."

The captain just grunted, peering at the damage. "What do you think done it, Bill?"

"Can't be sure," Bill replied honestly.

"Well," the captain began, as though he meant to go on, but he didn't. For a moment, he just looked at the hole, thinking.

"Well?" Byron pressed.

"*Well,*" the captain said, annoyed, "I'm not too proud to admit when I'm wrong." He glanced over at Bill. "Bill's right. If this ain't accidental, could mean someone has designs on us." Just like that, he went from lazy and smiling to crisp and in command. He rolled out from under the cart and got to his feet, brushing himself off. "All right, boys! Let's form it up!"

He swung into the saddle as Bill and Byron scrambled out from under the cart.

And that was it. That was when the shot went up, and there hadn't been any need for the unseen adversary to cause a distraction, because the company had distracted themselves.

The captain's horse reared up, as startled as the rest of them, and as the captain was thrown from his saddle, Bill wondered if tonight was going to be his last. It wouldn't be, but he'd never leave it behind. Before it was all over, he'd have come back to it enough times in his dreams that a part of him would wish it *had* all ended there.

It would've been easier that way.

CHAPTER THREE

G OOD NIGHT" WAS what Silva had said, but Carpenter had known better. He was accustomed to it, and he liked to think there wasn't much left behind his own eyelids that could take him by surprise. This couldn't be blamed on Oceana, or even on Penelope. In his dreams he didn't see his mare, and he didn't see his wife. He didn't dream about colic or tuberculosis, and he didn't even dream of Seven Pines. Just the weeks and months that had led up to it had been enough. By the time McClellan and the battle came, there hadn't been much left to take from him, and what he'd kept he could live without: thudding hooves, booming shots, thundering cannons.

Those were familiar, certainly. But the captain falling from his horse that night in April, all those years ago—that was when things *really* started to change.

Carpenter could stand over his horse, watching her suffer, and she would go. He could sit by his wife's bed, watching her drown on dry land, and *she* would go.

People liked to talk about ghosts coming back to get you, but he didn't hold with that. He'd never seen a ghost, but there were memories that wouldn't die.

One day, maybe soon, they'd be nailing his cold body inside a coffin, and on each blow of that hammer, he'd only hear the muskets and smell the powder. If someone sang a hymn, he'd hear a bugle. He'd still see sabers catching the light and Byron breathing his last in the mud.

There wouldn't be another dawn for Byron, but for Carpenter—for him, that sun just kept coming.

The only surprise was that each day he made it out of bed.

There was barely a hint of dawn yet, and even if the lodge didn't have any real whiskey, at least they had eggs. After that, Carpenter went outside to go through his saddlebags, wondering what was worth carrying. On this terrain he might do fifteen miles in a day if all went well. He'd want a walking stick by the end of it, but he thought it might be nice to trim one up along the way, rather than try to buy something here.

He carried his saddlebags out of the stable and knelt to see what he could live without. He had to bring the weight down; it couldn't all come along.

Even in the dim, hazy light, the birds were starting to sing.

The letters from Penelope would come. And his hat. And his bedroll. His shotgun? That, he'd just as soon leave behind. It was heavy, and he didn't plan on killing any birds between here and Antelope Valley. Unless antelope were birds, but he was fairly sure they weren't.

He came up with the sifting pan he'd packed at the last minute, just before leaving Richmond for good. He'd thought he might give it a try when he got here.

He shook his head, wondering if a horse had kicked him in the head and he just hadn't noticed. He didn't need the money; he'd just thought it might be interesting to try.

Something to do.

Maria was there, watching him. He returned the staghound's gaze, and Silva emerged from the lodge in his shirtsleeves with his hat and a tin cup. The morning chill didn't seem to bother him. He stood on the porch a moment, looking a good deal more sensible without that silly gun on his hip.

He put his hat on his head and descended the steps, peering out at the dawn breaking behind the trees. Maria went to his side and sat, tongue hanging out, not a care in the world.

"Good morning," he said.

"Morning," Carpenter replied, watching the curtains fall back into place at the window at the corner of the house where someone had been watching until just a moment ago. "You know that fellow?"

"I haven't had a good look at him." Silva didn't look.

"You didn't make his acquaintance like you made mine?"

"I did not."

Carpenter finished lightening his saddlebags and got to his feet with a groan. "Is that why you want company? Worried about him?"

Silva looked genuinely startled. Now he looked up at the window, then back at Carpenter.

"That had not crossed my mind." It really hadn't, but the notion clearly shook him. It was a sign of nerves, the way he rubbed the staghound's head with his free hand. "You think I should worry?"

"I'm trying to think as little as possible," Carpenter said, and grunted as he shouldered his saddlebags. He donned his own hat and tipped it. "But even my old eyes can see he's watching you. It's none of my business. Good luck."

"Journey safely," Silva replied.

THE JOURNEY WOULD be safe enough; it just wouldn't be easy. There had been a time when something like this would've been a mere inconvenience, but there had been an awful lot of soft living since then. Thirty years ago, it would have taken some doing to convince Carpenter how much work it was to build and run a factory; it had been the labor of his life, and he'd done most of it in a chair, with ink on his fingers instead of dirt.

He didn't need his bandanna; the reddish dust of the road was easily kicked up by hooves, but a man's boots hardly stirred it. The winding road was lined on either side with some of the finest timber he had ever seen, and by the sound of things, these woods were swarming with deer and all manner of life.

There was just enough breeze to feel good, and that went nicely with the serenading from the birds. At least for now, just short of the mountains, the going was easy. A little harder terrain would have been welcome; his mind was too free to wander this way.

The hoofbeats were still a long way off, but in the quiet, they were unmissable. He was barely into his second mile. When they were near enough, Carpenter moved to the side and mopped his brow, then rested his hands on the saddlebags draped around his shoulders.

He had to squint, but it could have been only the young man from the lodge. He'd been dressed like a cowhand, and he still was, but that wasn't the way he'd carried himself.

He was riding in a hurry. Carpenter moved off the trail and into the thick ferns, raising a hand in greeting as the young fellow approached.

The young man waved and slowed to a trot.

"Morning," he called out, looking down at Carpenter as he passed.

"Same to you."

"You all right?"

"I'm fine," Carpenter replied, though the hoofbeats probably drowned his words out as the rider went to a gallop and disappeared around the bend.

The birds went back to singing, the deer started to move again, and Carpenter got to walking. It was still none of his business, though now that he'd had a look at him up close, the boy looked a little familiar.

THE WAGON WAS worse than the horse, because it moved much more slowly, giving Carpenter longer to stroll, knowing that it was coming.

When Silva's wagon finally rolled up behind him, Carpenter could no longer politely ignore it. Dressed in a fresh beige suit and looking more or less at ease, Silva halted his team. Beside him, neatly bundled, waited the things Carpenter had tried to leave behind, even his saddle.

That had been the only thing it really pained him to leave.

He didn't say anything for a moment, instead rubbing his chin.

"If you're going to Antelope Valley, I can take these things there. I can leave them with the sheriff for you to collect."

Carpenter scowled, eyeing Maria, who was up there beside her master, panting at him expectantly.

"For God's sake," he muttered. Silva got up and offered a hand. Carpenter took it and clambered stiffly up to sit beside him, catching a glimpse of the crates stacked in the back, under the canvas hood. He put down his saddlebags to scratch the staghound, and Silva picked up the reins to drive on.

The way grew steeper, and the ride grew slower and bumpier as the sun went higher. Silva's horses were strong and tenacious, and doing well. A big hawk wheeled above the treetops, and as the warmth of the day came on, Maria drew back from the two men and jumped into the shade of the covered wagon.

There was no one else on the trail, and that was just as well. The elevation was enough that the pass was treacherous on either side, so having to go around another coach or wagon would have been troublesome.

The afternoon sun caught on a pond off in the trees, and they stopped and unhitched the horses to lead them down and water them. The shade was merciful, and the water was cool and clear.

Carpenter paused, watching Maria sniff about energetically. He moved some fallen pine needles aside with his boot, revealing tracks in the dirt. He took off his hat and crouched for a closer look. Silva was at the water's edge with the horses.

"What's wrong?" he called out.

"Wolves, I expect," Carpenter replied. He put his hat back on and climbed back to the road, looking in either direction. He'd ridden his share of lonely trails, but never without the hoofbeats of his mount to fill the air. Now there was such a silence that the silence itself seemed loud. Except for the quiet ringing in his ears, but he barely noticed that anymore. It had been there a long time.

When Silva returned with the horses, Carpenter was in the shadow of the wagon, leaning against it to smoke. "You're sure you don't know that boy, the cowhand?" he asked.

Silva got the horses hitched and used a handkerchief with his initials on it to mop his brow.

"I didn't see his face. I don't believe I know him."

"Then why'd he do this to your wagon?"

Frowning, Silva joined him and leaned over to look. Carpenter pointed to the gouges on the wheel. Even after several minutes of looking, he still wasn't sure exactly what sort of tool the boy must have used. It didn't look like the work of a hatchet or a saw. Had he really sat down here last night for an hour with a buck knife?

Silva had never looked particularly cheerful, but now he looked particularly stony.

"I give it five miles." Carpenter rubbed his face. "If we're lucky."

"We should go on, then." Silva didn't hesitate. "Best if we get away from the wolves."

"You're armed."

"It's not me I'm worried about. It's Maria. She's brave enough to get into trouble."

"*Brave*'s just another word for *stupid*," Carpenter pointed out. "Tie her up. Your load's too heavy. If this goes, you'll lose the axle." He sighed and knelt, peering at the wheels. "One wheel, I can fix. All this?" He pointed at the underside of the carriage. "I don't know. Even if I could, it could take days."

"It's that bad?"

It was; there was no question. Was Silva blind? But Carpenter didn't ask that; he just nodded and let his eyes do the talking.

Silva put his hands on his hips and bit his lip, gazing at the ground.

"There's metal back here that you're carrying," Carpenter said, tapping the side of the wagon. "It better not be gold, because if it is and someone out there knows it, we may as well just cut our own throats and save everyone a little time."

Silva snorted. "It isn't gold."

"Is it valuable enough that someone wants to cripple you out here?" He watched the hawk in the air for a moment. "So they can bushwhack you in peace?"

There was no uncertainty, and Carpenter felt one corner of his mouth turn up in something like a smile. Someone had designs on this wagon, to state the matter in the captain's parlance.

The other man just shook his head and unknotted one of the ties for the cover. He pulled it back and lifted the lid of one of the crates, revealing metal objects nestled in straw.

"My cargo is not a secret, Mr. Carpenter. Steel components," he said. "Enough to assemble a hundred rifles. My factory will have everything I need except for the means to do the metal work myself. I'll need these rifles to raise the capital for that."

"You're opening a factory?"

Silva just took a document from his pocket and handed it over.

Carpenter accepted it, but didn't unfold it.

"I don't want to know about your business," he said, and handed it back. "Not really. But if there's a bullet on the way, I wouldn't mind knowing it's coming. For the sake of my nerves," he added dryly.

Silva didn't ask questions, and he didn't try to drown him in small talk. Carpenter appreciated that, and he'd have truly liked to return the favor, but this was a little much to let go.

"I am not a popular man in Antelope Valley," the shorter man replied, putting it back in his pocket. "This letter is from General Anderson. The Army supports the construction of my factory. I already have orders to fill. But there are men in Antelope Valley that do not support my business."

Carpenter frowned. That didn't seem right; what did anyone in Antelope Valley care about some rifles? Or a factory? They ought to have been busy finding gold and getting rich up there. A wagon full of metal parts didn't seem like much of a target for outlaws.

"Were you going to mention that?" Carpenter asked, more curious than bothered.

"These men aren't going to *attack* me," Silva replied, taking off his hat and running a hand through his hair. "They're content to be a nuisance."

That seemed naive. Carpenter stared at him for a moment, then leaned over for a second look at the wheel.

"Let me see that letter."

Silva gave it up readily, and it was exactly what he said it was. It seemed like the last thing anyone would ever bother to forge, not that Carpenter was any authority.

"I design firearms, Mr. Carpenter. It's not a secret." He indicated the gleaming pistol on his belt.

"I thought that was jewelry."

One corner of Silva's mouth twitched upward. "I also have the role of the salesman. A sample product should look impressive."

"Do you want to impress me or my wife?"

"I don't know. Is she pretty?"

Carpenter caught himself there. He clapped Silva on the shoulder and stepped back, eyeing the nearby trees. They'd need wood.

"You ever manage a factory before?" he asked, unable to help himself.

"I expect my business partner to handle that." That was for the best. Silva wasn't cut out for it. "Have you?"

"As a matter of fact, I have."

"Making what?"

"Tables and chairs."

Silva raised an eyebrow. "Would that make you a sort of, you know, carpenter?"

Carpenter ignored that. "Do you have a saw?"

CHAPTER FOUR

THE WORK WAS tedious but not difficult. It took all the daylight, and a little of the evening, working by lamplight. Carpenter might've reinforced the wheel more quickly, but he wanted to be certain it would hold. If one wheel gave under the weight of all those metal parts, they'd be lucky if they didn't have to build a whole new wagon.

That was no position to be in if Silva really did have enemies. Of course, if someone had a grievance with Silva, it wouldn't much matter if the wagon had wheels or not. Although it didn't take a great general to beat Carpenter at chess, he seemed reasonably bright. Why was he traveling alone? Did he really *believe* it when he said he didn't think anyone truly meant him harm?

Because the state of the axle suggested that he'd misread something, somewhere along the line. No—he knew. Carpenter had seen Silva at the lodge, his worry and preoccupation. The younger man wasn't fooling himself or anyone.

"You're certain someone did that deliberately?" Silva asked from the other side of the fire, jerking his chin at the wagon.

It wasn't worth lying to make the other man feel better. It wouldn't work in any case; Silva wasn't as naive as he seemed.

"Can't imagine a wheel coming by that damage honestly," Carpenter replied, flat on his back, with Maria curled up at his side. The staghound's warmth was welcome as the night chill set in, and Silva seemed a little bitter about it, but it stood to reason. Carpenter was bigger and taller; of course the dog would choose the warmer of the two.

Or not; she got up and went back to Silva. Carpenter put his hat over his eyes.

"If you're worried . . . ," Silva began, no doubt intending to say something to the effect that he wouldn't be offended if Carpenter chose to go his own way.

"Do I look worried?"

Silva stoked the fire with a branch, then broke it in half and tossed it in. The man wasn't much good with a saw, but he was a fair enough cook with a camp stove. He stroked Maria's side fondly.

"You aren't looking for gold in Antelope Valley?" Silva said after a moment.

"I have friends that settled there. My company from the war."

"From before you were a factory man."

"That's right."

"Which side did you fight on, Mr. Carpenter?"

"I don't see that it matters," he replied.

"I would tell you that it does," Silva shot back, "though I venture I can know the reply from just your way of speaking."

"I don't take kindly to that, Mr. Silva," Carpenter noted tiredly.

"Then I apologize."

"And I accept. Go to sleep. If we're going to be shot tomorrow, might as well be rested."

"Or sick from whiskey."

"So you do have some sense." Carpenter muttered. He just put his hand out blindly, and Silva passed him the bottle.

If not for the wolves to think about, it might have been a pleasant night, even on the ground, even knowing what was coming when the dawn would bring tomorrow's troubles. Carpenter had spent more than his share of nights on the ground as a younger man, and he could dream there the same as anyplace else. Of course, in his dreams at least he knew what he was up against. On the night of April 16, 1862, that shot in the dark had denied him any chance he might have had of sleeping or dreaming that night.

Another man had slept, though, gone away to dreamland. And Carpenter had been the one to send him.

That shot was so loud that the moon had come out as though to see what all the commotion was about. The only sound louder was that of the captain's body crashing to the ground, or perhaps that note quite specific to his skull meeting that rock.

Bill had been wearing the uniform for months, and he knew chaos by sight. Even as the men shouted and ran and the transformation overtook that one quiet stretch of Virginia road where in the space of a heartbeat everything could turn to hell—there was one thing that wasn't moving, and that was the man who was meant to lead them.

There was a second shot, but only the one. It wasn't good sense or restraint that was to thank for that; it was the moon. If the moon had stayed hidden, they never would've known what they were up against. No, it wasn't sense. Nothing so elegant.

It was just surprise.

The men there, up on the embankment at the side of the road—and there were *plenty* of them tucked in those trees and those shrubs—were not Yankee soldiers. They were, however, well armed.

Bill had been knocked over in the scramble, and Byron had caught him by the elbow. He was in the act of helping him up when it became apparent what had occurred, and like everyone else on both sides, he went perfectly still. It was a lot of puzzled, unlucky men, most of them a good way from home, all of them turned into nothing more than a pack of statues.

Joe was over there near the captain, holding the horse's reins so it wouldn't step on the fallen man, but he was too afraid to move to do anything more than that.

The enemy, if that was what they should be called, was clustered on the south side of the road, just spread out enough to look frightening. There were a handful of white faces in there, and it was mainly the white hands that were holding the rifles. The colored folk, women too, were armed as well, and from a distance of fifteen feet, a sickle was probably more useful than a smoothbore Springfield.

Certainly more useful than Bill's, which was unloaded, and in the back of one of the carts.

He had never fired it. And he never would.

That was then, years ago. A place and a time that was only real behind closed eyes, but now it was time for Carpenter's eyes to open. He didn't want to open them; the waking world wasn't any better, but he didn't see that he had much choice.

For a man who cut such an elegant figure, Silva didn't have much talent for stealth. He made as much noise as a team of hungry mules when he tried to creep away from the camp.

Carpenter lifted his hat and opened one eye, peering in the bright starlight. After a moment's deliberation, he got up, scratched Maria behind her ears, and went into the shadows.

It was good manners, not to mention simple decency, not to ask questions about another man you weren't well acquainted with. Carpenter had enough business of his own; there wasn't any sense in trying to get his hands into anyone else's.

But polite manners were for polite times. Now it was obvious that young fellow had been watching Silva, and there hadn't been anyone else to sabotage the wagon. Whatever was waiting for them on the trail ahead wasn't likely to be half as polite as Carpenter liked to be.

Silva got a spade from the wagon, and a small bundle, and went into the trees with his appalling imitation of quiet. Carpenter trailed him, doing a better imitation of himself ten or twenty years prior, when he'd had a truly light step. Wearing a uniform hadn't taught him that—war had been anything but quiet—but as a boy he'd spent enough of his time hunting to make sure there was soup over the fire that something like this was no challenge, even forty years later.

Silva found a startlingly ugly tree, and Carpenter watched in silence as he dug a shallow hole, buried the bundle, and covered it.

CHAPTER FIVE

T HE SUN DRAGGED itself tiredly over the horizon,
and the birds got to shouting at one another
while a stiff breeze rustled the pines. Carpenter did
what he always did in the morning, giving his sore
back and joints their due. Between a dream without
pain and the waking world and its aches, he knew
which he preferred.

After the best breakfast he had ever had on the trail,
Carpenter resigned himself and opened his mouth.

"You can turn back," he told Silva as they got the
team ready. The horses were a good deal better
rested than either man, but they still struggled with
this burden. What Silva needed was a few oxen for
this trail, but there was no money in mentioning that
now. "Their notion would have been for you to break
down yesterday. They'll be coming on this way now.
Can't say exactly when, but if we keep on west, we'll
meet them."

"I have a great deal tied up in Antelope Valley,"

Silva replied, unperturbed. He climbed into the driver's seat and picked up the reins. "I can't let myself be frightened off."

"It ain't about being scared," Carpenter pointed out. "There's no sense in it, walking into trouble when you got no cause to."

"If anyone wanted me dead, I would be. And if you thought you were in danger, you wouldn't be along."

"My wife is gone," Carpenter told him frankly, tossing his bedroll into the wagon. "I have lived my life, and not all that well. Only kin I got left is at the end of this trail. Might as well go. You'll understand when you get to my age, and you're tired and sore all the time. A bullet isn't the worst thing I can think of."

Silva snorted, then pointed at the wagon. Maria jumped up obediently. "You'll forgive me, Mr. Carpenter. I did not know of your woes. I'd have brought my violin."

"You should worry about your own." He climbed up to the wagon. "Or did I figure you wrong, and you actually know how to use that pistol?"

"The bullets come from the narrow end if my memory serves me rightly."

"I admit my mistake," Carpenter said dryly, handing him the reins. "Just tell me before you shoot them all, so I can cover my delicate ears."

It wasn't even an hour before there was distant dust in the air, rising over the trees. It was a sure sign of mounted men.

"We've been seen." Silva's voice was calm, but he'd taken a hand off the reins to rub Maria's head for comfort. "Are they coming?"

"No. They didn't think they'd find us moving. They thought we'd be broken down, I'm sure."

"We're making excellent time."

"I'd hate to be late for an ambush," Carpenter said

tiredly. "That would be rude. You could build your factory somewhere else."

"I could do even better and just build it in Mexico."

"It'll be there that they hold us up." Carpenter pointed ahead. The trail rose steeply, curling around the mountain, into a particularly thick cluster of tall trees. If there were riders here for them, they'd take their horses around the rock face and return on foot. That tight pass was the perfect place to make a play for travelers.

"Are you speaking from experience as a highwayman?" Silva asked curiously, though he didn't slow down. Maria raised her head, but stopped short of growling.

"I speak from my experience of knowing my own name and how to walk in a straight line."

"Did you get those marks on your back by walking in a straight line?"

"As a matter of fact I did," Carpenter replied, surprised and a little annoyed. It was true they'd bathed in a stream yesterday, but he'd made a point not to show his back. So Silva didn't want to notice what someone had done to his wagon, but he took note when another man had taken lashes. "And I was glad to have them."

"That seems like an unusual thing to say."

"The alternative was to hang by the neck until dead." Carpenter reached over and took the reins, bringing the wagon to a halt. The worst part of the pass was just ahead.

"And why would anyone want to hang you, Mr. Carpenter?"

Silva was unbelievable; he'd keep chatting until he was old and gray, or dead with a bullet, rather than think about the moment he was living in. The men who had sabotaged his wagon were concealed up ahead and he knew it, even if he liked to behave as though he didn't.

"Cowardice," Carpenter replied, dropping the reins and climbing down from the wagon.

Silva looked startled, but Carpenter ignored him, pulling his shotgun from its sheath. He cradled it in his arms and took a few steps forward. "You may as well come on out," he called.

Silva had stiffened, but at least he didn't panic. The growl in Maria's throat was low. Carpenter glanced back and caught the other man's eye, indicating the dog. Silva grabbed her with one hand and rested the other on his pistol, but Carpenter gave a little shake of his head.

"While I'm still young," he added, addressing the shadowed road ahead. "If it's not too much trouble."

Today there were two hawks in the sky, but no deer in the woods. That alone would've been telling, even if they hadn't had every reason to know this was coming.

"I would just as soon stay where I am," a voice replied from somewhere off to the right.

"Would that be because you enjoy the shade?" Carpenter replied, raising his voice to make sure they all heard him. "Or because you are one of these men of the notion that you cut a better figure without a hole in you?"

"What is your name?" the hidden man shouted.

"Why do you want to know that?" Carpenter shouted back.

"Because I do not know who you are!" the voice replied, indignant.

Carpenter took another step forward. "I'm the man you're going to regret you tried to rob," he roared, pulling back both the shotgun's hammers. "That is, if you live long enough."

It was a beautiful day to look at, though not for

standing in the sun, but that was what he did. There
had only been one voice, but there were certainly more
men. That watcher at the lodge hadn't ridden ahead to
report to nobody; he had been sent by *someone*.
Maybe this fellow out there in the trees.

It was too hot to wait any longer. After another
minute, Carpenter put his shotgun over his shoulder
and returned to the wagon.

"They're gone," he said, and it wasn't worth the effort to try to hide how much that surprised him. Those
men had had them dead to rights. If they'd wanted this
wagon of rifle parts, there wasn't a thing that could've
stopped them from taking it. What they'd have done
with it—that was less obvious. Why would anyone
bother to steal this? They wouldn't. No, it was whatever Silva had buried the night before that they were
after. Carpenter had never reckoned himself a genius,
but that much was fairly clear.

"Do you want to be shot?" Silva asked after a moment, letting go of Maria and picking up the reins.

"Not in particular. But if I'm going to be, might as
well be on my feet."

The other man let out a long breath. "What would
you have done if they had opened fire?"

"Died," Carpenter replied, settling tiredly in his
seat. He broke the shotgun open and showed Silva
that both barrels were empty. "I expect."

"To what end?" Silva was baffled.

"Maybe you'd realize what a fool you are and try
to run away."

"You went out with an empty scattergun to threaten
a band of robbers, and *I'm* the fool?"

Carpenter rubbed his eyes and adjusted his hat.
"That's the long and short of it."

CHAPTER SIX

"M R. KARR IS my partner. He has property and a claim outside town, but he has experience with this work," Silva said, adding more wood to the fire. Clouds had come late in the day, and that made for a conspicuously dark night. Carpenter added some wood as well; there was something about that extra layer of shadow that made it seem wise to build up the fire a little higher. Or at least it was easier to credit it to shadows than to lingering apprehension from the confrontation on the road.

"Where is he now?" he asked.

"There, in the valley. He's supervising the work-men. The materials for the factory were ready before I left. By now it should be all but complete. We've already had one setback with Mr. Orr."

"Who's he?" Carpenter asked.

Silva was chatty, but it wasn't him talking right now; it was his nerves. It was best just to let him, and there was no sense blaming him for it. Anyone would have been rattled by what had happened, but Silva had more than that to grapple with. He had to come to grips with his beliefs and the knowledge of how wrong they'd been. It was a hell of a thing to go to war and see those things done, things that no one ought to do, but it hadn't taken Carpenter completely by surprise.

Silva, though? A fellow like him wouldn't expect people to actually *do* something to him. Now he had to live in a world that wasn't the same as the one he'd lived in a little while ago. Or maybe Silva already knew how things were and was just giving a convincing performance of ignorance.

"He would've been our third partner, but he's fallen ill. He has a very large family, and they were to be half my workforce. The sooner he's back on his feet, the sooner we will be able to achieve full production. I was traveling alone, Mr. Carpenter. But I'm not alone."

"Good," Carpenter grunted, trying to get comfortable beside the flames, but comfort was like Silva's civilized world. It might've been real at one time, but it wasn't now, and it never would be again.

"Don't worry. Maria won't let us be killed in our sleep."

Carpenter wasn't convinced that was true. The staghound was too friendly and agreeable for her own good, or for Silva's. Anyone with a bit of meat could probably buy her silence.

Best not to mention that. Silva worked hard to hide it, but he was more worried than Carpenter, which was telling. He'd said himself that if these men wanted them dead, they would have simply killed him. If that was true, what did he have to worry about tonight? It would be no easier for an enemy to creep up in the dark than it would've been to just shoot them both a few hours ago. No one was coming tonight; Silva could sleep soundly.

But he wouldn't.

Carpenter sat up and looked at the staghound, who was dozing. Silva was lost in thought, and he couldn't hear the distant wolves. Their howls were faint and mingled with the wind, but Carpenter's ears were a good deal better than his eyes.

Well, they were a long way off.

They *would* come, though, and he would worry about them when they did. Going to sleep wasn't the same as going to the gallows, even if there were nights when it was no more appealing. You came back from sleep, at least most of the time.

Wolves would have the decency to show you their teeth, and whatever they had in mind, they wouldn't drag it out. People, on the other hand—well, there wasn't any getting around it. Dogs barked, birds sang, and people did the things that people liked to do.

The captain had always liked the sound of his own voice, and to his credit, nobody else had ever seemed to mind it much. On May 9, 1862, he'd gotten to put it to use for something more than giving orders and trying to put men at ease.

In fact it might've been the first time he ever put himself forth to be so cross. The first time he ever raised his voice this way, and not just him.

The sweltering courthouse had been packed with people, so many that it was hard to know who they were all supposed to be, but now Carpenter was there again, and it was as real as it had ever been.

There were Joe and Yates and Isaiah. Fred too. The chaplain, Roy Brown, and a few of the others. O'Doul had not come along. They had all chosen to be there; none were required except the captain. By choice they had come to swelter in this place, and at least one of them would go on to swelter even in his dreams.

The captain, his head still swathed in bandages, stood out there alone, and Bill couldn't see the wooden floor and the tables and the chairs because they weren't really there. They might all have been wearing the same color and speaking, but this was nothing as civilized as a meeting. It was a battle, and the tobacco smoke that choked the place might as well have been cannon smoke.

And like a grand barrage dying away, so did the captain's voice as he finished.

"For God's sake," he roared, but that was where it ended. There must have been more he meant to say, but he didn't do it. Probably because he could see what Bill could: that no one was really listening. There was only so much you could tell by looking at a man's back.

So the captain stood out there by himself, staring down the supposed tribunal, which was *not* a mere three men, but probably closer to twenty. It was best not to think about, let alone wonder aloud, where all these officers had come from to sweat in this place when McClellan was still on his way, same as he ever was.

But they weren't here to wait for McClellan; they were here to hang Bill.

It was always a bit of a surprise that no matter how stubbornly a man found himself living in the past, it wasn't any good at all at stopping the future from coming.

S o it was no surprise that in the morning, Silva was dragging his feet. This would be the final day on the trail; there wasn't much ground left to cover, and anyone in the world would know at a glance that Silva was in no hurry to get where they were going.

He'd been this way at the lodge as well. He could smile and be friendly, but something was missing, and now Carpenter knew why: the other man didn't know what to expect, but he *did* know he wasn't going to like it. Why was he going through with it, then? Did he think that if he pretended to be invincible, things would just work out in his favor? Was that how he'd gotten along until now?

Silva stood at the wagon in the hazy morning light, his waistcoat open and his hair disheveled. He was looking at Carpenter's empty shotgun, which was back in its worn sheath.

Carpenter settled the straps of his suspenders and rolled up his sleeves, watching the other man. What was he thinking about? That a scattergun would do him more good than the letter in his pocket? He hoped not; the gun was nearly as long as Silva was tall.

"There's always a way," Carpenter said, kicking a little more dirt over the fire and picking up his bedroll and hat. "But sometimes you have to give up ground." Silva turned to look at him, and Carpenter just met his eyes. "It's all right," he said simply.

For a moment, it looked like Silva intended to argue. Then he shook his head and turned away from the shotgun.

"I expect you're right, Mr. Carpenter," he said.

There weren't any hawks in the sky today, just the sun and its blinding light spilling over the pines. It had been a long, slow climb, but they were deep in the mountains now. Carpenter kept his eyes open for every glimpse of the distant snowcapped peaks that the trees would give him. This journey had been supposed to be about the past, but instead there was something new.

It wasn't Virginia, which he knew he'd miss, but he could sit and look at these mountains all day.

There was still enough light to see by when they arrived, but Antelope Valley wasn't much to look at. It *was* a valley, or that was what some would've called it. Carpenter called it the most asinine place to build a town he had ever seen. It had obviously lasted this way for a couple years, but he was ready to wager that the first big rains they had would wash away the entire street with a landslide. Or if there was a big snow in the mountains and it all melted, that would be just as bad.

He hoped Silva was building his factory on higher ground.

There were people down there, though not as many as he'd expected. This place was supposed to be in a boom, but who'd have thought a boom would be this quiet? Even the smells of woodsmoke and horses were faint. The wind carried just a hint of music. The air should've been a miasma of awful smells, and there should have been half a dozen rowdy joints to keep the miners and prospectors amused.

But it was almost peaceful.

Silva stopped the wagon; a single rider was making his way up the trail.

The rider drew up in front of them, a man like Carpenter in age but closer to Silva in size. He'd done away with his jacket and collar, and his dark shirt was damp with sweat. He'd shaved, though, and on the whole, he looked good.

He obviously intended to say something, but he was just looking at Carpenter, who tipped his hat.

"Hello, Roy."

"Your acquaintance?" Silva looked surprised. And then there was a hint of panic—and then resignation.

"Well, he was supposed to be our chaplain," Carpenter said mildly, ignoring those flickers that he'd seen going across the other man's face. "But he was more of a wet nurse. Kept us fed when we had no supplies. Talent for fishing. There's something in the good book about that, isn't there, Reverend?"

"You know," Roy said dryly, "I believe there is. It's good to see you, Bill." What he said was friendly enough, but he wasn't smiling. "I got no good news for you, Mr. Silva."

"I've grown accustomed to that, Reverend."

"There wasn't anything anyone could do. Your property—by the time we knew there was a fire . . ." He left it at that, shaking his head. "Ain't much left of your cabin, son."

Silva's face didn't change; there was a slight bob of his throat as he swallowed. Then he nodded. "Lightning, I suppose?"

"I could not say," Roy said, face flat. "And Mr. Orr has passed."

That got more of a reaction. Silva straightened, and he lost some color in his face. "Was that lightning as well?" he asked after a moment, and Roy scowled at him.

"For God's sake, the man was ill. Has been for two months. Have some respect."

Silva's eye twitched, but he said nothing to that.

"Thought it might be easier to hear it now," Roy grumbled, squeezing his reins. "Rather than ride up to a pile of ashes."

"Thank you."

"You are welcome." No real condolences. No offer of help.

"What about me?" Carpenter asked mildly, and Roy gave him a funny look.

"You're welcome too, Bill."

"That's decent of you."

"What have you done with yourself?"

"Parsons and I built our factory. The first one back then." He shrugged. "Now there's four or five others within a mile. We sold a lot of tables."

"That's real good to hear. I know the captain mentioned you were doing well. And Penelope?"

"Well," Carpenter said, leaning forward and rubbing his hands together, "she went on ahead."

"I'm real sorry."

"Oh, I don't expect it'll be long till it's our turn."

"That's true enough. Gentlemen." Roy tipped his hat and rode on. Silva didn't reply or turn to watch him go. A minute or two passed as they sat, looking down at the town.

"Lightning," Carpenter mused finally.

Silva took a deep breath. "Perhaps I'll just pretend that it was," he said, rubbing the staghound's back. "I was going to try to build Maria a house," he said, glancing at Carpenter. "I've never made a thing with my hands, but I thought I was up to it. I had the lumber ready and everything else. I suppose they burned too, I'll find."

"There's always more lumber," Carpenter told him. "You won't run out of that."

"Oh, I know. It's time I'm thinking about."

With that, he picked up the reins and took them into town.

There were no surprises waiting. Carpenter didn't need all the details to know it stood to reason that no one wanted to look Silva in the eye. And no one could be particularly curious about Carpenter: a big older man humbly dressed. They'd think he was just another prospector, here for the Antelope Valley's bounty of gold.

But where were the real prospectors?

"You were correct," Silva said as they drew up outside the hotel.

"First time for everything." Carpenter picked up his things and climbed down. "About which part?"

"You survived the ride."

"Wonders never cease." He put his saddlebags over his shoulder. "If a bullet puts you in an early grave, that's the cost of doing business. But don't let your backbone put you there. The money's only good if you're around to collect it."

Silva just glanced at him, then at Maria. "I don't know that it's entirely up to me," he replied. "I was glad to meet you, Mr. Carpenter."

Silva tipped his hat, and Carpenter did the same.

This was something Carpenter had looked forward to. It didn't take many nights on the ground to remind him what he'd taken for granted in Richmond: above all else, his feather bed and his wife. He knew which he missed more of the two, but with the noises his back had started to make, he would settle for having a bed.

The room was rough and overpriced but clean.

On the long ride west, Carpenter had fancifully considered how he might go about building a cottage here if things played out in such a way that he was inclined to stay. Now there was no fancy left in him, only the truth. His building days might not be over just yet, but he wouldn't be building any houses. He'd made peace with the gray at his temples and in his beard, and now it was time to make peace with paying other men to do the things he'd once have done himself.

The hotel's parlor was filling up as the sun got down low, and no one paid him any mind. The whiskey wasn't half as good as whatever Silva had had in his wagon, but it was a hundred times better than that swill they'd tried to give him at the lodge.

"Did you drive in with that factory man?" the barman asked, offering the bottle.

Carpenter leaned over the bar to be sure there wasn't a better bottle in hiding. When there wasn't, he accepted a second glass. "He was kind enough to let me ride rather than see me walk. I lost my horse."

The barman nodded, looking sympathetic.

"Of course," Carpenter went on, taking a sip, "that other fellow lost his home. He's got no luck to speak of, does he?"

"No brains, more like. On account he can't see he's got no friends. Apart from the dog." That was what the man said, but the look on his face didn't go with the words. He had no grievance with Silva. All he had was pity. "It's a handsome dog, though," he added after a moment.

"He's a fool all right," Carpenter agreed, glancing at the door. "I suppose if the factory doesn't pick up, he can make his fortune in gold. They say all you need is a pan in this camp."

"We all could," the barman snorted, stepping away to pour for another man. "We could pan until we're all as gray as you are. Wouldn't find no gold."

Carpenter paused, about to drink. He set the glass down and opened his mouth, but a hand fell on his shoulder. He turned to see a man he knew well, even with that mustache, which he certainly hadn't had twenty years ago.

"Get your rifle, Joe. I believe there's a weasel on your face," Carpenter told him.

Joe Fisher groaned. "You got old, Bill. But you ain't grown up none."

"I have a razor. I could be prevailed upon to allow you to borrow it," Carpenter went on.

"I have my own. Edith *likes* it," Joe added, touching the mustache self-consciously.

"But does she like so *much* of it?"

"Why don't you worry about your own wife, Bill?"

"Don't see what good it would do. She's dead."

That stopped him. "I'm sorry to hear that. Penelope was a find. You did better than any of us."

Carpenter snorted and got to his feet. "It happens to the best of us. I'm glad to see you, Joe."

He looked better than he ever had. Better dressed, better fed, and better groomed, even with half his face hidden.

They shook hands, but Carpenter wasn't satisfied with that. He embraced the other man, who put up with it stoically.

"I didn't think from your letters that you were inclined to join us," Joe said, stepping back and looking Carpenter up and down. "Making too much money in Richmond. What did you do with it all? Those boots are the same ones you wore on the march."

"I would have loved to come with you." It was true. "But you know she couldn't leave." Penelope had too much family, too many ties to just drag her out of Richmond. He'd always been a bit wistful about the others, about the way they'd all stayed together after the war, their families and all.

Things were different now. He was alone, and though there was no good reason he shouldn't have a few more decent years in him, there wouldn't be many more long journeys. Just coming this far was enough to make him feel like he had one foot in the grave. It had been a long time since he'd been this tired.

"I know," Joe said. "You missed some good times, Bill. And some bad. But that's just the way of it."

"Even after all this time, you still don't want to do honest work?" Carpenter eyed the badge on Joe's chest.

"No one changes that much. I'm not here because

I missed you. The captain wants you to have dinner at the house."

"I didn't write him I was coming. How's he know I'm here?" Carpenter finished his whiskey.

"Must have seen you coming in."

"Must have. Well." He put the glass down. "I suppose I'll make room for him on my crowded itinerary."

CHAPTER SEVEN

CARPENTER'S ITINERARY WASN'T crowded, but the captain's house was.

It was well outside town, high above it, and overlooking it without being too obvious about it. What *was* obvious was how much the man must have spent to build it. Though it was all a single floor, it was sprawled over the ground, finer than it needed to be, but maybe not bigger.

It was full of children. Seventeen by Carpenter's count, and the youngest of them had to be at least ten years old. Not just children, though.

In addition to Joe Fisher and his wife, Reverend Brown was there, and the others. Isaiah, O'Doul, and even Fred. Even in his wildest dreams, Carpenter would never have thought a reunion could be this way. All of them still here, all of them whole and doing well. Fred had put on a bit of paunch, and Isaiah's nose was as red as blood, but they were all still on their feet, surrounded by their families. It was nothing short of a miracle.

The men rushed to him with such warmth and familiarity that their wives and children were left in shock. They all stared, uncomprehending. That stood to reason; if any of the old boys were inclined to tell stories, they probably wouldn't tell the ones about Carpenter. Their wives and children simply didn't know who he was.

That suited him.

"Lord Almighty, Bill," Captain Hale said, entering the foyer. "I never saw a man look taller after this many years. Most of us are starting to shrink."

Hale hadn't shrunk, at least not his middle. His hair was white, though he seemed spry enough. A fair number of these children were his, a lot of daughters.

"Might be I just stand straighter than you remember." Carpenter took his hand and shook.

"I'm so proud that Richmond went well for you."

"I can tell you, Captain, I didn't have anything like this." He gestured at the grand house.

"We're real sorry about Penelope," said Isaiah, his hat in his hand.

"Thank you."

Hale beckoned. "Bill, we'd have eaten an hour ago if not for you. How about we sit?"

It was a sight.

There were lamps outside the house to light up the flower beds, which were full of blooms. Each one of the children at the table wore clothes that had to have cost more than all the men's uniforms in the war combined. There was more food in one dish than the dozen of them had shared in a day.

Carpenter had never been good with names or faces, and tonight would be his worst night yet. He would remember Captain Hale's new wife, who was a startling beauty half his age, but the rest he wasn't so sure about. The wives he would learn eventually. The children's names he might learn if he lived to be a hundred.

It was a cool night with a good breeze through the open windows, just enough to make the smell of the food seem to fill the house. Strange things had come and gone in his time, but he'd never lived in a moment that didn't feel quite real until now.

"What we found," Carpenter replied to Joe, "was that you could do more work if you didn't do it all yourself. If we made the legs in our building, and Pierre made the tabletops at his—well, in the end it meant we were able to move more that way. Later on we bought out Pierre's factory. Now the company has quite a few, not just in Richmond. I was more lucky than smart. They don't need me anymore."

"That's a hell of a thing," Joe said, shaking his head. "Of all of us here, you were the one to strike gold."

That might be, but Carpenter didn't want gold. He wanted his wife, but no sense talking about it. It wasn't fair to have what he didn't want and not what he did. He couldn't get Penelope back, and he couldn't get rid of what he knew. He had a thick skull, or at least several people had said so over the years, but that meant that once something got in, it was there to stay. This was no different.

It was very quiet; even the children listened when Carpenter spoke. He was a curiosity. It wasn't just his height; it was his clothes and how familiar all the men were with him.

A board creaked, and he looked up to see a boy in the doorway, leaning. Carpenter hadn't seen him when he came into the house, but he must have been there. He was the boy who'd been at the lodge and on the trail; there was no mistake. Now he was dressed like he belonged in this house.

"Bill Carpenter," he said.

Carpenter paused in the act of pulling a roll apart. "That's right. I remember you. I'm glad you made it here safe, son."

"You the same coward that killed my uncle Byron?"

Hale choked and put down his wineglass, glaring at the boy. He cleared his throat. "Bill, I'll introduce my oldest, since he hasn't got the manners to do it himself. This is William."

"I'm glad to meet you," Carpenter said evenly.

The boy just stood there, wearing his fine suit as though he'd been born in it. He was so tall that he looked older, but he couldn't be more than seventeen.

"Answer my question," he replied, glaring without blinking.

"I will apologize, Mr. Carpenter," Hale's wife cut in. "He's been in this humor ever since he rode back in."

Carpenter saw the look that passed between Hale and Joe, and Mrs. Hale twitched as her husband touched her thigh.

"That's all right," Carpenter said before anyone else could speak up. "My humor's no better. I'm sorry, son. But I never killed anyone. I can swear to that."

William straightened up, and Joe immediately leaned back in his chair, blocking his path. It wasn't clear what the boy had intended, but that stopped him. William was sore about something—that much was clear—but it couldn't have had anything to do with Carpenter.

"Will, I told you a hundred times you got to watch what you say," Joe warned.

Hale groaned. "Maybe it's not him that needs to speak more careful." He leaned forward, looking up and down the table. "Lord, have mercy. Who told the boy about Byron?"

A moment went by. Carpenter kept his eyes on his plate, not out of politeness, but because he didn't have to look. Of those still living, O'Doul was the only one who might've told the kid something like that. Byron and O'Doul had always been close, and he'd never understood. Even after the dust settled and it all came out, it just hadn't mattered. O'Doul felt the way that he felt, and that was all right.

Carpenter didn't blame him.

Hale put his face in his hand. "O'Doul, if you want to tell my son something that ain't none of his business, can't you at least tell him the truth?"

"Sit," Joe said firmly to the boy.

After a moment, William did so. His mother let out her breath, and some of the others started to eat again, however hesitantly.

Hale picked up his wine again and finished it off. "It was supposed to be a nice night."

"It still is," Carpenter said, shrugging. "The past knocks on the door all the time. No need to let it in if you don't want to. Hell, I been hearing that knock close on twenty years."

"I wish it was that simple, Bill. But I have my constituency to think about," Hale said dryly, gesturing at the others and their families. "Can't let it hang, or William'll just sit and grind his teeth all night." He glanced at the maid. "I suppose we'd better have more wine, if not for them, then for me."

"Or just get the whiskey," Fred said bitterly.

Joe snorted. "Bring it all out, Captain."

"I can't even have a meal without putting you out, sir," Carpenter said.

"There are worse things than a story at dinner, Bill. Even if it ain't the one like to bring the most

cheer. I take a stroll that way once in a while myself."
He sighed. "I just don't like to go that far back."

"Tell the story, Mr. Hale," one of Fred's sons said.

"Yes," Isaiah's wife agreed, eyes bright.

"It ain't a good one," Joe warned, glancing at Carpenter. For what? Permission?

"I've heard worse," Carpenter said lightly.

"Reckon you have." Hale shook his head and rested his chin on his fist, looking out over everyone at the table. "Been a long time since I heard anyone say Byron's name. Strange thing. I scarcely even think about him anymore." He rubbed his face and straightened up. "Sounds all wrong when I say it like that."

"I do," O'Doul said, taking a bottle from the tray as the maid returned.

The captain didn't reply to that. It was obvious he would have liked to let it lie, but there were too many people at the table, and all of them were looking at him expectantly.

"I can tell it," Reverend Brown volunteered.

"No." Just like that, Hale's exhaustion left him, and he smiled. "It's all right. My younger brother, Byron, was with us. This was only a month or so before Seven Pines, I guess. We were withdrawn from the peninsula, and we had some trouble a week or so earlier in travel. That was when we lost Tucker."

Reverend Brown was the only one who lifted his glass. Tucker hadn't been a popular man, but Carpenter still felt a chill at the mention of his name. "Trouble" was the word the captain had chosen for what had happened, but trouble didn't do it justice.

"We were in camp up by that white birch creek. It was us, and the Fifth, and the cavalry out of Baton Rouge, and some of General Johnston's irregulars. There was a pair of Yankee spies that sneaked in, and through the grace of God, they mistook our grain for powder. Now," Hale added firmly, seeing the look on Carpenter's face, "if Bill were telling the story, he'd tell you they weren't spies at all, and they weren't confused about anything. That they were hungry, and that grain was all they wanted. But he's wrong. Dead wrong. They were Yankee spies, and they wanted our powder."

"They were children," Carpenter said. "Can't argue that, can you?"

"They were young, but so were we, and it was war. Ain't nobody a child then, not with McClellan on his way. And of all the people to find those two, it was Bill. And Byron."

"Wasn't even their watch," Joe said bitterly.

That was true; it hadn't been. They'd just been strolling, but Byron's ears had been sharp. Sometimes it was better not to notice everything.

"They confronted them, and all they had to do was raise the alarm. But Bill didn't want to do that," Hale said with a very direct look that Carpenter didn't have any difficulty matching, "though I don't know that was Bill's fault. It was the timing. That's what it was. Not a month earlier, we were camped with Pierre's men, and they had caught some deserters, and Bill didn't like the way they treated their prisoners. He was afraid that if these two spies were taken it would be the same. So he wanted them to leave. Quietly."

"Letting spies go isn't cowardice," one of the wives piped up. "It's treason."

"He didn't think they were spies," Joe grunted, pouring more whiskey.

Carpenter helped himself to some as well. It was miraculous how quickly an evening could take a turn. He would have his memories for life, and rumors—rumors were almost as long-lived. But he'd never heard it told this way.

It wasn't as bad as he might have expected. At

least not for him. Carpenter made a point not to look at William or O'Doul.

The weather was perfect, but it suddenly felt like the dead of winter, and that wouldn't change. No one was eating, so there was no clinking of cutlery to disturb the silence. Not even the owls were making themselves heard out in the dark.

"Were they or weren't they?" Mrs. Hale demanded.

"We'll never know, ma'am," Carpenter told her frankly.

"Byron had a little more sense than Bill did. He called out, and one of those two had a pistol, and he brought it out. Bill had his rifle, though, so it might've gone either way." Joe gave a little shrug and scratched his chin.

"And everyone heard Byron shout, so everyone saw what happened," the reverend said. Not *everyone*, no—but enough people, certainly.

"That boy was going to shoot Byron, but Bill had his rifle on him, so he didn't."

Carpenter remembered the standoff. Hale hadn't been there himself, though most of the men at this table had.

So far, the tale matched his memories. The captain's whiskey was awfully good, but Carpenter didn't taste it, though he was drinking it like water.

"And then he did what he did. With every eye in four companies watching." Hale shrugged, eyeing his wineglass. "He threw his rifle down."

Nobody said anything, but the looks on their faces were enough.

"And he did something even more interesting," O'Doul said, though without any real malice. "He told them he wasn't going to shoot them."

"Only these two, they weren't as compassionate, and that one with the pistol went to kill old Bill,"

Hale said quickly. "And Byron, being Byron, went and tried to push him out of the way. They only got loose the one bullet before they were shot down, the both of them Yankee spies. Byron was dead before he hit the ground, and so were they, and that was all. Bill didn't *kill* Byron." He glared at O'Doul, then looked at William, who was rapt. "You hear that, Will?"

"Yes, sir," the boy replied.

"He tried to do those spies a kindness, and Byron paid for it with everyone watching. And there were a few of them that didn't take kindly to it." Hale looked distant. "They took him all the way to Richmond and saw him charged. Most wasteful thing you ever saw. Twenty men at least, and at least as many officers in Richmond all stopped what they're doing because a few real cowards saw Bill act a fool and wanted . . ." He shrugged. "I don't know what they wanted. Revenge? Justice? I never could understand why they wanted to see one of our own hang. *Bill* wasn't the spy, for God's sake. Took me and Joe, and . . . Isaiah, and the reverend, and damn near half of us a whole week to make that tribunal understand."

"If the trial had gone any longer, we'd have missed Seven Pines," Carpenter pointed out, smiling back at Joe.

"And then there'd be even more of us at this table," Joe remarked. "And not quite so many under the dirt."

"Joe Fisher," he wife chided, pinching him. "Have respect."

"Got none left, darling."

"We did, at the end, make them see. Old Bill didn't hang." Hale held up his empty glass in a mock toast. "Closest thing to a victory I ever had to my name as an officer."

"Why?" William asked, baffled. "He don't seem concerned by it. Does *he* even remember Uncle Byron?"

Joe about spat his drink out. "Oh, I reckon he does," he told the boy.

Carpenter just rubbed his eyes.

"He does," Hale agreed. "Show the boy sometime, Bill. Just not when we're eating."

"Show me what?"

"Take your elbow off the table," Mrs. Hale said, moving William's arm for him, but he just glared at Carpenter.

"Show me *what*, Bill Carpenter?"

"Can't you just be easy, Will? The man took twenty lashes."

A few of the men winced at the captain's words, and the wives all went pale. Carpenter wasn't going to say it, but the truth was that he didn't think about it much. Not these days.

But he couldn't forget, and no one would let him. Even someone as polite as Silva had noticed the state of his back.

"That one from the fort died after ten strokes. You remember that, Joe?" Roy asked.

"I do, Reverend."

"That son of a gun wasn't half Bill's size, though," O'Doul cut in, "and that fellow that lashed him was bigger than the one what hit Bill."

"Gentlemen," Mrs. Hale said, arching an eyebrow. "The story is over. Do we need to dwell on whippings?"

Her husband was about to agree, but William spoke up. "The story ain't over. Father still hasn't told why he went to fight for this man," he said.

"We *all* fought for him, Will," Joe said, setting his whiskey glass down. "Why? Why else *would* you fight? For anyone but your family? That's what we were, and that's what we are. Because it's what you *do*, son. You think Bill wouldn't have done the same for us?"

"Don't look like that," Hale said sharply, seeing William's scowl. "Every word Joe said is true."

The boy just shook his head in disgust. Then he leaned back and snorted, crossing his arms.

"Of all the men to share a name with," he said.

Joe glanced at Hale, annoyed, but then that went away, replaced with a smile. "Enough," he said. "It's enough. I want pie."

So did Carpenter; it was over there on the sideboard waiting, but everyone had been too arrested by the account of his disgrace. After the war, it had clung to him in Richmond, and it was no surprise that it would have to cling to him here as well.

The years made it easier to live with.

"No," Hale replied, stopping the maid with a look. "No, not enough. Not yet. William, nothing is shared. Only given. Would you like to know why I named you after this man?"

The boy rolled his eyes. "Oh, I know. He saved your life. Or something like that. Is that it?"

Hale and Carpenter exchanged a look.

"Not that I recall," Carpenter said.

"Nor I."

"The captain saved my life with the tribunal," Carpenter told the boy. "I never saved his. I did poison him once, though it was not my intent."

"We learned not to let Bill cook fairly early," Isaiah explained.

"I believe I mentioned it earlier, that we had difficulty on the march to Richmond in the summer, a few weeks before the battle," Hale said, speaking over Joe's laughter. "We were ambushed, after a fashion. There were escaped slaves making north, and they believed we were there for them. We were not, but they didn't know that. They got the jump on us in the road."

For just a moment, the silence had been gone, but just like that it was back. Carpenter didn't like this story any more than the last one.

"My horse startled, and I fell and hit my head on a rock. Joe took a bullet right away. They realized their mistake the moment they came at us, but we didn't know what was happening. There were eighty of us, and about the same of them. We were soldiers, and armed, and they . . . were armed as well, but they were not soldiers. I was out cold. That left Tucker."

A few of the men groaned. No one really had a grudge with Tucker, or ever had. He just wasn't meant to lead people—that was all. They'd known it back then as well as they knew it now.

"There were some whites with them, and Tucker didn't want to let them go."

"Nor should he," one of the other boys piped up, one of Isaiah's sons.

"Our numbers were even," Hale explained patiently. "But scrapping over some runners wouldn't have helped us beat the Yankees. We'd have licked them." He shrugged. "No question of that. But how many people wouldn't be at this table?" He gestured at them all. "Which one of us would have caught a bullet? I was lying in the road; I might've been trampled. Anyone with sense knew it wasn't a fight worth having. Tucker, though." He shook his head. "Tucker didn't have no sense."

"We all knew it, but Bill was the one who did something about it," Joe said. "Knocked Tucker flat before he could give the order. Talked those runners into backing down and going on their way. They was as relieved to go as we was to let them. The captain was laid out. If Bill hadn't've done it, someone would've fired. Maybe Tucker, maybe them. But Bill stopped it. Walked out there with his hands up. Talbot died from his wound in the starting of it, but the rest of us are sitting here because Bill didn't let Tucker give that order."

"Which is the reason Bill couldn't hang for what happened with Byron," Reverend Brown added. "They wanted to charge him with cowardice, and we all knew that wasn't true. There was nothing cowardly in anything he did. He made a mistake, that's all."

"Byron had a lot of friends," Hale said bitterly. "And it got around, what happened, more lies than truths, I'm sure. But no matter what anyone says, old Bill's no coward. He's just soft. I don't know if that's any better, but it ain't for me to judge. Or if it is, then I forgive it, because there's no sense doing otherwise."

"Surprised you could survive as a factory boss," O'Doul said, sounding more tired than vicious. "Didn't you ever have to fire a man?"

"Never much minded firing," Carpenter replied absently, his eyes on the pie. "It's shooting that I don't care for."

"Do you understand, William?" Joe asked.

"Understand what?" the boy asked obstinately.

"That Bill is one of us," Hale said. "One of the smarter ones too, if his fortunes are anything to judge by. The man made his way proper, even if he don't show it off."

A moment went by; then the boy smiled.

"Fair enough. Been a long time since you told me a story, Pa. I apologize, Mr. Carpenter." He glanced across the table. "Were you there, then? At Seven Pines?"

The hush over the table deepened. There had been a few skirmishes, but Seven Pines was the only battle they had all fought together. No one really *wanted* it brought up, but it had a way of happening around Bill. It probably did for the rest as well.

"He was," Hale told William. "With his back still bleeding. But Bill did his job. He *always* did his job."

"Well, all right." After a moment, William shrugged. "I got a brother that's soft. I love him anyway."

One of the other boys threw a roll at him, and Hale relaxed.

"You all right there, Bill?" He clapped Carpenter on the shoulder.

"I don't know, sir. Now that all my business is in the street, I'm inclined to leave town."

Hale just laughed.

CHAPTER EIGHT

A SHOT SPLIT the night. Then another.

"He's got a good eye," Carpenter observed, taking a drink from the ladle. He was at the well behind Hale's house, in his beautiful garden. A row of columns flanked a pathway that led to a firepit, past which the boys were shooting the empty wine bottles from dinner.

William hadn't missed one yet.

Hale was just a few steps away, watching the others.

"He didn't get it from me," the captain said.

Carpenter pulled up another bucket and dipped the ladle again. He'd had too much whiskey; if he didn't drink this water now, his head would kill him in the morning, if nothing else did first.

"I saw you kill two Yankees with two bullets," he said, "as I recall. With that Navy six you won in Charlotte."

"Hell, Bill. They weren't but ten feet away."

Carpenter shrugged and drank. "Two more than I ever killed."

It was just the two of them.

"Is Yates still with you?" he asked Hale.

"Of course. He's on business, or he'd have been here tonight, I'm sure. He'll be mighty pleased you've come home to us, Bill."

"I sure would like to see him again."

"You weren't going to leave, were you?" Hale asked.

"I certainly was."

"After you ate my food?"

"Seemed you have plenty," Carpenter pointed out.

Hale snorted and joined him, perching on the well with a groan. "Well, I can't let you go, Bill. I still think of you as a friend, so it wouldn't be right. Not before I have a word with you about the company you're keeping."

"Who do you mean?" Carpenter winced as another shot went echoing up and down the valley. The fire in the pit was built so hot that the embers were floating up as high as the treetops, glowing all the way. It was a touch foolish; you could start a fire this way when things were dry.

"That skinny Mexican boy, Silva."

"He seems all right. Wouldn't let an old man walk the trail alone. He let me ride with him." Carpenter smiled. "Even offered to shoot my horse for me. If that isn't kindness, I don't know what is."

"He ain't what he seems like."

"None of us are," he reminded the captain.

"He wants all this for himself." Hale made a sweeping gesture. "I warned him to move on along to somewhere else."

"What right do you have to do that?"

"Every right. I built this town, Bill. This ain't the

place for him. I have told him. Everyone sees it but him. He won't succeed. He'll never get his factory built, never do what he thinks he wants to do."

Carpenter scratched his chin; he needed a shave. "Seems to me there are a few that could use the work," he said hesitantly. "Men to build it up, work the factory, move the guns. He said something about metal works as well."

The captain waved a hand. "Even if it was all up and running, he can't be trusted. A man like that."

"Like what?"

"He's not one of us, Bill."

"A soldier? I think he has too much sense for that."

"He's of low moral character," Hale said, annoyed. "You haven't seen it like we have."

"What's he done?"

"Were you introduced to O'Doul's oldest? Fiona?"

Carpenter squinted, trying to remember, but the whiskey was making it difficult. "Blue flowers in her hair," he guessed.

"That's her. Silva made overtures for some time."

"Was she inclined toward him?"

"Very much."

Carpenter held back a yawn. William probably hadn't cared for that.

"But he only led her on," Hale went on. "He did not make an offer of marriage. There was some impropriety."

Carpenter was taken aback. He was beginning to understand the captain's desire to find flaws in Silva's character, but was that really the worst he could come up with? It wasn't even a genuine scandal. And purely on intuition, he had a suspicion that Silva had only backed away because O'Doul had probably threatened him. O'Doul was a solid, reliable man who had never been afraid of hard work. He was the sort of fellow Carpenter looked for when it was time to hire. But he wasn't an easy man to get along with, and Carpenter doubted that part of him had changed.

"For God's sake, that's nothing you and I didn't do a dozen times or more when we were younger," Carpenter told him. "Are we of low character?"

"We're grown," Hale replied. "Would we engage in that behavior now, Bill?"

"I like to think not."

The captain nodded sagely. "He ain't right for this town, this place. I am truly sorry he did not take my advice." For a moment he was drowned out by laughter from the children, who were now gathered around the firepit. Carpenter couldn't see what was happening over there, but it sounded like a nice time.

"He's a clever man," Hale admitted, watching the children. "I have to hand him that much. Coming up with them rifles. They will sell. Two-thirds the cost of a Winchester, and very nearly as good. But all those brains he has," he said, glancing over at Carpenter, "and no sense."

Carpenter snorted, nodding. "You're right about that."

"I'm glad you're here, Bill. They're good boys, but Joe's the only one I can trust not to smoke next to the powder. We can use your help."

"With what?"

"With business, of course. You were a factory man. You've got a good head for it."

Carpenter looked up at the stars, grimacing. "You thinking of opening a factory, Captain?"

"It worked for you, didn't it?"

"I suppose it did."

"You had better stay here with us tonight, Bill. Comfort starts to mean something when you get to our age."

"Best tuck me in, then," Carpenter replied, getting to his feet. "I'm not thirsty anymore. In fact, I'm nearly drowned." That wasn't a lie; he really should have put a stop to the whiskey earlier.

The women gathered up the children, and the men got the horses. One by one, they made off for their own homes, some taking the time to speak to Carpenter, some just going ahead.

O'Doul made his way over, brushing a firefly from his shirt and taking off his hat. He stood in front of Carpenter, chewing his lip. "I owe you an apology, Bill."

"It's all right."

"Then you accept?"

"Of course I do."

"I don't remember telling the boy," O'Doul said, leaning in close and shaking Carpenter's hand. "But I have no doubt that I did. Maybe I was at drink. I would not lie on you sober, Bill."

"I know." Carpenter squeezed his shoulder.

He'd been looking forward to that feather bed in the hotel, but Hale's house was just as good, if not better. Lacy curtains framed the windows of the guest room, and the bed was covered with a fine thick quilt. It looked so good that Carpenter felt a touch of the closest thing to temper that he had in decades. It really was uncanny, the way these things tended to play out.

The bed called to him.

But he went to the window, opened it, and climbed out into the night.

CHAPTER NINE

T HE WALK BACK to town in the dark was more
  treacherous than it was difficult, and those third
and fourth glasses of whiskey were no help at all.
Carpenter wanted to move faster, but it wasn't safe,
and with the men still trickling out of Hale's property
with their families, he couldn't use the road.

Branches snapped and pine needles slipped under
his boots as he picked his way downhill, guided by
the glow of town and the faint music on the breeze.
The night was at least cool, if not exactly pleasant.

It was really something, what Hale had built here.
Not the house; there were big, fine houses wherever
you went. But to have kept them all together this way,
and for so long, it really was an accomplishment.
Captain Hale never had led them to any victories, but
that was no fault of his. He *had* kept most of them
alive. And now he was keeping them together.

During the war, no one could have asked for a better leader. And even now it was probably difficult not to feel the same way about the man.

There was a fight in the street when Carpenter came out of the trees, brushing himself off, and no one noticed. One fight, and hardly anyone watching. A few girls gazed from a balcony, visibly bored. If there was gold in this valley, there would be full streets right now, commerce still going strong, and those girls would not have been idle.

Silva wasn't in the taproom in the hotel, though there *was* a man handing a tiny piece of gold to the barman. There was gold, then. Just not enough of it. No amount would ever be enough to keep everyone happy, but it wouldn't take much to keep a camp like this alive. Still, it seemed like even that was too much to ask for.

Upstairs, Carpenter paused on the landing to look down the hallway lined with doors. Silva's room was the third on the right, next door to his own. He had no house to sleep in, after all.

Below, someone laughed loudly.

Carpenter's one goal for the day had been to find and purchase a new horse, but that hadn't happened.

The sounds of the fight outside were gone; it was over, and he hoped both men still had their lives. He'd thrown more than his share of punches in his time, so he didn't know why it bothered him so much to see it this way. Maybe it was because things just weren't quite the same as he remembered. In his mind, folks might fight over money, or a girl, and there wasn't really any helping it.

Now it seemed they all wanted to fight over an insult, or just because life wasn't going their way. That was harder to understand.

He went quietly to his room and took the chair from the table, carrying it out into the hall. He set it down gently and took a seat. It wasn't long before he was shifting around and leaning the chair back on two legs so he could rest his back against the wall. Comfort wasn't an option, so he'd have to find a way to wait that wouldn't leave him walking like a hunchback if morning came and he was still alive to see it.

The town grew quieter, and it wasn't particularly late. These buildings were all but a year or two old, and well-built. Hale had made a real effort in Antelope Valley, and the expense must have been considerable.

But there weren't enough people or enough prospectors to give it what it needed. It wouldn't be enough for someone to just find a little gold and spark a rush. They'd need a reason to stay. This was rich land, but would those prospectors stay for that when they could chase gold elsewhere? *Someone* must have found something to start all this; maybe that fellow had just kept all the luck for himself.

THREE FULL HOURS passed before he showed up. Carpenter opened his eyes, though he hadn't been dozing. There wasn't any danger of that in a wooden chair in a hallway. There'd been a time when he could have slept anywhere, and that had been his greatest advantage during his days in uniform, but too many years had passed since then.

There were only two lamps in the hall, but he'd have known Joe Fisher anywhere.

He straightened up, the chair creaking in the thick silence.

Joe's face was hidden in shadow, but there was no mystery about what sort of look would be on it. He'd believed Carpenter was at the house up on the hill, fast asleep in Hale's guest room.

Joe could have, if he'd chosen to, turned around and gone back down the stairs. Carpenter would've preferred that; it would have allowed him to go to his bed.

But he didn't. Joe moved forward, treading lightly, though the boards underfoot squealed anyway. As he came closer, the lamplight caught on the old Navy pistol at his hip. And the handle of a sizable buck knife. He hadn't been wearing either of them a few hours ago.

His hand wasn't on the gun; it was on the knife.

Carpenter got stiffly to his feet, stretching and stepping into the center of the hall. Joe stopped just a few paces away, glancing at Silva's door.

"I expected Fred," Carpenter said, stifling a yawn. Fred was . . . Well, Fred was the type for this sort of thing. Or maybe not; maybe it was better if the sheriff was the one to do it.

Joe had thoughtfully taken off his badge for this errand.

"Figures the only part of you ain't soft is your head," Joe replied, glancing at the door. "He in there?"

"I suspect."

"How about you go on to bed, Bill? It's late. Or early, rather."

Carpenter sighed. "I could." He hooked his fingers into his belt and returned the other man's gaze. "But I don't know that I could sleep."

"I *am* an elected official. Suppose I was issuing you an order," Joe said quietly, though his heart wasn't in it.

"Is it a lawful one?"

"You planning on pulling on me, Bill?"

"I suppose I could." He frowned and patted himself down. "If I had a pistol, that is. But wouldn't you know it, Joe? I'm unarmed." Carpenter spread his hands and smiled. "How's that for luck?"

"I'd say that what I know of your life, you best not talk about luck. You already had your share."

"No argument from me."

The door opened, startling them both. Silva peered out, a little blearily.

"Mr. Carpenter," he said, turning to squint at Joe. "And Mr. Fisher. Sheriff Fisher," he amended.

Joe's jaw went tight, and a muscle throbbed in his cheek. "Evening, Mr. Silva," he said.

That was all the time it took for Silva to wake up. The bleariness was gone, and nothing was lost on him. Questions could swim around in swarms like fish, and they could go away just as quickly, all at once, and all in a flash of glittery scales—and then it was as though they'd never been there to begin with. Clarity was what Carpenter had wanted, and now that he had it, it would've been nice to just give it back.

"Is everything all right?" Silva asked, a look of placid neutrality taking over his face. The man didn't have an ounce of sense, but he had at least a little nerve.

"Joe's an old friend of mine. So are his friends," Carpenter said, "as it happens. We fought the blue bellies together, in years back. Though it could be said that we didn't do a particularly good job of it."

"I see," Silva replied. There wasn't any alarm in his eyes. Just a little more melancholy than before. "It's good to have friends, Mr. Carpenter."

"It certainly is. I apologize for disturbing you. Me and Joe are just having a little trouble falling asleep, that's all."

He looked at Joe, but the other man didn't say a word. Silva stood in his doorway, holding his lamp.

"I wonder that I won't have trouble sleeping now myself," he said after a moment of the terrible silence. Awkwardness was a pest, a stubborn animal that would creep into your house and you'd have to tire yourself shooing it out. This wasn't awkwardness, though. It was something a little more dangerous.

Carpenter kept his eyes on Joe, but the sheriff wasn't moving his hands.

"Seeing that we're all awake," he said, watching the way Silva was working so hard to keep still, "and the bar is closed, do you have any more of that whiskey? I know you do, Mr. Silva. What do you say, Joe? How about a drink?"

Joe let his breath out and put his hands on his hips. "Hell, Bill. When'd you ever know me to turn that down?"

"Oh, I don't know, Joe. Sometimes you don't know a man as well as you think."

"May I dress?" Silva asked dryly. Without waiting for an answer, he shut the door. Joe took a step back, putting his hand on his pistol, but he was just being careful.

Silva wasn't the type to shoot through a door, though it wasn't the worst thing he could've tried.

As the moments passed, neither of them made a sound. Carpenter just waited, and Joe watched him with a new look, one he'd never worn before. They'd walked more than one patrol together, after all. It felt like that, only they weren't wearing gray now, as they let the time pass.

"Don't tell William," Carpenter said after a moment, "but you know it don't bother me, what I did. Or what I didn't do."

Joe's brows rose. "Is that so?"

"It bothers me that it was so sudden." Carpenter rubbed his cheek, then hooked his thumb back into his belt. "I don't know that Byron ever really knew it. You saw."

"I did."

And he'd been the one to tell Hale what had happened. Joe must have given the captain a narrative that was friendly to him, or Carpenter wouldn't have been here now.

When the door opened, Silva was halfway presentable and carrying a bottle by the neck.

His pistol, polished metal and pearl handles shining, was on his belt. That didn't seem to bother Joe.

"It wouldn't be good manners to talk here," Silva told them, "with everyone sleeping. Shall we take the air?"

"Might as well," Carpenter replied, struggling with another yawn.

"Lie down," Silva said quietly to Maria, who was just behind him, still in the room. She obediently padded to a little nest of blankets on the floor and curled up. "After you, Sheriff," Silva went on, gesturing graciously.

Joe's smile was a work in progress, on its way to becoming a smirk, but he stopped it there and shook his head, making for the stairs.

They followed him out of the hotel to find that the night's chill had set in fully. Joe's horse was just up the street, tied up outside the hardware store.

The sheriff took a few steps into the empty street. There weren't many lights in the dark. Someone, voice slurred by drink, was talking in one of the alleys. The wind rustled the pines and stirred up the dry dust. The stars were out, and half the moon with them.

"When exactly did you all settle here?" Carpenter asked Joe, taking in the camp. He could see it as it must have begun, and that wasn't so different from how it was now.

"At the beginning."

"That long, and all these people have stayed even

when the gold ain't coming," he said, looking up and down the street. It wasn't a great many people, but for a town where the prospect had never come to anything? Were they holding out, keeping their faith in their claims? "That is a wonder, isn't it?"

"Beautiful country," Silva replied, watching the treetops sway, the dark mountaintops rearing up behind them. "Why would anyone want to leave?"

He offered his bottle of Overholt to Carpenter, who passed it along to Joe.

"How about this way?" the sheriff suggested, taking a drink and gesturing with the bottle. Carpenter was going to say something, but Silva just started to walk, and he thought better of it. It was best not to be more of a busybody than he already was.

"You fought together," Silva said, accepting the bottle back from Joe as they strolled.

Someone was watching from a window above the bank, but Carpenter wasn't worried about anyone like that. It was someone a little closer that he needed to keep his eye on.

"We did," Joe replied, his thumb tracing the handle of his knife.

Silva clearly wasn't as worried about courtesy as he had been in the past. He was ready to indulge his curiosity, and who could blame him? He'd come back here to a crowd of enemies and the news that they'd burned his home and everything in it. It was a miracle he had any manners left at all.

"Where?" he asked.

"Here and there. The big one wasn't far from Richmond," Carpenter told him.

"What was it like?"

"Like any other fight," Joe replied without hesitation. He paused, squinting into the alley between the feed seller and the barber. Even without the tin on his chest, a little of the sheriff in him could bubble up to the surface.

Even on a night like this.

"Waste of time, waste of men," Carpenter said to Silva. "Nobody won, everybody lost. McClellan didn't reach the city. Close as the federals ever got, as a matter of fact."

Joe just shook his head.

"That laundry was shut up just like that during the day," Carpenter said, pointing at the dark building. "What's the matter there? Even if there's no gold, it ain't as though we don't all wear clothes."

"Empty. There were two families who opened it," Silva said, swinging the whiskey bottle at his side.

"Chinamen," Joe noted.

"They ran a good business. A pleasure to deal with. Then they left."

"Weren't right for the town," Joe said tiredly.

"Who *is* right for the town?" Carpenter asked curiously.

"You are, Bill. In fact, there's a need, a real need, for a man who works with his hands, with the wood. Putting things together," Joe said dryly. "Like tables and chairs. There's a word for it."

"There *is* such a word," Silva agreed.

"Very funny, boys."

They had reached the end of the street. Silva paused in the middle of the road, which would quickly become no more than a trail.

"I still need a horse," Carpenter said.

"Take one of mine," Silva replied.

"Don't you need them for your wagon?"

"No, they've served that purpose. That's my land up there, Mr. Carpenter." Silva pointed, and Carpenter looked, but trees blocked the view. Silva had a plot similar to Hale's: above the town, but with more timber for privacy.

"Anything left of your house?"

"Not worth keeping," Silva said, stepping off the trail and going into the trees. "No gold, but there is a hot spring. I've become attached to that."

"You want to stay over a spring?" Joe asked tiredly.

Silva hadn't said one word about what had brought him to Antelope Valley. He had made plans for firearms, and he had been to school. He had a little money, though Carpenter sensed it wasn't as much as people might think from looking at him. He had a letter from the Army for an order of rifles, enough of them to make the job worthwhile. He had prospects, and he had manners.

That was all Carpenter knew. He accepted the bottle and pretended to drink, then gave it to Joe, who didn't pretend.

The pine needles rustled quietly underfoot. It was a change for the better. There were some comforts and conveniences in the city, but there were also noise and smells and no peace.

There wasn't peace here, either.

Joe's body language was giving him away. The charade of civility couldn't go on.

Carpenter looked back, but the lights of the settlement were already blocked by the trees.

They crested a rise, and below lay a clearing with a small pool, the reflection of the moon making a white disk on the still surface.

"Is that the spring?" Carpenter asked.

"That's just standing water." Silva gazed down at it. "We aren't on my property yet. Does this location suit your purposes, Sheriff?"

Joe's hand was resting on the handle of his Navy.

"It'll have to," he said, taking a step to his right. "Is that one of yours? You invent that shooter, Mr. Silva?"

Silva didn't move toward his gun. "I did."

"Then why are you selling rifles?"

"It's a prototype, Sheriff. It is neither practical nor profitable to produce."

"Does it at least shoot straight?"

"You'll know in a moment. Is this the best time for these questions?"

"I can't ask a dead man," Joe pointed out.

"Get more use out of a rifle," Carpenter said mildly. "Can't put dinner on the table with that," he added, indicating Joe's Navy with his eyes.

"Just watch me, Bill. I'm about to."

"He's quicker than you, Joe." Was he? Probably not, but Joe didn't know that.

"I ain't as old as you, Bill."

"Nor as smart." Carpenter stepped between them, truly taken aback. Had Joe really intended to pull? Even in front of him? His intent at the hotel had been clear, but that should have gone away as soon as he saw he was exposed. What was this? What was he thinking?

He was thinking that it didn't matter, and he was right. He was the sheriff, and who was Carpenter? An old friend, yes. Beyond that?

Nobody.

"What's the matter with you, Joe? You really want to kill a man because you don't like him?"

The other man looked set. "I don't want to, not in particular. I have to."

"Mr. Carpenter," Silva warned.

"Quiet," Carpenter said without looking back.

"Oh, stop it, your holiness," Joe groaned.

"I can't tell which of you has less brains," Carpenter hissed at Joe. "You boys for bothering this man for no good reason, or *you* for not knowing when you're beat," he snarled at Silva.

He was about to go on, and no doubt to raise his voice considerably, but something caught his eye. Joe looked as well, and Silva couldn't help but do the same. For a moment Joe and Silva both forgot their guns.

A stag had emerged from the trees down by the water, intending to drink. It would've been a fine animal under any circumstances, but this one wasn't normal. Its coat was white, and under the harsh naked moonlight, it shone so brightly that Carpenter almost had to squint at the silvery glow.

He'd heard of animals like this, but this one had to be one in a million.

For a moment, no one spoke. They watched in silence as it moved closer to the water.

Carpenter had forgotten whatever he'd been about to say. He might've stood and watched all night if Joe hadn't spoken.

"I wager that skin is worth a hundred dollars," he said under his breath. "The head, twice that or more."

Carpenter smiled. "Glad I don't need the money, then."

"I do," Joe replied, and Carpenter looked over sharply. His friend had forgotten about Silva, and he looked pained. "Could use one of your rifles right now," he whispered to Silva, who grinned.

That was easy to say, but they were at least eighty yards from the animal. The stag was drinking in peace.

Carpenter envied that. "Well?" he muttered to Joe, glancing at the knife on his belt. "You want to use that for what it's meant for? Make a dollar honestly? Or does that offend your delicate sensibilities?"

"Age has not made you more agreeable, Bill." The sheriff's voice was tight.

"Why should it have? Or do you have pressing business elsewhere?"

"I have pressing business here."

"Then shoot me and get on with it," Carpenter said impatiently.

Joe glared at him, then looked back down at the stag. He shook his head in disgust. "You going to help me, Bill?"

"Of course. You won't get but one shot."

Joe glanced down at his Navy. It was only a thirty-six. It might do if he was close enough. It would have to be a good shot, though. Then he looked past Carpenter.

"How about it, Silva?" Joe asked. "If I only get the one shot, it should come from yours."

"I'm flattered that you trust my design."

"I trust a bigger bullet."

Joe put his hand out. Carpenter had been about to take a drink from the whiskey bottle, but he stopped. Silva's smile stayed in place.

"It wouldn't be very neighborly of me to say no, would it?" He drew the gun and offered the handle.

"I'll return it," Joe promised wryly, taking the larger pistol and tucking it into his belt.

"Right behind that front leg," Carpenter told him.

"I know how to kill a deer, Bill."

"I'd expect you to. But I'd also expect you not to build a gold town in a valley with no gold," he added. "And here we are."

"Ought've just shot you both," Joe grumbled. "You stay here, Silva. You make more noise than a column of blue bellies. Go left, Bill."

"I know how to stalk a deer, Joe," Carpenter replied, imitating the other man's voice.

"Yet you can't put down your own damn horse?" Joe whispered back, struggling out of his boots.

Carpenter didn't say anything to that, but he took his own boots off, handed the bottle to Silva, and crept into the trees. He scooped up a handful of needles and crushed them, rubbing the scent on his hands as he felt his way down the slope.

Joe was off to his right, making a wider circle and even less noise. It had been a long time since either had had reason reason to move quietly, but it wasn't a skill one could forget, even if he wanted to.

The stag looked up from the pool, but not toward either of them. Something else had caught its attention.

Joe was within ten yards, but he was still creeping forward, so it wasn't close enough. Apparently he didn't feel quite as cocky as he had acted in front of Silva.

Carpenter was a little farther back, but there was less cover for him. He couldn't go any nearer without being smelled or seen. And if the wind changed, the stag would bolt at once. There wasn't much time.

Joe stopped, leaning against a tree and laying Silva's revolver over his arm. It wouldn't be an easy shot with a pistol, but it was feasible.

Carpenter put a hand up, and Joe returned the signal. Gently, he used his foot to find a small stick on the ground and eased out from behind his tree. With painstaking slowness, he let his weight down. The stick broke.

The stag went rigid and looked straight at him, presenting its left flank to Joe.

Then there was no sign of it, as though it had never been there, vanishing into the trees so quickly that it left stars in Capenter's eyes, and nothing but a silent curtain of pine needles floating to the ground like snowflakes as the hoofbeats faded away.

Shaking off his surprise, Carpenter went out into

the open as Joe did the same, looking wistfully after the stag, which was now long gone.

Carpenter had given Joe the best shot he could hope for, but the sheriff hadn't taken it. Carpenter just looked at him, puzzled. The other man gave him a scowl.

"Handsome animal," Joe said after a moment. "It would be a waste to kill it."

He whirled and brought up the pistol, taking aim at the object sailing toward him, but for a second time, he didn't fire. Joe snatched the whiskey bottle out of the air, but it hadn't been flung at him with malice; it had only been tossed.

Silva came out of the woods, carrying their boots. "More like you didn't want us to see you miss," he said.

"Am I the wisest man to provoke?" Joe asked, irked.

"If not the wisest, then at least the ugliest."

"I liked that stag more than I like you, Silva."

"You'll shoot an unarmed man?"

"Depends what his mouth's doing."

Silva just threw the boots on the ground and looked expectant.

After a moment, Joe lowered the pistol's hammer and twirled it idly on his finger.

"That's the second time you've lost your nerve tonight, Joe," Carpenter remarked. "How long before they start calling *you* soft?"

"I've been called worse," Joe replied, going up to Silva, who stood his ground. "Better soft than dead. Or deaf." He held out the pistol. Without hesitation, Silva took it, then the bottle as well.

"You know, Joe," Carpenter said, beginning to pull on his boots, "I've had this dream."

"Yeah?" Joe was standing in shadow; they couldn't see his face as he picked up his own boots.

"I wake up in my bed, in my house. It's only me."
Carpenter straightened up and faced him. "Penelope
ain't there. I'm always by myself." He shook his head.
"I've had this dream half a dozen times at least. I have
a lot of dreams like that. Over and over."

"The same ones?" Joe asked, still standing in the
dark. Silva took a drink from the bottle, saying nothing, though his left hand was still on his belt, right
next to the gun.

Carpenter nodded. "They don't seem to change,
and they don't get no easier. I get up, and I get dressed.
And I have breakfast."

"You don't cook it, do you? That's how you'd know
it was a dream," Joe pointed out.

"No, I don't cook it," Carpenter went on impatiently,
scowling at him. "And I remember Byron, and I know
that it would be all right if I could tell him. If I could
tell him why I did what I did. Why that was the way it
had to be. If he knew, he wouldn't mind."

"Wouldn't mind being dead?"

"He wouldn't," Carpenter told him flatly. "And in
my dream, I finish eating, and I go out and start my
walk, because it ain't that far. And I'm in the best humor I've ever been in, because everything else . . ." He
trailed off, gesturing toward his head. "Everything
else is getting old, but my memory's still good. I remember what it's like to wake up like we did." He
paused. "Do what we did." Then he smiled. "So I
never did mind going to the factory, but it's different in
the dream. I'm so happy."

"Why are you happy in the dream, Bill?" Joe asked
tiredly.

"Because I know that when I get to the factory,
Byron's going to be there. And I'll tell him. I'll tell
him everything, and then he'll know."

"Yeah?"

Carpenter nodded. "So I walk to work, and I go in, and I go up the stairs to the office."

Joe put his hands on his hips and waited. "And then what?"

Carpenter shrugged. "And that's always when morning comes."

Silva held out the bottle to Joe, who didn't take it. After a moment, the sheriff just turned and started away.

"Does Mr. Silva need to mind his back with you?" Carpenter called after him.

Joe stopped. "Bill, do you really believe that tonight I came to take his life?" He looked back over his shoulder. "I came to save it. To make him understand, because he don't." He pointed at Silva, who didn't react. "He never should have come back. He *needs* to understand. You both do, by the look of it."

That was all he had to say.

They watched him go. Carpenter knelt at the edge of the water to take a drink, and after a while, Silva joined him, sitting down on the smooth rocks. There were some clouds in the sky now, and the stars didn't seem quite as bright.

Silva toyed with the bottle in his hands, which was still half full. "Do you believe him?" he asked.

About not being at the hotel to murder him? Carpenter shook the water from his hands and sat back, looking up. "Do *you*?" he asked.

CHAPTER TEN

I N RICHMOND, DAWN liked to creep around as though it had something to hide. In Antelope Valley, it came in a flood. One moment there were a murky haze and the sounds of a few hesitant birds, and the next it was as bright as noon.

The bed in the hotel lived up to Carpenter's expectations, and leaving it was as difficult as putting Oceana down. His back, his head, and general principle were just a few of the reasons he had not to hurry, but the noise of the settlement rising with the sun wouldn't let him go on as he was. His dreams were as reliable as the sunrise, but at the moment, they were the least of his worries.

So as he had many times before, he shook them off and turned his back.

The canteen downstairs wasn't as full as it should've been, but there were enough men in it that it took him a moment to spot Hale. He was at the counter drinking coffee and waiting. It was telling, the way they all stayed away from him. He was a gregarious fellow and the town's patron. These people should have flocked to him, and normally they would have, but they knew this wasn't a good time.

Carpenter paused on the steps as a boy passed with a basket of fragrant herbs. A coach rattled past outside, sending a pale mist of dust through the open doors, and a man in a white suit scowled and tried to brush it off, to no avail. This wasn't Richmond.

Joints creaking, Carpenter put his hand on the bannister and made his way down.

"Morning, Bill."

"Morning." Carpenter helped himself to a cup, and held it out to the man with the coffee, who filled it. "Nice day to be alive."

"You reckon?" Hale was controlling himself with some effort, and it was a sight to see. He'd once been well acquainted with his temper. Not with controlling it, but with the thing itself. It seemed these last years had changed that, and now he was fumbling for what had once been instinct. That was for the best; bluster hadn't ever done much for Carpenter, and these days it would do even less.

"I am at a loss," Hale announced. "Bill, I can't tell if you are a changed man or if change has never touched you. You always did things to take me by surprise. And you still do."

"That ain't my intent." Carpenter blew on his coffee, wincing as someone outside the hotel shouted and pain shot through his head. It wasn't just the pain; his stomach was unsettled as well. Maybe it was time for a break from the whiskey.

"Well, what *is* your intent, Bill?"

"I'm retired. I don't need one."

"Some might call that rude."

"Good Lord. Look at me," Carpenter said, annoyed. "What the hell do I care what people call it?"

The other man stiffened. "Have I offended you somehow, Bill? Did you not receive my invitations for you to join us? To share in what we had? Is my house not comfortable enough for you? Is there someplace in the road where I fell short as your friend?"

"Never once."

"Then *why* do you want to come here just to spit in my face?" he snarled.

Carpenter took a drink. "I ain't done that yet."

People were gathering outside, across and down the street a little. Carpenter couldn't see what was so interesting to them, though.

Hale shook his head in disgust. "I'm a simple man, Bill. I don't understand it. And I don't like it."

"I was just thinking the same thing." Carpenter squeezed the bridge of his nose, clenching his jaw while his belly tossed and turned. "Why send Joe? Why not Fred? He wouldn't have had the sense to listen to me and see reason. On your word he'd have just slit my throat as well, and you'd have two fewer things to trouble you today."

Hale ignored the question. "I am asking you to help me understand. Asking as your friend. Mayhaps you *don't* want to be my friend and do the things that you should, but you can still talk like my friend, and that means talking straight. You can do that much for me, can't you?"

"Why can't you just let him build his factory?" Carpenter asked directly.

Hale twitched, but he didn't hesitate long. "Why can't you just let him leave?"

"I ain't what's stopping him leaving." It was as though the coffee had gravel in it. It *was* strong, though. He snorted. "I'm pushing him as hard as you are."

"If a man won't leave your house of his own accord, even *you* would lay hands on him," Hale said.

"I would, and I have before," Carpenter replied, unperturbed by the insult. "Only one difference, Captain. This valley don't belong to me." He finished his coffee. "Or to you."

Another hesitation, this one a little longer. Then Hale broke into a smile. "Bill," he said, shaking his head. Then he leaned forward and struck him on the arm in a friendly fashion. "Bill, that may be, but what kind of men would we be if we let a man like that stay and do as he pleased? The things he's done. It's only his good grace that Joe doesn't act in his capacity as sheriff and hang him from the neck in the street."

"What's he done now?" Carpenter asked, catching the eye of the owner. He looked meaningfully at a plate of food that a prospector was eating. His stomach was still in a bad state, but he had to eat regardless. Age had taken enough of his strength from him already; this wasn't the time to let any more of it go.

"He took advantage of Abigail Manley. And, I hear it tell, the widow Miller."

"I thought it was O'Doul's daughter that he had led on."

"He's guilty of that as well."

"When were these allegations made?"

"Just this morning."

"Just this morning," Carpenter echoed, looking out the window. So that was the reason for the crowd that was gathering out there around the newspaperman.

"Bill, you know these things ain't always talked about when they occur. You understand that, I know."

Carpenter nodded. "I understand a lot of things."

"You want to defend a man like that?"

"Have I defended him yet?" Carpenter asked, and Hale shrank from his gaze. "Even one time?"

"You certainly have," the other man replied, remembering himself. Hale straightened on his stool and looked around, but everyone was being very careful not to look at them. "On the road. You showed more spine in that exchange than you have in the rest of your life combined."

The barman, with an astounding lack of sense, chose that moment to deliver his breakfast. Bill accepted the plate, fork, and knife and began to cut his eggs and sausage, not looking at Hale.

"Where did you hear about that exchange?" he asked curiously, as though he wasn't well aware that last night he'd dined with the very men who had tried for Silva on the trail. In fact, Isaiah had been the one doing the shouting. Carpenter was still a little irked that he hadn't recognized the man's voice at the time. Though Isaiah hadn't recognized his, either. Or had he? Was *that* why they hadn't made their move? "Are you keeping company with bandits and bushwhackers? Weren't you just now telling me about Silva's low character? You tell the tale almost as though you were there yourself." He didn't wait for Hale to say anything. "You don't understand what I'm doing?" He shook his head. "*I'm* the one who doesn't understand. Why are you going this far?"

"There's nothing I won't do for my family, Bill. You would do the same."

Carpenter nodded, taking a bite of his food. That was true, most likely.

It still didn't make sense. A factory would hurt no one. Silva and his ambitions were no possible threat to Hale and his, and in fact they were essential. Getting rid of Silva was contrary to Hale's interests. Was he so bullheaded that he couldn't see that? He had invested in this settlement, and he wanted to let it dry up and die? Over some sort of grudge, one Carpenter still didn't fully comprehend? It didn't feel right.

"Bill," Hale said at last, sighing, "it may be that if this place doesn't agree with you, you ought as well go on yourself. It was good seeing you."

"And you," Carpenter replied immediately, putting down his utensils and twisting to offer his hand. "And the rest. You don't know what it means to me to see that you're all well. And that you've done well."

"We'll do better yet. I wish you could be here to share in it. But I suppose you can't." Hale got to his feet with a groan and picked up his hat, laying money on the bar. "Whenever you do get settled, wherever that may be, write me, Bill."

He took Carpenter's hand, and they shook.

A handsome gray mare was waiting for Hale outside. Carpenter watched him climb into the saddle, and then went back to his breakfast. Behind him, the men at the nearest table were talking about some quartz that had been found at the north end of the valley, on another man's claim.

It was always possible that there *was* gold here, and the problem was that no one had found it yet. But if that was the case, how had Hale known to build here?

The newspaperman had gone back into his shop, and the crowd he'd attracted was dispersing. The mission of smearing Silva's name further was accomplished for the morning. Carpenter wondered how much Hale had paid the newspaperman for this favor.

He finished his meal and left the hotel, stepping into the street and shielding his eyes against the sun, avoiding the mud as another coach passed. A preacher, one with only a tent, was accosting people at the far end of the street. He'd have to preach from sunup to sundown if he wanted to compete with Reverend

Brown, who had money, Hale's support, and an actual church.

Was that what the Almighty had in mind? Competition?

Carpenter bumped his hat against his thigh to get some of the dust off it, then put it on. There was only one man louder than the preacher: one finely dressed, advertising the superiority of the girls at his establishment and assuring the passing prospectors that the joint down the street couldn't possibly compare. That there were only two such places here said something about the stalled growth of the settlement.

How long did Carpenter have to get out of town? It was difficult to say, but the count had begun.

The same count that had been under way for Silva for a while now, it seemed. That gave it all an element of urgency that explained some of what Carpenter was feeling.

But not all of it.

Relaxed as he had wanted to appear, it wasn't just a guilty conscience that had brought Hale to the hotel this morning. Time wasn't running out only for Carpenter and Silva; it was for Hale as well. His sense of urgency made that clear.

What wasn't clear was why.

Carpenter looked to the west. Past the town, past the pines, the mountains were still there. The peaks were covered in snow, no doubt cold and crisp. Down here, it was just hot and dusty, and that wasn't likely to change.

He sighed and trudged across the street, pulling open the door of the general store and going in. The shopkeeper kept a good shop, neat and clean, though tellingly empty.

"Morning," he said.

"Morning," Carpenter replied, his eyes going over

it all. Three full barrels of pickaxes, and there were at least three more in the hardware tent two doors down. Sifters and spades. It was only morning, but it felt like the sun was already setting on Antelope Valley.

He bought some of the man's best tobacco and rolled a smoke, which he lit. "Who's the best man to buy a horse from?" he asked.

"That would be Mr. Hale," the shopkeeper replied at once, absently rubbing at a stain on his waistcoat. "He keeps them on Mr. Brown's property. You won't find better near here."

"No doubt."

"Though you may have to wait to do business. Some of Mr. Hale's men rode out early this morning."

"Going where?"

"Hardly my business." The other man shrugged. "To the south."

Carpenter took that in. After a moment, he picked up a Spencer rifle and looked it over.

"That fellow," he said, glancing at the door. "The one they talk about. Building the factory."

"Mr. Silva. I don't know him."

And he didn't want to talk about him. "Where was his plot for the factory?"

"Just north of town. Quarter mile up the trail. Or road, rather."

Carpenter sighed and laid the rifle back down.

"Too costly for you?" the shopkeeper asked.

"In a manner of speaking." He pushed it away. "That, and my eyes aren't what they used to be."

CHAPTER ELEVEN

S ILVA WASN'T AT the hotel, but his wagon was, and
his horses.

Maria was there, though. Carpenter could hear
the clicking of her claws as she padded around rest-
lessly on the other side of the door.

Leaving his things in his own room, he instructed
the barman to let the dog outside and feed her something if no one else did within the hour. That done,
he ventured out again to a street that was doing its
best impression of bustling as the day wore on.

Isaiah was outside the other hotel, the one beside
the barbershop, his feet on the table and a glass in his
hand. It was a posture to which he appeared accustomed.

He watched Carpenter, but didn't call out or wave.
He was wearing a gun, but unlike Joe, it wasn't the
same one he'd had during the war. It was bigger and
looked well used.

Carpenter nodded to him, but kept walking. He'd

caught a glimpse of Joe in the sheriff's office. Who had ridden out, then? Fred? O'Doul? John hadn't been at dinner last night, but he was still around somewhere. And Yates. Carpenter still hadn't seen Yates.

Hale's riders had gone south, according to the shopkeeper. Carpenter trudged north. The mud of the street quickly gave way to the dust of the trail, though someone had gone to some effort to make it easily passable. That had probably been Silva or his business partner, anticipating shipments of goods and hoping for easy travel.

This was where the dust was worst, and he pulled up his bandanna.

The sounds of the settlement, however pitiful, faded behind him and were replaced by the wind and what sounded like a good-sized stream. It was an up-hill journey, though not a cruel one. Occasional rustles in the woods always made him look, hoping for a glance of that stag from the night before, but he wouldn't get another look at that animal. It had seen the danger, and it had fled, as anything unburdened by pride or other foolishness would.

The breeze didn't make the sun any less blistering, and he wiped his face with his bandanna and pulled the brim of his hat low over his eyes.

It wasn't quite as far as the shopkeeper believed. Silva's land was more or less level, but it still needed work. As for the factory, there wasn't one. Massive stacks of timber waited, some with dewy spiderwebs gleaming between them. It was all untouched, and there were still a few tree stumps left to be removed. Mounds of dirt and gravel had been prepared, but not yet put to use smoothing and strengthening the trail for the wagons that would have to come and go.

A shadow passed as he went into the midst of the

building materials. He looked up in alarm, but there weren't any buzzards in the air, only hawks.

Silva wasn't a corpse, but he was sitting as still as one, perched on some of the timber.

He still wore his clothes from the night before, though it was a relief to see he had his hat on.

Carpenter didn't say anything, but he didn't have to wait long.

"My partner, Mr. Karr, has not appeared in town," Silva said.

"Does he have a family?"

"He does."

"Then he's doing right by them." If someone had to choose between angering Silva and angering Hale, anyone with any sense would side with Hale. Silva's partner wasn't doing anything surprising, and he likely had more sense than Silva himself.

After a moment, Silva nodded. Then he smiled and looked down at Carpenter.

"You have a charitable way of regarding people," he said.

"I *say* charitable things," Carpenter corrected him, folding his arms. "But I'm thinking the same thing as everyone else. More times than not anyways."

"No sign of our workers, and not an ounce of progress."

Carpenter could see that for himself. Would it be wise to mention the latest slander against Silva? He probably didn't know about it yet, but it would do nothing to improve his already bleak way of looking at things.

"You ought to get out of the sun," he suggested instead.

"I brought provisions." Silva held up his bottle.

That would not help. "A picnic alone? You might have invited me."

"Mr. Carpenter, as your friend, I believe I have an interest in your well-being. Particularly after you helped me last night. Is being in my company advantageous to you in any way? I think not."

That wasn't unreasonable. Silva squinted up at the hawks for a moment, then lowered himself to the ground, leaving the bottle behind. He walked through the weeds to join Carpenter in the middle of it all.

"It doesn't look like much," he said, gazing around at the raw materials. "For an endeavor that's taken years from me."

It was hard to know what to say to that. A pair of squirrels was running along the top of the nearest stack of timber, oblivious to the hawks.

"There are those who find me tolerable."

Silva turned, taken aback. He raised an eyebrow. "Your pardon, Mr. Carpenter?"

"They tolerate me. Out of what I guess you might call a sense of obligation. And there are those who don't." He shrugged. "Because of the things that I've done, and most of all the things I ain't done. Being a coward, being soft, and not being what they all thought I ought to be. And so on." He waved a hand. "My wife was the only person who ever saw all that, and not only did she not despise it—she preferred it. Or so she always said."

Silva was at a loss for words, but Carpenter wasn't fishing for a reply.

"I used to be afraid of losing her. Now she's gone." Carpenter rubbed at his cheek, which still needed a shave. "And the sun keeps on coming up. It don't matter why. Let it go."

The other man laughed bitterly. "My house is ashes, Mr. Carpenter. My cargo? Vanished. Stolen from the middle of camp." He shook his head. "My time? Worthless. My partner gone. My money." He snorted and gestured at the nearest pile of timber. "You're looking at it. My prospects? Even my—" And he stopped there, taking a deep breath through his nose. He'd been about to say something about the girl, O'Doul's daughter.

"I know."

"I have *nothing*," Silva snarled.

"I'm no different." Carpenter started to roll a smoke. He smiled at Silva. "And it's all right. You understand? It's all right."

Silva shook his head, jaw clenched. "No, Mr. Carpenter. It is not right."

And Carpenter hadn't meant to say that it was, at least not that exactly, but he didn't get the chance to go on. Silva's posture had changed, and the look on his face had, if it was possible, gotten even colder.

A minute ago the heat of the sun had been a nuisance. Now it felt very far off.

Carpenter turned to see William standing fairly close by with a pistol in his hand. The gun looked comfortable there, and last night he'd seen for himself that the boy knew how it was used.

There were two others with him: one who'd been around the house at dinner, but not at the table—his name was Perkins—and another Carpenter had never seen before, both fairly young and thankfully unarmed. It stood to reason: Hale's men from the war, his friends, his inner circle—none of them were getting any younger. His daughters hadn't looked likely to be much help on the farm. He had only the one son, William, so he had to employ some help.

That was who these men were.

"Howdy, Will," Carpenter said. "Does your pa know you're here?"

At first the gun hadn't been aimed at anyone, but

the boy didn't hesitate. He lifted it, pointing it squarely at Silva.

"You put that down," William told him.

Silva hadn't moved, but he was getting ready to. There was no fear in him. And why would there be? Fear was for men with something to lose. William didn't have a clue what he was doing. No doubt he thought he did, but that could be said of any boy his age.

It took everything Carpenter had not to open his mouth, but he didn't have to. Silva saw the look on his face. William was only a boy, and his pa did *not* know he was here. Hale wasn't the man Carpenter remembered, but he hadn't gone so low that he would send his own blood on a dirty errand like this.

Silva spread his hands just enough that one of the men was able to take the pistol from his holster and tuck it into his own belt.

"Something you want to tell me?" William asked. "Mr. Silva?"

Silva's eyes lingered on Carpenter's face, and a little reason seemed to return to them. He looked at the man who'd taken his pistol.

"Thurgood," he said. "Hale won't like this."

"What he don't like is that you're still here," the man replied.

"Don't you ignore me," William warned.

"Are you here to murder me, Will?" Silva asked tiredly.

"If I wanted to do that, I'd've just shot you five minutes ago," the boy replied, nodding to Perkins, who put his fist in Silva's kidney hard enough to send him to his knees in the dirt, groaning. "I just want you gone, and you're dragging your feet. You need a push." The words sounded rehearsed.

William snapped the pistol around to Carpenter as he started to move forward.

"Now, you just stay on back, Mr. Carpenter," he said. "This is not your business."

Carpenter stopped, but Perkins didn't. He grabbed Silva, and Thurgood hit him in the face, spotting the dirt and the weeds with drops of blood.

"This is a mistake," Carpenter told them, his eye twitching.

"The mistake was my pa naming me after you, and not just putting a bullet in this damn Mexican," William said frankly.

Silva tried to resist, and Perkins just threw him to the ground. Thurgood stepped in and delivered a vicious kick to his ribs. Silva had been stoic as the blows rained on him, and all but silent, but now he cried out.

"For God's sake, the point's made," Carpenter snapped. "It ain't needed! I had him sold. We were about to go!"

"Didn't sound sold to me," the boy said, glancing back, but only for a moment, to see Silva shield his head from another kick. "And why would I trust you to do anything, old fellow? I seen you on the trail. You couldn't even put down your own horse. What good are you?"

Silva was on his hands and knees, bloody and covered in dirt. Perkins and Thurgood stood over him, looking questioningly at William. They might have been reasonably good hands on the estate, but they were not the most attentive men.

Silva was attentive, though. He'd been watching Perkins' right boot since the first kick landed, and so had Carpenter, with a churning stomach and sweat like ice.

There had been a chance when Silva gave up his

pistol. He'd seen what Carpenter had: that William was young and stupid, and that it didn't have to be like they all thought it did. But that moment had come and gone, and now they were living in a different one.

There was no look, and no words from Carpenter could change it now. It was like the forest knew; the animals had all shut up, and even the sun didn't want to look.

The clouds moved in, Silva saw his chance, and he took it. He snatched Perkins' boot knife and rammed it into the other man's thigh, twisting sharply.

William flinched and whirled at the cry of agony, and Carpenter knocked the pistol from his hand. There wasn't time to think about it, and that was the worst feeling he'd ever known. Nothing was easier than acting without thinking, but there was always a bill to pay, and bringing it to account was never as easy as racking it up.

But he'd done it before, and he did it now. Carpenter struck with his fist, sending William crashing to the ground.

Thurgood reached for Silva's pistol in his belt, but Silva kicked his feet from under him, and Carpenter was there in time for a kick of his own, which sent the gun tumbling away through the bloody weeds.

Perkins pulled the knife from his leg and slashed at Silva, who narrowly avoided the blade, spilling to the ground. Carpenter swung at Thurgood, who ducked and hit back, doubling him over, then clubbing him full in the back with both fists to knock him flat.

Choking on the dust, Carpenter tried to get up as Perkins lunged for Silva, falling on top of him with the knife. Silva caught his wrist and kept the blade away, but he was in a sorry state from the beating, and he would not win a contest of strength.

William stirred, groaning.

Thurgood knocked Carpenter onto his back and straddled him, delivering a punch with everything he had, then another.

Perkins had both hands on the knife, pressing down with his strength and his weight. Arms quivering, Silva held the point away from his chest by only inches. He shifted his body and twisted his shoulders. The knife plunged into the dirt, and he struck the other man with his elbow, snatching up a fistful of dirt and flinging it at Thurgood, who flinched and looked away.

Carpenter shoved him off and rose, spitting blood. Thurgood scrambled up, pulling a hunting knife off his hip and getting ready, shaking the stars from his eyes.

Silva put his whole body into a punch that sent Perkins stumbling into a stack of lumber hard enough to daze him.

"I thought you were supposed to be soft," Thurgood said.

"I am," Carpenter replied, arduously lifting Silva's pistol, which he'd taken from the ground. "That's why you're still breathing, son."

That stopped him.

Perkins was straightening up, and Carpenter swung the barrel over to him.

"Are you finished?" he asked thickly, then leaned over to spit blood.

Perkins didn't reply, but William was starting to sit up.

The ground was rolling like the ocean, and one moment there were four men, and the next there were eight as the world swam and blurred in Carpenter's eyes. He stood taller and kept the pistol steady.

"I would take the boy and go," he said, hoping none of them had the notion that even without having his skull rattled, Carpenter had about as much chance of hitting anyone with a pistol as he had of being elected president. "If I had any sense," he added.

Thurgood still had his knife in his hand, and he hadn't made his mind up yet. Perkins had, though. Without a word, he pulled his bandanna tight around his wounded leg and limped over to William.

Silva got upright, his shirt and waistcoat open and torn, his eye swelling shut, and blood dripping from his chin. Carpenter knew he couldn't look much better.

"Go on," he said, no malice in the words as he lowered the pistol.

Thurgood's fingers opened, then curled tightly around the handle of his knife. He didn't like to lose a fight. Carpenter would have liked to explain to him that nobody did, and further that it didn't matter, at the end of the day. They were all in pain and bleeding. Everyone had lost, and no one had won, or if they had, it was only in that they were still alive. There was no profit in this for anyone and, above all, no meaning. Only suffering.

But Thurgood wouldn't understand any of that. All he knew was that he'd come off worse in a tangle with a dandy and an old coward. He probably didn't know which was worse: being on the wrong side of the gun, or that Carpenter hadn't used it. Dirt in the eyes didn't matter.

It was pride that blinded him.

"Our business ain't finished," he said to Carpenter.

"I thought your business was with him," Carpenter replied tiredly, glancing at Silva.

Thurgood didn't reply to that. He shoved his knife back in its sheath and went to Perkins, who was supporting William. The boy didn't look so good. Carpenter swallowed. He hadn't thought about it, hadn't planned it. There hadn't been time.

But he'd hit the boy the only way he knew how, and that was fairly hard.

CHAPTER TWELVE

W HEN HE COULD hear the hoofbeats of the horses departing, Carpenter staggered into the shade of the stacked lumber, and that was where his strength gave out. He fell against the beams and sagged to the ground.

Gingerly, Silva joined him with a groan.

Carpenter put the gun on the ground between them, and with what looked like a mighty effort, the other man picked it up and pushed it into his holster. He leaned back and probed around his mouth, then spat out more blood.

The shade had lost some of its rarity; overhead, the clouds were getting thicker. The birds had more sense than the men, and they had all cleared off without making any fuss.

A squirrel watched curiously from the top of the lumber pile, sitting beside the whiskey bottle, which was now out of reach for two men profoundly disinclined to stand up. Carpenter had been feeling his age for years, but never quite like this. Throwing punches had never been exactly easy, but just now it had been as though he'd been throwing them through molasses. He couldn't possibly have many left in him. Or maybe he just hoped he didn't.

"I offered to make him a partner," Silva said after a moment, tenderly rubbing his chin.

"Who?" Carpenter asked, closing his eyes.

"Hale."

"Yeah?"

"I showed him my plan. For the metal works and all of it. What we stood to earn." Silva sighed. "He would not have it, though. Would not meet me as an equal, would not talk business. It offended him that I even approached him." There was a click, and Carpenter opened one eye to see Silva checking his watch. It was broken. "It was my intent to be courteous."

"Would you have drawn on the boy?"

"I don't know. I wanted to."

Silva couldn't be blamed for that, though even if he'd been fast enough, that would've been his life. Any chance he might've had of leaving Antelope Valley alive would've been gone, and there was nothing in it for him. Silva thought the weight of his failure here was as bad it could get, but he was wrong about that. So far he wasn't dragging anything new behind his conscience, and even if he didn't appreciate that for the blessing it was, it made his burden lighter.

"I'd like to shoot his father too," Silva added.

It wouldn't help, though.

He was staring at the lumber and the tools. "There would've been profit in the very first order," he mused. "All this would've been paid back and more. Not much more, but it was solid. The plan was solid."

"Did Hale see that?"

"Oh, I think he did."

"That's a pity," Carpenter said, though the words didn't quite do it justice. They both fell silent after that. Even the sun's lackadaisical pace looked dizzying as it crept across the sky behind the darkening curtain of clouds. The business of walking back to town, readying the wagon, and departing would not be an easy one. Just the thought of getting up seemed out of reach. Sitting there was the best he could hope for, but at least it was beautiful country to look at.

"What if someone did find gold here? Wouldn't that be something?" Carpenter asked.

Silva wasn't listening.

"Maria's hungry by now," he said after a little while.

"Might as well go, then."

"Might as well."

Silva dragged himself to his feet and offered his hand, and Carpenter wasn't too proud to take it. His head was light, but he was no longer seeing double.

"Should have brought the dog," Carpenter noted.

"I had a notion this was coming." Silva halfheartedly tried to put himself in order, but it was a lost cause. "Best if she wasn't here when it did."

"And they call me soft."

"She is the only good thing left in my life," Silva said earnestly, pointing a warning finger at him. "Do not make light of that."

"I would never. I'm just glad you make mention of your life," Carpenter said, staggering toward the trail. "I was worried you'd forgotten about it. It should mean something to you that you still have it. If it's all the same to you, I'd like to see you keep it. If you can be bothered."

"His intent was not to murder me."

Carpenter wasn't so sure about that, but he held his tongue.

"I could not help but notice, Mr. Carpenter, young

William's familiarity with you," Silva remarked as they walked, or more accurately shambled, toward town.

"I wouldn't call it that. I only met him last night."

"Then Mr. Hale and these men are your friends. I had that notion yesterday from the sheriff and from your intimacy with the reverend. I'd hoped it wasn't true."

Carpenter chose his words carefully, or tried to. Then he thought better of it. "It is," he replied.

"These are the men you knew in the war."

"That's right."

"Do you plan to fall in with them?"

"Don't know that I could," Carpenter replied, "even if I wanted to."

"I understand."

Carpenter doubted that.

"Will you see to the wagon?" Silva asked, though it must have pained him. It was his pride; no one was free of it. The one thing he wanted even less than running away was to be *seen* running away, but embarrassment was survivable. Being strung up wasn't.

"Yes," Carpenter told him. "Of course."

And Silva could gather Maria and his things. There wasn't enough of the day left to put as much distance between themselves and the town as Carpenter would have liked, but there was no sense being sore about it. They would go as far as they could before making camp.

And after that? It was easier not to think about it. Easier than walking uphill, at any rate. He wiped his brow, and his hand came away with as much crusted blood as sweat. The pain wasn't anything to bother him; after the lashes during the war, nothing else had ever seemed to matter much. The sun was different, though. If it decided to peek out from behind the clouds, this would be a short walk.

But the clouds held, and as he had for more than fifty years, Carpenter put one foot in front of the other.

The music came first, and nothing followed it. As they climbed the final slope that would bring them into view of the settlement proper, there were only the distant notes of the pianoforte. There were no voices, or none loud enough to be heard this far off.

And that wasn't right. The day was ending; the prospectors stubborn enough to ply their trade in Antelope Valley relied on daylight for their work. They would be returning to the settlement, the whiskey, the girls, and the bunkhouses.

And they likely were, but they were doing it quietly. Were there any secrets in Antelope Valley? Probably not, except what in the world an antelope was. The people knew of Hale, they knew of Silva, and they knew of the trouble between them. They were also, by the sound of things, hoping to stay out of it. No one could find fault with that, particularly when they likely had no reason to disbelieve the nonsense everyone else was repeating. As far as they were concerned, Silva was every inch the scoundrel he was rumored to be. The truth had no value to them, and there was no help to be found in it. The only recourse was to go, and quickly, before someone had the brilliant notion of endearing himself to Hale by doing something foolish.

What little sound there was went away as they came into view, shambling onto the road like two men walking in their sleep.

Reverend Brown was there with his Bible under his arm, outside the sheriff's office. He said nothing; he just looked on with no expression. Slow and steady, the sun was well on its way. Carpenter couldn't see especially well in the fading light, but he could feel the eyes on them.

They split without a word, Carpenter making for the corner to go to the stable and Silva going into the hotel.

The boy who was supposed to be minding the hay and the water wasn't there. No one was, and there were two horses tied up, but they weren't Silva's. There was no sign of the wagon. It wasn't coincidence; you couldn't very well misplace something that size. Carpenter had been struggling to keep his breakfast down all morning, and now it only got more difficult. So they'd taken Silva's cargo, then come back and taken the wagon and team for good measure.

The quiet pressed on him from all sides. Naively, he had believed that he understood. The people who lived in this settlement weren't blind or deaf. They weren't holding their breath and standing back in shame, waiting for Silva to go on his way.

No one had thrown dirt in *Carpenter's* eyes. This was his doing and no one else's. Which was worse? That Hale had gotten older and let go of the rope? That the man might act against Silva and against his own interests?

Or that he wouldn't?

Carpenter slipped out of the stable and moved quietly to the hotel, sidling along the rear of the building and keeping out of sight. Was anyone looking? It was difficult to be sure, but it was time to make a change. Speaking softly and giving the benefit of the doubt hadn't accomplished anything but getting the two of them beaten into the dirt.

He paused alongside a window and tapped on the glass. After a moment, the curious barman opened it, and Carpenter looked past him. There were men drinking, but none that he recognized.

Seeing who it was, the barman's face went blank.

"Wait," Carpenter told him quickly. "These two

mares," he said, pointing at the stable. "They're yours?"

The man nodded.

"Sell them to me."

Even if the man couldn't have been blamed for his uncertainty, time still meant something. It had been foolish to assume that Hale would be content to simply watch the two of them drag themselves out of Antelope Valley in disgrace.

The owner hesitated, and as he did, the hush inside the hotel crept out through the window like a fine mist. They both felt it. The owner turned, and Carpenter leaned in to see what all the men were looking up at.

Silva came into view at the top of the stairs with something in his arms.

"Please," Carpenter hissed at the owner, who looked back with wide eyes and skin as white as chalk.

The quiet had woven itself into a prickly blanket of dead silence, broken only by those faint notes from the taproom of the joint down the street. Carpenter's eyes weren't what they'd once been, but he could still see that Silva wasn't carrying his belongings. He recognized Maria's fur, and the still, limp way the staghound lay in Silva's arms.

Silva reached the bottom of the stairs, and without a look for the men at the tables, he left the hotel.

Carpenter grabbed for the owner, who dodged away and slammed the window shut hard enough to crack it. Swearing, Carpenter hurried down the alley, back toward the street, but halted.

Joe Fisher was there with Isaiah beside him, striding into the street.

There was no sign of Reverend Brown now.

There was no sunlight to catch on it, but Joe's star still shone dully in the gathering twilight.

Silva paused on the porch with Maria in his arms, his eyes on Joe. Silva hadn't noticed Fred yet, but he was there around the corner of the general store. And if Fred was there, O'Doul wouldn't be far away, probably upstairs or even on the roof. Normally it would have been Isaiah on the roof with his Henry rifle, but today he was in the street. The years had taken a great deal from them, but they likely still remembered how to do this much.

Now Carpenter could clearly see the handle of the knife still buried in the dog's breast. It wasn't Joe's knife, but at this point, it didn't really matter whose it was.

Joe didn't look entirely sure of himself, and that was fair enough. Silva was a sight with his worn and bloody clothes and carrying the dead dog.

There were too many faces at the windows; Carpenter tried to stay in the shadows, but it wasn't dark yet, and it wasn't easy for a man his size to go unseen. He eyed the stable door, but getting in there without being noticed would never happen as long as the town was as still and quiet as a grave. Even a sneeze would carry like a gunshot.

Silva stood his ground on the porch and stared at Joe.

"Are you here to bring the man who killed my dog to justice?" he asked after a moment, a new look on his face, one that Joe evidently didn't like.

The sheriff shifted his feet. "No," he called back. "Can't say that I am."

"Then what is your business?" There wasn't even the slightest hint of fear on Silva's face or in his voice.

Joe hesitated. "You are," he said finally, not looking very happy about it. His eyes darted left and up, looking for reassurance or possibly for Carpenter. Joe had never been one for nerves. He wasn't afraid of Silva as a man; he just had no stomach for this business. All the same, that brought his apprehension out, and now he'd given away where O'Doul was hiding.

"I was just about to leave," Silva was saying coldly, "without the expectation of return. I would much prefer if you did not detain me."

"So would I," Joe replied. "But it's what you did to Will Hale. You gave that boy a beating, Silva."

Chickens were clucking in a coop behind one of the buildings, and a dog whined.

"Do I look to you, sir, like a man who has *given* a beating?" Silva bit out through his teeth.

Joe started to say something, but the other man cut him off.

"I suppose I *might* explain to you," Silva said, raising his voice, "what a fair fight is. I'd be wasting my breath, though, wouldn't I? You wouldn't know the meaning of the word 'fair.'"

Carpenter paused at the corner and peered out.

Blood from Maria's body had traced red lines across Silva's forearms, and it dripped and hung in sticky strings.

Joe wasn't blind or stupid, but Isaiah was both.

"Just come on, now," Isaiah said, beckoning. "To the jail."

Joe might well have done the right thing in that moment, but the moment got away from him.

"What you done to the boy ain't right," Isaiah went on, all but shouting the words. His outrage was as real as the gilding on Hale's garden columns, but that wasn't important. His notion was to have everyone in town hear him. Maybe they'd already paraded Perkins, Thurgood, and William through this street to set the stage.

"In other words," Silva said, dust swirling around his ankles, "you mean to say that you want justice."

Slowly, he knelt and laid out the body of the staghound. Then he got to his feet and stepped over her, down the steps, which creaked noisily.

He didn't walk toward Joe and Isaiah. Silva might never have been a soldier, but he had to know he was surrounded. He had to know these men wouldn't face him head-on, not even two to one.

He saw Carpenter in the shadows, and his look didn't pass along anything Carpenter didn't already know. He could step out and confess that he had been the one to strike down the boy. It wouldn't change a thing, certainly not what was about to happen. Silva knew it, and he wanted Carpenter to stay right where he was. And that was rational; Silva was a largely rational man.

One man was already about to be shot dead in the street. Making it two wouldn't accomplish anything.

"Don't do nothing you'll regret, Silva," Joe warned.

Silva cocked his head. "Why not?" he demanded, sweeping out an arm at Maria. "You already have. And you seem none the worse for wear."

"I am sorry about the dog," Joe said, clearly meaning it. It must have been Fred who'd done it; there was no one else who would have. Fred had always been one for sending messages. It hadn't been good business during the war, and it wasn't good business now. The man was older but not smarter.

As Carpenter made up his mind, he decided the same could probably be said of him.

The stillness was broken by sudden laughter from inside one of the buildings, but it was quickly cut off. Everyone looked, and as they did, Carpenter stepped back into the gloom and got moving. As he slipped between the empty barrels, squeezing through the alleys, the voices in the street carried clearly. He could hear every word, even if he didn't care to.

He stopped for a moment, thinking fast. He was

behind the sheriff's office and jail. There was no one inside.

The quiet stretched like taut wire, all but humming in the air.

"You are sorry, Sheriff? No," Silva called out. "But you will be."

Carpenter couldn't see Silva's face, but he knew exactly what look was on it. He'd known other men to wear that face, the mask of someone who was ready to kill. None of them had worn it well. It could happen to anyone. There was no time left.

He picked up a board. Fred, poised at the corner of the alley with his rifle, turned to look back. The board splintered over his head, and he crumpled to the ground. Carpenter dropped the pieces and clambered onto the nearest windowsill to bang on the side of the building with his fist.

Beams creaked, and the barrel of a rifle appeared over the roof. Carpenter seized it and pulled, bringing O'Doul right over. The other man splashed into the mud. Carpenter jerked him to his feet and wrapped his arm around his throat as the other man cried out in pain. Something was wrong with O'Doul's leg, but Carpenter's sympathy had gone away to the same place that all his time had. The other man struggled, but people called Carpenter soft, not weak. He kept his grip and took up the rifle, dragging O'Doul into the street.

"Joe," he called out.

Carpenter wouldn't have thought it was possible, but the sheriff somehow came to look even more miserable.

"Damn it all to hell, Bill," he snarled.

Isaiah started to take aim, but Carpenter laid his commandeered rifle over O'Doul's shoulder, and that gave Isaiah pause. Red-faced, O'Doul was still trying to swear, but Carpenter didn't give him enough breath to do it, and he kept moving toward Silva.

"You can't put him in jail, Joe."

"I'm the sheriff, Bill. I can put anyone in jail."

"Even if they ain't the one that done it?"

"I saw the boy's face, Bill."

"So did I when I hit him," Carpenter snapped. "All Mr. Silva did was receive a beating, unprovoked."

"Then maybe I'll put you both in jail," Joe said, his hand hovering by his revolver. "Just to be safe. Until we can get it figured."

"I'd prefer you didn't," Carpenter told him honestly. "I don't like your jail. It's too hot in there."

For a moment, Joe looked puzzled. Then he turned to look in panic at the smoke rising from the jail. With only matches, Carpenter hadn't been able to set a very large fire. He'd worried it wouldn't spread quickly enough to do him any good, but it looked as though it had finally started to catch.

He shoved O'Doul away and threw down the rifle, then dragged Silva toward the stable.

O'Doul twisted around and fired, the slug sending wood chips flying from the doors. Carpenter shouldered through, pulling his shaving knife and cutting the two horses free.

For just a moment, Silva was undecided, standing inside the door with his revolver in his hand. Then he stuffed it back in its holster and leapt into the saddle.

They burst into the open. Carpenter kicked the mare's flanks and got low, urging her to a dead run with Silva thundering just behind. For once the red dust could do them a favor, covering their escape. The wind took Carpenter's hat, but he didn't mind leaving that behind.

They got clear of the town and rode for the trail.

A shot split the air, and he looked back to see Silva

and his horse tumble to the ground. There was a glimpse of O'Doul with his rifle, and Carpenter reined in at once, dismounting and ducking as another bullet sailed past. It was the horse that was shot. Carpenter took Silva's hands and helped him from under the writhing body, reaching for his own reins, but the skittish mare was already galloping away.

Swearing, he pushed Silva ahead of him, off the trail and into the ferns on foot. They slipped and skidded down a slope of smooth rocks and vines, nearly crashing headlong into a tree as big around as an outhouse.

Carpenter looked back, and the blood in his ears made it difficult to hear anything but the thudding of his own heartbeat, but he didn't have to hear them to know they were coming.

PART TWO

---◇---

THE WOLVES AND THE WIDOWERS

CHAPTER THIRTEEN

To stand as he had at the lodge after putting Oceana down and look along the road to Antelope Valley and know how far there was to go, and how his old joints would fare and everything else that went with it—that had really been something. It was also nothing. And it had been nothing in the past, the long marches in his gray wool uniform. The miles had come and gone as easily as the hours of the day, all these years.

It had never occurred to him before, but one of these miles, sooner or later, would be his last. That thought wasn't particularly distressing. He'd just always thought that last mile, if it had to come, would come in Virginia.

Carpenter reached back to help Silva, and they clambered up the rocks. They were deep in the trees, but the moon had come out to light the way, or at least try.

"Is this enough?" Silva asked, looking down in the

gulley and breathing raggedly, as he had been for the past hour.

It was all Carpenter could do not to wheeze.

"Better to keep on a little while yet," he replied. Of Hale's men he wasn't aware of any who could track with any reliability apart from Yates, but those were only the ones he knew of; there could easily be someone else. Even if the pair of them had the energy and the inclination, neither had the expertise to conceal the signs of their passing. If someone with any skill at all wanted to follow, he would have no difficulty.

The way wasn't easy. Uphill was a struggle, and downhill was treacherous with all the rocks, which for all the magnificent size were none too steady.

Silva eyed Carpenter for only a moment before shaking his head. "No farther. You won't last, Mr. Carpenter."

"As long as I wasn't the one to say it first."

"I'm not completely without society."

Silva helped him sit down against the stone; they were nearly at the top of the hill, with quite the gulley stretching out below, covered in pines and boulders. At least if someone was coming from that way, they might be able to see him.

Carpenter took deep breaths, and only now that he'd stopped moving did the pain in his body become fully apparent. His battered face was the least of his worries; it was soreness and bruises elsewhere that were going to make it torture just to get up in the morning.

All that time he'd spent looking forward to a feather bed, and he'd gotten what? A few hours in it at most? Well, there was no blaming anyone for that. This was all his own doing.

He patted himself down and came up with his tobacco, but he'd used all of his matches to start the fire. Sighing, he put the bag back, only for Silva to produce matches of his own.

"So you are good for something," Carpenter grunted, rolling a smoke.

"That's what I was really thinking about, you know. At the factory." The place that had been *meant* to be a factory. "What I would do when I left this place."

"I knew you knew you were licked." If Carpenter still had it in him to be upset, that was what would have bothered him. William hadn't needed to beat anyone; Silva would've been gone by evening of his own accord.

"I considered it," Silva went on. "And I was nearly ready. The only thing that made me think I could do it was that I'd have Maria with me."

Now he had to start over without her. Carpenter liked dogs as much as the next man, and he sympathized, but he couldn't really share the other man's anguish. He was just too cold, perhaps. All he could see was that they had their lives, and they were lucky to have that much. Mourning the dog didn't seem like the best use of their time, but Carpenter hadn't been her master. He'd met other folks like that, folks who got stuck on their dogs the way he was still stuck on his late wife. He didn't understand it, but there was no sense holding it against them.

He passed Silva the cigarette. They'd found a good stream an hour back and drunk deeply, but they had nothing to carry water with. He licked his lips and looked up at the moon, listening to the wind and the owls. The light of the cigarette might give them away, but it was a chance they were taking. There was no part of Carpenter's body that didn't hurt after the long day, and it was hard not to feel as though a bullet to the head would have been a mercy.

Silva wasn't the only one with nowhere to go, after all.

"I suppose I owe you thanks," the shorter man said.

"Maybe," Carpenter replied, trying to get comfortable, though he knew it was impossible. "If I'd left you be, your troubles would be over."

"That they would," Silva grumbled, puffing. "I still have my patent." He sighed. "It will be a long road, though." He didn't mean the walk; he meant the work.

Carpenter had been thinking about it was well, unable to help himself. All the labor that had been needed for Silva's dream of a factory, and now he wasn't just going to have to do it again; he was starting from a debt. A debt of time and money that wouldn't be settled quickly.

"There's some justice, though," Carpenter told him. "Unless they find gold and soon, it'll dry up. Hale will have his palace all to himself. There'll be no camp, no people, and no living for him."

"He's a fool, sure enough," Silva agreed. "He could have made an investment and had a handsome percentage of my profit without lifting a finger. It would not have been a fortune this year or next." He shook his head. "But in some time . . ."

"I know. You have family?"

"I do."

"They have money?"

Silva nodded. "I don't want it, though."

"That's fair." Carpenter glanced down the hill and put out the cigarette. "Though it don't matter if they catch up to us." He pointed. "That is north. We covered, oh, seven or eight miles, I think."

"Then Howard's lodge would be to the southeast."

"A long way, my friend."

Silva shrugged. "It is necessary."

Carpenter hadn't forgotten when Silva had slipped away to bury that parcel when they'd been on the trail. The other man wanted to collect it.

"Although it would be wise not to go too promptly," Silva added, looking thoughtful. "It was just as I thought. The boy was sent to spy on me. The lodge may be watched. If I were to appear there too quickly, that could be a mistake."

"What did you really do to offend him? For him to have such a grudge?"

"A grudge?" Silva looked taken aback. "I don't believe he has one."

That wasn't the answer Carpenter had hoped for, and it probably wasn't true. If Hale hadn't borne a grudge against Silva before, he certainly would *now*.

NOTHING CAME IN the night but hunger, bad dreams, and a chill that made the bones ache.

Getting upright in the morning was even worse than expected. It was painful on a good day; now it was agony, but Carpenter kept his swearing to a minimum as he picked his way down the slope.

The wisest course would be to take a long and leisurely path past Antelope Valley, with plenty of ground to spare. It would cost them some time, but it was best if they could follow the river for as much of that journey as possible. They needed the water, and it would remove all the challenge in navigating. On the other hand, it was the first thing anyone would expect.

The clouds returned much thicker, and with them a misty rain. It was midmorning when they reached the river, which was wide and frothy, tumbling over the mossy rocks. Tiny lizards crept about on the smooth stones of the bank, and they found a spot shielded by a stone overhang. It was too soon to think they weren't being followed, but both men were far too hungry to care.

Silva wasn't overly attached to his broken watch, so it was a simple matter to turn the front cover into four reasonably good fishing hooks. Worms were plentiful, and once the bait was in the water, they set about quarreling over how best to go about getting small game. Silva wanted to design and build an elaborate contraption with some sort of gate, while Carpenter didn't understand why they couldn't just gather some milkweed to make lines for simple snares.

"We can carry the trap," Silva explained as they smoked, watching the strings trailing into the water, "and bait it with fish anywhere. With your snares, we have to find dens."

"Ideally," Carpenter replied, rubbing his arms and shivering.

"I don't know how," Silva said, giving him a funny look.

"I do."

There was a pause. "Oh," Silva replied, taking the cigarette. Carpenter went back to trimming the bark from the green branches he'd cut, and sharpening the ends. The fish were visible under the surface, so it was no surprise that it didn't take long for them to start biting.

"Figures we'd be the ones to find gold here," he muttered, bringing the first up out of the water, held tightly in his hand. He showed it to Silva, who admired the bright golden scales.

"Pretty," the other man admitted.

"Are you as good at cooking fish as you are at your trail food?"

Silva's disgusted expression was the only answer

that was needed. Carpenter sighed and laid the skewers aside to set about the cleaning himself. Silva made another face when Carpenter threw the guts into the fire. There was no choice; they'd bring wolves otherwise. The fire itself wouldn't give them away, though. Not with this hazy curtain of rain to camouflage it.

Soon the fish were over the flames, and the hooks were back in the water. They were trout, according to Silva, and they were about the best fish Carpenter had ever tasted, though his hunger likely played a role in that valuation.

"You're a fair cook," Silva confessed as they ate.

It didn't take much expertise to turn the skewers so the fish wouldn't burn, but Carpenter wasn't going to point that out.

"Suppose I have to be," he said, yawning. "My wife's gone, and I haven't even got my good looks to fall back on." He probed tenderly at his swollen eye. Silva smirked. "You aren't so pretty anymore, neither," Carpenter pointed out.

The other man touched his own chest, frowning as he probed at his ribs. "That may be. I'm just fortunate to be whole."

That was a sensible way of looking at it.

There was another fish on, but only one out of four. Carpenter left the line where it was. He'd pull them in when they'd all been taken.

"More fortunate than that boy," Silva added. "You left half his teeth on the ground."

"I know," Carpenter replied, grimacing.

"Nothing he didn't bring on himself," Silva assured him.

"You think your son wouldn't do something foolish to impress his pa?"

"I like to think my son would have more intelligence."

"How much intelligence did you have at that age?" Carpenter asked.

"Less than I have now, but that's a strange thing to say." Silva handed the cigarette back, "as I could not say that I feel unduly burdened by cleverness. At the moment."

"Cleverness is easy on the back. As burdens go."

Silva grinned.

THE TEMPTATION TO sloth was strong, but when the rain stopped, they got back on the move. It was frustrating not to know if they weren't being pursued due to a lack of means or a lack of inclination. If there was no desire to give chase, that was one thing. If there was unfinished business and Hale simply lacked a tracker to lead his men into the wilderness, that was another matter.

It was a forest like none Carpenter had ever seen before, with vast trees and mountain slopes covered with boulders the size of houses. The sun emerged to warm the ground and light up the path with a scattered speckling of gold over the ever-present carpet of pine needles.

They crested a rise, coming into something like a clearing and nearly stumbling over a cluster of mushrooms that stood as tall as their ankles. Carpenter considered the position of the sun, then looked ahead.

"How fine should we cut it when we get to the camp?" he asked Silva. "Simpler to take it on the north."

"I'll defer to you, Mr. Carpenter. I'm a poor navigator at the best of times."

He sighed. "Then, though I don't care for any more nights than necessary on the ground, I would say we take our time. Hope that Hale loses interest, if he is keeping an eye out. Or that be believes we've gotten past him."

"Seems reasonable."

The sun brought heat with it, and by late afternoon, the bubbling of the river was too much to resist. It was a narrow stretch with a good deal of the water in rocky shallows. It was a good place to stop and bathe, and nice enough to look at that it wouldn't have been half bad just to sit idle.

As they climbed out to dry and dress, Carpenter stopped in his tracks.

"What's the matter?" Silva joined him, wiping water out of his eyes.

"My eyes are even worse than I thought." Carpenter pointed to a small pile of stones. It must have been there all along; they had walked right past it, more interested in the cool water of the river than anything else. "Savages, you think?"

Silva shook his head. "Prospector. To show that he's already panned here."

"I thought they used flags."

"They're meant to. Only, there shouldn't be any claims here. This is all the commissioner's land."

"That won't stop anyone."

"Clearly. We had best be wary; whoever put this here is in violation of one law already. He might see fit to violate another."

He was right. They had strolled along without a care, but no matter how much it might seem they were the only two men in these mountains, they most certainly were not. Still, they were better off to follow the water in the open than to go creeping through the brush.

Some half a mile down, they paused again. Though the breeze tried gamely, it couldn't completely carry the smell away.

Silva covered his mouth with his shirt, but Carpenter didn't. It was an unmistakable odor. He'd spent long enough at war to know a rotting body when he smelled one.

"Must we?" Silva asked, following his gaze into the trees.

"Might as well," Carpenter replied.

CHAPTER FOURTEEN

T HERE WASN'T MUCH left of him.
Wolves had done for the rest, and done it thoroughly enough that there was no telling what had killed him. Perhaps he had worked too hard, or been injured and succumbed to sickness. Or maybe the wolves themselves had done it. The poor fellow had had no weapon to defend himself by the look of things, but if it was men who had done this, they might have taken it. He did have a piece of paper crudely drawn on with charcoal. Carpenter couldn't make sense of it, but he put it in his pocket anyway.

"Wait a minute," Carpenter said, hefting a small bag. "My mistake. He wasn't robbed."

Silva was holding his distance and his nose. Carpenter threw him the bag, which he caught.

Silva pulled the strings and opened it, looking surprised. "Gold," he said. "Not as much as it looks like, though. There's stone here as well."

"Still enough to make a man curious."

One of the man's canvas bags was still intact, likely because there hadn't been any food in it.

"The only thing I'm curious about is how long you want to linger," Silva said.

"We still have to bury him."

"There's a time to stop being decent."

"Maybe so, but this ain't it."

Silva groaned and joined him, picking up the prospector's shovel. "Here?" he asked, irked.

"Go down a bit. The earth will be softer." Carpenter pointed.

"At once, sir," Silva replied dryly.

A burial was necessary, and a marker. That was all, though. They would still take what might be useful. The trek ahead would be long, and making it with nothing but a shaving knife would likely make it feel a good deal longer. Carpenter had no particular compunction about robbing the dead man under the circumstances; he wasn't superstitious.

Silva dug, and Carpenter used the line he'd woven on the way for snares to tie a cross for the prospector. An hour later the work was done, though the flies still gathered in the air.

Together, they considered the grave.

There was an obligation to say something, but nothing came to mind. Carpenter was no preacher, and he'd never been especially pious. Silva seemed to be of the same mind.

"Lonely way to die," Carpenter murmured after a minute, wiping his brow.

Silva just nodded.

They returned to the water, where the fresh air and the breeze carried away the worst of the smell, though it still lingered about the canvas bag. They had taken a sack of tobacco from the dead man, among other things, and Carpenter hoped the odor wouldn't stay tenaciously enough to deter them from smoking it.

There were rabbit dens under some of the smaller trees, and the prospector had had wire in his pockets, so there was no more need for milkweed. Carpenter tied snares and placed them, then rejoined Silva at the edge of the water, perching on a rock still warm from the sun, which was getting low.

"We haven't made but five miles today," he noted.

"If that," Silva agreed, resting his chin on his hands and staring at the distant peaks.

Carpenter considered this side of the river, then the other. There weren't any markers here.

After several minutes, he got to his feet and rolled up his trouser legs. Silva looked on curiously as he took the prospector's pan from the bag and waded out, feeling with his toes for promising gravel.

The truth was, he'd always wanted to try it. It wasn't as though he'd get a better chance.

He got a bit of gravel and went about the business of sloshing the water from side to side.

Unable to help himself, Silva waded out curiously for a closer look.

"Is this what it is?" he asked, unimpressed. "This is what they all come all this way for?"

"You want to do it a certain way," Carpenter murmured distractedly. He switched to sloshing in a circular motion.

"Why?"

"The gold is heavy. This will keep it at the bottom. We get rid of the rest."

"I know *that* much, Mr. Carpenter." Of course he did; he'd been to school.

Carpenter carried the pan back to a rock and set it down, picking out some of the larger stones.

"To do this all day," Silva said, shaking his head. "I know they do, but I don't believe I could."

"All day. But with method," Carpenter explained. "To determine where the real gold is."

"How, though? *That* part, I don't fully understand."

"If I knew that, I might have tried my hand at it."

"At your age?"

"Why not? Gold will do that to a man."

Together, they poked through the silt and fine gravel that remained in the bottom of the pan.

"This is good," Carpenter noted. "Black sand."

"It's not sand. It's metal."

"Is it? I only know that it means we did it right."

"Tedious work, isn't it?"

"Yes, but look there." Carpenter indicated with a dripping finger. There was a tiny glimmer in the dirty water. He scooped it out, and separated the tiny piece of gold from the sand. It was hardly larger than a few grains of the sand, but it was unquestionably gold.

"Well," Silva said.

"Isn't it something?"

"It really is."

Carpenter peered past him. "And upstream, somewhere, there's a meaningful deposit." He snorted and shook his head. "Finding it, though . . ."

"Shall we try again?" Silva asked, taking the pan, not bothering to hide the eagerness on his face. Panning wouldn't make him rich, but it was a novel diversion for a while.

Birds erupted from the trees, and the crack of a rifle shot was what had made them do it.

The bullet struck the pan, sending it spinning in the air, sand and water flying.

Silva was faster to act than Carpenter was, pulling him down to the stream and behind a boulder. Silva held his pistol above the water but didn't lean out to look. The shot had come from upriver, in the trees on the south side. The shooter had to be some distance off, or he wouldn't have missed.

The pan struck the water, and Silva pointed. Carpenter wasn't inclined to make it a debate.

Silva rose, firing rapidly as Carpenter made a run for it, splashing through the shallows and onto the bank. He snatched up what he could of their belongings on his way to shelter behind a thick tree.

Another shot came from the rifle, but Silva scrambled out of the river unscathed.

They plunged into the trees, making as fast as possible for better cover. It had been naive to think that because no pursuer had caught up to them at once there was no pursuit. Giving in to laziness and following the water had been bad enough; giving in to sloth and simply waiting to be killed had been nothing short of an invitation to that bullet.

Carpenter would never know if he'd really been foolish enough to think they were safe or if he had just convinced himself that they ought to be. It was too easy to let suspicions lie, to tell himself that the details didn't matter when the bullets were flying.

The truth was what it had always been, what should have been obvious to him from the beginning: Hale hadn't meant to run Silva out of town. That had not been anyone's goal, and it hurt that Carpenter had allowed himself to believe it. Of course, if merely convincing Silva to leave had been the intent, they would have made no effort to stop him. There would have been no need for jailing him.

And *certainly* no cause for pursuing him. But here Carpenter and Silva were, crashing over loose, crumbling rocks that threatened to send them tumbling down slopes, scratched and cut every step of the way by sharp branches because all of those things were preferable to the alternative.

Silva had never been meant to leave Antelope Valley.

Carpenter lost his footing, but caught a sturdy branch and stayed on his feet, staggering down the hill and into a clearing. Silva was already there, tipping the spent cartridges out of his pistol, but he had no more. Even if he had, they wouldn't have done any good.

It was hard to know who was out there. Whoever it was, they had poor judgment to have attempted that shot, and they had made very poor time in their pursuit. But in the end, despite those things, they would still be soldiers, or men who had been at one time. Their slow pace suggested more of them, not fewer.

There was nothing as obvious as crashing footsteps to give away their pursuers, but all the birds had gone quiet, and a new sound rose up over the distant rushing of the river. They stumbled to a halt, gasping for breath and looking up in wonder.

The howling was such a powerful chorus that Carpenter wouldn't have thought there could possibly have been so many wolves in the world.

CHAPTER FIFTEEN

T HE MOON HUNG in the air all but full, taunting them.

Never had Carpenter covered so much ground on foot, even as a young man, even during the war. At least in the war, they had marched like civilized people. This mad, ragged dash across the mountains was another matter entirely, and it didn't suit him.

Silva fared little better. He was younger but not stronger.

The howling had died down hours ago, and Carpenter was more worried about bullets now. Fred *had* to be behind that rifle; he was the only one foolish enough to ruin everything with a greedy shot. It might have been Isaiah with him or O'Doul, or the both of them, or even John as well. It wouldn't have been Hale's younger hired men; clearly his true intent wasn't known to them or even to his own son. William *had* tried in good faith to drive Silva out. He'd taken his father's words at face value.

No, the only ones Hale would have trusted enough for this work were his *own* men, the ones he had known a long time. That was good; even the youngest of them was over forty, so they couldn't be making much better time than Carpenter and Silva.

They found a shallow brook and waded upstream for at least three hundred yards before continuing into the brush. That would stand a good chance of shaking off their followers, at least for a while.

With the sun down, it wasn't long until the cold set in, but it was only after they finally stopped moving that they started to shiver. Not a word had passed between them since the river, but Carpenter considered it a point of pride that he wasn't groaning in pain with every move he made. He settled on the pine needles and put his back against a tree. He didn't know how many days this body had left in it, but if they were days like this one, it wouldn't be many.

Silva was just a shape in the dark. A fire was out of the question. A smoke, though? He didn't have the strength to roll it.

"I take it they want what you buried," he said finally. "Was that why William was watching you?"

"No. He wouldn't have ridden on, if so. He was just to let his father know that I really had come back."

"What did you bury?"

"My patent. Plans. Some money." Silva sighed, propping his feet up against another tree. "It's the patent he wants."

Carpenter put his face in his hands and rubbed.

Driving Silva out and putting a stop to the factory had never been to Hale's advantage; of course he'd never really wanted it gone.

He'd wanted it to be *his*.

"It don't make sense," Carpenter groaned, running his hand through his hair. "Why?"

"There is only one reason, Mr. Carpenter."

"I know that." He sighed. "He made money after the war. I know he did."

"I can never know for certain," Silva replied. "My inference was that he overplayed."

"I wrote to the man. He wrote to me."

"I am sure he mentioned only his successes. Hale is a vain man, Mr. Carpenter."

That much he'd already known. He grimaced.

"I believe he looked to the west and he saw the gold, the camps, and the profits flowing, but did not understand. These men are not uncommon. They see the success of others and attempt to duplicate it without ever properly understanding why it came about." He hesitated for a moment. "I wonder if Mr. Hale, in his haste, did not wish to wait for credible intelligence of a likely gold deposit."

It took Carpenter a moment to take his meaning. "You want to say that instead of following the prospectors to Antelope Valley, he incited them to go in the first place?"

"He may have had a rumor," Silva suggested, "or something to that effect to guide him."

"He gambled and lost," Carpenter growled. "I can believe it. The man always was the worst card player that God ever cursed this earth with. What I can't believe is that he's doing *this*."

"He's your friend."

"That ain't the point. You want to tell me he's a common *robber*."

Silva snapped the branch he'd been toying with. "I don't have to tell you," he said quietly, and that was true enough.

Carpenter had seen all of the signs for himself. It was pathetic that it had taken him this long to look at it with clear eyes, but now that he had, he couldn't find it in himself to be surprised.

The urgency in the things that Hale had done: Carpenter had noted it before, and he hadn't been wrong.

"He owes money," he said.

"I expect he does," Silva replied.

"To someone who puts the fear of God in him."

"Or the fear of something more meaningful. And immediate."

Carpenter groaned. Silva let out something that might have been a laugh.

"You look as though *you're* the one who's had his house burned." A pause. "And his hound butchered."

Carpenter swallowed. "You're butchering my memories, Silva. And they have some value for me. Or I should say that they did."

The other man grunted noncommittally, but he understood even if he wouldn't say so. The shadows of the past stretched so long that the present was lost in them. The two of them hadn't eaten, and they carried nothing helpful with them. Nothing to make a snare with, and nothing for fishing, not that Carpenter had any intention of going back to the river. Hunger and thirst weren't the foremost things on his mind, but they would be soon. The growling of his belly wouldn't let him forget it, and Silva was no better off.

"Hale's foolishness and his debt became my misfortune," the younger man mused.

Carpenter didn't reply to that. It was succinct, and though he didn't take kindly to it, it was true.

"How far do you suppose I'll have to go," Silva went on, "to be away from him and all this?"

"I couldn't tell you." There had been a time when he'd have had an answer, but that was behind him. Tonight he'd opened his eyes to all of it, and it was as though he didn't know anything at all. Of all the men to give advice, he would be the last.

"You're his friend, aren't you?" Silva pressed.

"Yes."

"If he's willing to turn on you, I suppose there is no saying how far he'll go. May I at least stop running once I reach the Atlantic?"

"To catch your breath, at least."

In fact, Hale probably didn't have the resources to pursue Silva very far or very effectively, but that wasn't really the problem. The problem was that the world was full of Hales, and if Silva wasn't welcome here, where *could* he go?

Silva drew his pistol and cocked it. He sat up, expression flat. "Come out," he said, his exhaustion thick in his voice.

It was disappointing how quickly Carpenter's flash of panic came and went. It was there and gone before he had time to think, leaving only something like resignation. He sat up a little, frowning as he followed the barrel of Silva's gun.

"I apologize" came a man's voice from the dark, and this man sounded every bit as worn-out as they were.

Silva kept the pistol up. It was empty of course, but this fellow didn't know that. He emerged from behind a tree, unnervingly close by. Carpenter hadn't even suspected there was anyone coming, but his blood was still pumping, and his breath still wasn't coming easy. To spend a day truly on the run was nothing to make light of even for a young man. For his part, he was just glad he'd made it this far.

"I shouldn't have approached," the man said.

"I would agree with that," Silva replied, rising to his feet and holding the gun at arm's length. What he was doing was wise: appearing strong and confident, and that took Carpenter aback. It wasn't that he was doing the sensible thing that was a surprise; it was that he had the energy to do it convincingly.

"It was just curiosity, I guess." The man came a little closer, and the moonlight found him. He was as grubby and worn as they were—no, he was worse off. Carpenter and Silva looked a fright after just two days, but this man must have been making his way for a good deal longer than that. Dark circles ringed his eyes, and he had the makings of a beard. It was difficult to know his age, or even guess it, but he had a bad limp.

"You understand," he said, peering at them in the dark. "Two voices, no fire."

"Are you alone, sir?" Carpenter asked.

"I believe he is," Silva replied.

"May I sit?" the stranger asked.

"Depends who's chasing you," Silva told him frankly. Carpenter couldn't disagree; it was the only reason this fellow might have been creeping through the woods in the dark rather than sitting beside his own fire.

The moonlight caught the tip of the rifle over the man's back, though he'd made no move toward it.

"Bounty hunters," he replied, "I expect."

That was a blunt and honest answer.

"For good reason?" Carpenter asked.

The stranger hesitated. "Yeah," he said after a moment. "I guess so."

"Thinking of robbing us?"

Silva snorted before the other man could answer. He put his pistol back in its holster. "We've nothing for him to take." He gestured in his gentlemanly way.

The stranger took off his things and settled beside them, taking a deep breath and looking over his shoulder. He began to rummage through his pack.

"Have you heard the wolves?" he asked.

"Now and then." Silva paused to listen for a moment. Hearing nothing, he went back to his place, sheltered behind boulders. "There must be quite a few."

"On all sides, feels like."

"Do you take precautions?"

The stranger shrugged, coming up with a package wrapped in paper. "Their dens are in these woods. We can't know where. That's what'll make the difference if they make a move or not." He smiled in the dark. "We may walk too near to one, never knowing what we were doing. Or we may not." He shrugged again, but there was no levity in it. His voice was melancholy. "Who can say? It's a gamble."

They watched him unwrap some hardtack. He took a bite, struggling a little with no water to soak it in; then he offered the package. Carpenter took a piece readily, and so did Silva.

"We're grateful," Carpenter said.

"Wolves have nothing to fear from us," Silva added.

"They don't know that. Even if they did, it wouldn't make any difference." The stranger cleared his throat absently. "It's what you do when someone comes for you. You bite."

Silva chewed and swallowed. "You seem to have a grasp of the animal."

The stranger chewed, regarding them in the gloom. "Is that what brings you here?" he asked finally. "Did you wander too near a den?"

"Could be," Carpenter murmured, looking up as something rustled in the dark. The stranger looked as well, but it was just the wind and the branches. "And you?"

The stranger finished his piece of hardtack.

"Maybe," he said after a moment, and as he folded the paper packet back over it, Carpenter saw that he was missing fingers from his right hand. He put the hardtack back in his bag and pulled the strings to close it tightly. "But I gave them cause. It's like you said. I've done wrong."

"What did you do?"

"What I thought was right," the stranger replied with a sigh, rising to his feet. He picked up his pack and put his rifle over his shoulder. "At the time. I'll go on now. It's for the best if you don't meet my friends."

"Nor you ours," Silva told him.

CHAPTER SIXTEEN

A SHARED BITE with a benign stranger was a reas-surance, but it wasn't a hot meal or a soft bed. The sun rose on Carpenter in such a state that he did not so much rise from his bed of pine needles, some five miles from the place where they had met the stranger, as drag himself from it.

The first creek they found was too meager to offer any fish, even if they had had the means to catch them, but the cool water was welcome. Bathing was all well and good, but what they really needed was a laundry. A discovery of a small supply of wild berries at midmorning was a windfall, but it wasn't enough. Carpenter hadn't been the most gregarious man to begin with, and he was well aware of the effect that hunger had on his disposition. It was going to be a curmudgeonly sort of day.

A few spiteful stones gave way, and he might have taken the sort of tumble that could leave a man with broken bones or worse, but Silva caught his arm.

"Did you use that language with your wife?" the younger man asked dryly, trying and failing to hide what an exertion it was to help lift a man of Carpenter's size.

Carpenter stopped swearing, which was good, because he was thoroughly winded. He groaned and sagged against a tree, then slid down to sit, wiping his brow. He took several breaths, peering up at the sun, which despite all these enormous trees still found ways to slip through and blind him painfully, joining the sweat stinging his gritty eyes. He wished he had his hat, which had been taken by the wind when they tried to flee the camp.

"You might make better time without me," he said, leaning back.

"That is a miraculous talent you have, Mr. Carpenter."

"Oh?"

"You saved my life." Silva turned his back on him and looked back down the hill they'd climbed. He'd been planning to go on, but instead he just looked over his shoulder and gestured vaguely at Carpenter. "This is what it's earned you. Half starved, and more than half done in, by the look of us. No prospect of anything good, certainly."

Even if he'd wanted to, Carpenter had a feeling that if he opened his mouth, the best he could do at the moment was wheeze.

"I haven't even thanked you. And I won't," Silva added. "Of course. You're a busybody."

"Is that my talent?" Carpenter managed at last.

"No, your talent is all that and no temper." Silva snorted. "It's really something, Mr. Carpenter."

"Oh, I'd have one," Carpenter replied grumpily, examining the calluses on his palms, "if I thought there was any use in it."

"There is a use. You feel better."

"How do you feel?"

"I'm angry."

"Does it help?"

Silva just walked over and put his hand out. Carpenter took it and let the younger man pull him up. Silva started to climb again, but Carpenter didn't.

"Can you walk?" Silva asked, looking back.

"We won't last without provisions," Carpenter told him. It was nothing Silva didn't already know, but one of them had to say it. They could stay alive out here a good while, but neither was really any good at fielding this country. That was obvious. They wouldn't starve or die of thirst, but they would be hungry, irritable, and ultimately careless. One of them would trip, or something else would happen. Things were already bad.

A sprained ankle or a cracked rib would bring certain finality to the matter. Going on like this could only end one way. If Silva knew it, he was leaning all his weight on the knowledge, pushing down with both hands, trying to keep it out of sight. The detail that they had no ultimate destination was secondary, because even if they had one . . .

Carpenter shook his head. "It ain't smart," he said honestly.

Silva, determined to be Silva, just put his hands on his hips. "When, Mr. Carpenter, have you known me to be smart? Or anything even resembling such a thing?"

It was a good point; they'd met when Silva had quite deliberately been returning to a town full of influential men who meant to kill him. He'd been traveling alone and evidently ready to put his faith in . . . what, exactly? In the letter that had been in his pocket? In the decency of men? In the hollow hope that ignoring a problem would make it go away? In that airy, theoretical notion that in a civilized world, men must behave in a civilized manner?

None of that was real, but apparently he'd believed in it just the same.

There was a word for that, but "smart" wasn't it.

"You are, though. And you know better," Carpenter told him frankly. There wasn't time for Silva's ego. "Is there anyone you can trust?"

"No more than I trust that fellow we met last night."

"He didn't stay but a minute. For a moment I thought I'd dreamed that."

"For that, you'd have to sleep."

"And you snore so loudly that no one could."

"The hunger's given you leave of your senses. You are hearing things, Mr. Carpenter."

"My senses are sharp, Mr. Silva. Particularly my sense for a man who doesn't want to answer a question."

Silva folded his arms and leaned against a tree, brushing a fly off his shoulder. "I had one friend in Antelope Valley, or one man that I would have liked to call such."

"Your business partner?"

Silva nodded, scowling. "Mr. Karr."

"You think Hale bought him?"

"I hope so. The alternative would be that he threatened him." Silva took a deep breath. "That would be a low thing to do. Mr. Karr has a wife and children, and I hold nothing against him for doing what was best for them. To cross Hale would be to sabotage his own interests, I know that. I know it," he repeated, though Carpenter hadn't said anything. It sounded as though the younger man had given this a fair amount of thought. Well, however betrayed he felt by this Mr. Karr, he seemed determined to be decent about it. That was admirable, at least.

"Does he have horses?" Carpenter asked.

"He does."

"Will he give them to us?"

"He owes me that much."

"But will he *give* them to us?"

"I pity him if he doesn't," Silva said, face bleak.

"Then we'd best call on him." That was enough self-indulgence; Carpenter got raggedly to his aching feet and took Silva's hand to clamber over the rocks. "Where is his property?"

"Northeast of the town proper."

That was convenient; they could pay him a visit without going either too far out of their way or too near to Antelope Valley.

"Turn us a touch south, then." Carpenter pointed.

"Oh, at once, Captain Carpenter."

"I was never an officer."

"I am surprised to hear that."

"Good Lord, why? I'm good at a lot of things, Silva. War ain't one of them."

Their new course mercifully gave them a few miles on ground that was nearly flat, but then it was back to seeking a pass on the slopes. They could have stopped and taken the time to gather some plants suitable to crafting snares or fishing lines with, but a little hunger felt like an appropriate price to pay for reaching their destination more quickly. Mr. Karr would have something to eat that they would not have to catch or snare, and he would part with it if he knew what was good for him. It was the least he could do for abandoning his partner, however difficult it might have been to blame him for doing so.

"Perhaps," Silva said, slightly short of breath as they picked their way through a particularly dense copse of trees, "Mr. Karr will see fit also to lend me a handful of cartridges. For my safe travels."

"You want to dig it up, then." Carpenter meant what Silva had buried along the trail.

"I must."

"He'll have people looking for it," Carpenter pointed out.

"Of that, I have no doubt." Silva slapped a buzzing insect and looked back. "And with enough time, they will find it."

He was right, but it was still a risk. If they could get some horses and ride away now, it was a safe bet that Hale would never catch up. His resources were limited; he didn't have *so* many men at his disposal, and did he even have money to pay them with? His desperation in the play he was making for Silva's factory suggested that he didn't.

Still, if Silva allowed his patent to fall into Hale's hands, that was trouble. Even if Silva could find the means to get the matter to a courtroom, was there even the slightest chance that a white judge would side with a Mexican over Hale? Small details like facts would be unlikely to get between Hale and his goal.

Silva just wanted the same thing he had from the very beginning: to keep what was his.

"All right," Carpenter said without much enthusiasm, climbing gamely after him.

"I don't need your blessing," Silva said, glancing over his shoulder. Then he stopped and looked back properly. "But I do appreciate it."

Carpenter would have liked to tell him that he was very welcome. That would have been the polite thing to do, and Silva was nothing if not polite.

But he wasn't very observant.

Not that Carpenter intended to be critical of that; he wasn't much better himself.

"I see that squint on you, Bill," Yates said. "I didn't take you for a blind man."

Carpenter sighed. Yates wasn't even hiding; he was right there in front of them, off to the right, leaning against a tree. And now that Carpenter was awake, there was someone else with him, a younger man he didn't recognize.

Yates wasn't aiming the rifle in his hands because he could see that he didn't need to. Time hadn't changed the look of him much, though there was a touch of gray in his short beard. It appeared he still liked to do and say everything as though there were all the time in the world.

The boy wasn't quite as relaxed. His pistol was in his hand, and there was a sheen of sweat on him that had nothing to do with the heavy pack he was carrying.

Carpenter had nothing to blame but his own inattention, though it was unlikely there was much that could've prevented this. Even at his best, he didn't have a prayer of evading Yates in the wilderness. Yates knew what he was doing, which made it all the stranger.

"Did you take that shot when we were in the river?" Carpenter asked, unable to help himself.

The other man twitched, but smiled wryly. "I only wanted to put it in your wing," he said, looking openly disgruntled. "Couldn't help but try. I thought I could make this a shorter trip, and you wouldn't mind. You've had worse, Bill."

"You used to have a bit more compassion," Carpenter said dryly. "That, and I never knew you to miss."

"Are *your* eyes as good as they used to be, Bill?"

"Yates, I'm lucky when someone writes big enough for me to read."

"Then you know just how it is."

"But you shot at me anyway," Carpenter accused. "You might have killed me."

"Sometimes greed gets the best of us, Bill. In my defense, it has been a long time since I've had to make a shot that counted for anything," he added.

"Duly noted."

"I do apologize," Silva cut in, giving Carpenter a look. "Is there something we can help you gentlemen with?" He brought an impressive amount of dignity to the words, given how dirty and disheveled the two of them were.

Yates didn't look happy to be there, and that wasn't quite right. He was Carpenter's age: too old to be tromping around the wilderness, and certainly chasing an old friend couldn't have been his *preferred* occupation. Yet he ought to have been able to find something in it, some bleak humor. He and Carpenter had always had that in common.

There was none. Yates wanted to look like his usual self, but there was nothing real about it. Even if he still always had a joke ready and a smile on, this wasn't the same man.

"You don't look so good, Silva." There wasn't any ill will in the words. They were true; there was no arguing with that. "Are you through running?"

CHAPTER SEVENTEEN

P LEASE, BILL." YATES gave him a patient look, and Carpenter sighed.

He turned his wrists so that his palms faced inward, and Yates wrapped the rope around them to bind his hands tightly. It had been worth a try; if they'd tied his hands with them held horizontally, Carpenter would have had enough slack left to get free.

But Yates knew that trick, and he was still sharp enough to look for it.

The young man's name was Rene, and he was another of the boys in Hale's employ. A few years ago, he probably wouldn't have been necessary, but though Yates seemed spry enough, it had to help him a great deal to have a pair of hands to haul the baggage.

It didn't feel good to come this far on foot, only to go back the same way. Yates and Rene couldn't have brought their horses any farther than the top of that first rise out of town, so they'd come a long way with their boots as well.

On the bright side, Carpenter had finally come to the place where he'd walked enough that he just didn't notice the pain in his feet anymore. It was a familiar feeling; he'd had it more than once on the march during the war. A man wasn't made to walk all day, and it was anyone's guess if it would be his feet or his knees that gave in first. For all his youth, Silva wasn't doing much better. Rene was the same.

Yates wasn't having any trouble, though. He was miserable, but not because of the exercise. He'd always been that sort: the one who ran the fastest, shot the straightest, and generally complained the least. Even when his luck turned bad, as it had after the war. He'd married, and Carpenter had never met her, but Hale had mentioned in a letter that she was really something. Things must have been all right for a while, then. But five or six years later, Hale mentioned that Yates had lost a little one.

And then a year or two on, the wife as well. All that, and still not a single letter from Yates himself. Carpenter had written him, though, and he remembered composing that letter. How he'd only done it because it seemed the decent thing to do, not because he understood. He hadn't understood, and worse, he hadn't expected he ever would. Penelope had still been with him then, and he hadn't even been able to imagine that the day might come when she wouldn't be.

With Yates, there wasn't any denying it. He'd had a hard run of things, but it looked as though Hale and the boys had stood with him through it.

Now, as Carpenter slogged through the pine needles with his eyes on Yates' back, he realized he was following in the other man's footsteps in more ways than one. Or he would have, if he hadn't met Silva. Yates had lost his wife and, for lack of other family, gone back to the boys. Carpenter hadn't given it any thought, but he'd done the exact same thing.

"You weren't at dinner the other night," he said.

"I was riding back from the Gray Hollow claim," Yates said over his shoulder. "It took so long because the assayer thought he found something, but when we looked closer, it wasn't nothing worth the time."

"You sure? Or did he tell you that so he could go back himself?" Carpenter asked.

"I don't believe so. If he did, that's the last mistake he'll ever make," Yates said lightly.

"Then there's nothing at Gray Hollow?" Silva asked.

"Don't look like it."

"That's a pity."

Yates glanced back and snorted. "That it is."

"About the only claim within ten miles that anyone was really sure about," Silva said to Carpenter. "Who owned it, Mr. Yates?"

"Wayne Palance."

"That's right, Mr. Palance. Has he been found, by chance?" Silva asked dryly.

"He has not," Yates replied, just as dryly.

"Where'd he go?" Carpenter asked.

"Who can say?" Silva replied, his eyes on Yates' back. "I'd hate to think someone did something untoward. Particularly if it was for nothing."

"You do hate to see that sort of thing happen."

So Yates was Hale's agent for seeking out the gold in Antelope Valley. Had he really killed a man because he thought his claim might be worth something, as Silva wanted to imply? Carpenter preferred to think that Yates wouldn't do that, but he'd also have preferred to think that Yates wouldn't shoot at him. Even just to put one in his wing.

That wasn't a good feeling, but of the four of them,

none could have been feeling worse than Rene. The boy kept his mouth shut and toiled along stoically, watching Carpenter and Silva, but it was as clear as day that this wasn't what he was here for.

"I guess I can't blame you for doing what the captain tells you," Carpenter said. "But it ain't right to bring the boy into it, Yates."

"The boy volunteered," Yates replied, taking a few big steps to scale a slope. He put his rifle in the crook of his arm and reached back to help Carpenter up. "Isn't that so, Rene?"

"I did, sir."

"Son, do you understand what's happening here? I can't imagine that you do. If you did, you wouldn't want no part of it," Carpenter said, disappointed.

"Mister, I understand that I need to do a good job for Mr. Hale," Rene said, only a little breathless. He had backbone at least, and there was no faulting him. He probably had a family to think about, brothers and sisters. Everybody needed money, and it was no surprise that the people of Antelope Valley were still under the mistaken impression that Hale had some.

The boy hadn't been to war, but Carpenter wouldn't be able to count on him losing his nerve if he had to shoot.

The going was even slower with four, and the daylight didn't wait for them. As the twilight came on, the trail grew more treacherous, not just for the two men with tied hands. Prisoners were harder to watch in poor light, and Yates was being careful. He called a halt well before it was fully dark.

Carpenter couldn't be pleased about his circumstances, but he didn't complain about a fire, a meal, and a chance to rest. He'd been through enough that having to eat with his hands tied was the least of the hardship.

"Do you really need to watch me so close?" he asked Yates. "I'm soft, remember?"

"You used to be, sure enough." Yates was on the other side of the fire, and he'd made a point to keep Rene close to him and far from Carpenter. He'd also tied a rope from Carpenter's right ankle to Silva's left, and done it with some impressive knots, a few of which were new to Carpenter. "I saw Will. That fist of yours ain't none too soft, Bill."

Carpenter glanced down at his scabbed knuckles. That was true enough. "I do regret that."

"I'll guess you only did what you had to. Will ain't stupid," Yates added. "But he ain't what you'd call a thinker."

"This from a man who's traded chasing gold for chasing men," Silva remarked.

"Well, men are a good deal easier to find," Carpenter said, taking a bite of bread. "By and large."

"Can you play the harmonica with your hands tied, Bill?"

"I did not know you played," Silva remarked, affecting a hurt look.

"I could, if it weren't in my saddlebags."

"And where are they?" Yates asked.

"My hotel room, I expect."

"You really did leave in a hurry."

"Well," Carpenter replied, settling back against his tree stump, "they *were* shooting at us."

Yates sighed. "Wasn't no call to hurt the dog. I liked that dog."

"So did I," Silva replied darkly.

"Hang it up, Silva," Yates told him, getting to his feet. He came around the fire and offered Carpenter his smoke. "Ain't no money in making it difficult." There wasn't any money in going quietly, either, but Carpenter didn't point that out. This was as close as

Yates would come to talking about what lay ahead, and Carpenter knew better than to ask.

"Beautiful country out here," he pointed out instead, taking in some smoke. "You wouldn't fault the man for not wanting to leave."

"Too many Yankees for my liking," Yates grumbled, going back to his spot across the fire and settling in. "And not enough gold."

"What would you do with it?"

"What?"

"The gold," Carpenter said. "If you had it."

Yates was taken aback, and for a moment he didn't say anything. "Hell," he muttered. "I don't know."

CHAPTER EIGHTEEN

IT WAS SOMETHING about the ropes on his wrists that put him in mind of it, though at the time it wasn't ropes but iron manacles. Still, at the feel of his hands being bound, that was where Carpenter's mind went. And wherever his brain staggered off to, his dreams would always follow.

But in the dreary, disappointing dreams that weren't dreams but just echoes of the past, the whip falling on his back didn't hurt so much. Even if it had, Carpenter was used to it. In fact, in the dream he didn't mind it at all. In the dream he knew the captain and the boys were there waiting for him when it was over, and there was a sense that the business was closed and the scales were balanced.

He knew it was only a dream, and that would've been all the more reason to stay there a little longer, but Yates wouldn't allow it. Camp was broken in the gray before dawn, and the march was back on, though one couldn't really march in the mountains. There was a clear sense of urgency in Yates, and Carpenter wasn't sure what to make of it. He had no plans to ask, but Yates fell back to go along beside him while Silva trailed behind, and Rene brought up the rear.

"I seen you panning in the river," Yates confided. "How did it look?"

"Just a few spots of color, that was all."

"Where'd you get the pan?"

It sounded as though Yates hadn't taken much of a look around after he missed his shot at the river. It was a fair question; he knew the two of them had gone on the run with nothing.

"There was a prospector who died. We found his body."

"Don't sound like that, Bill. I'd rob a dead man too in your place. Where was he?"

"In from the bank a bit, fifty yards or so. Near where the water bends around the tall rocks, the two of them, reddish and sharp."

Yates had seen them as well; it was a pretty view from that point.

"Had he found anything?"

"Only some dust," Carpenter told him. "He might have hidden something else, I suppose."

"Did you take it?"

"That really would be stealing. We took what we could use."

"Is there anything that can get you off that high horse?"

"If there was, you'd know it by now. That fellow used stones as markers, but I didn't see many holes. I'm no miner. I don't know what he was up to. Look in my pocket." Carpenter indicated his shirt, and Yates obligingly took out the folded piece of paper. He put his rifle over his shoulder and unfolded the paper curiously.

"Well," he said, brows rising. There was no mistaking the way he looked at it or the way he spoke when he talked about gold. Yates had never struck Carpenter as greedy; or rather, he'd never shown any real ambition beyond a desire to win the war and settle down. He'd gotten half of what he wanted.

"Can you make sense of it?"

Yates halted and turned around. "Hold on, Rene. Bill, is this meant to be the river?" He indicated it on the crude map.

"Has to be."

Silva caught up, awkwardly wiping his brow. It was still early, but already it was getting warm. Carpenter pointed to a pine needle stuck to the other man's neck, and Silva irritably brushed it off.

Rene reached them, pistol in hand, though he wasn't pointing it at anyone. He took his role as Silva's guard seriously; Hale would have been proud. An earnest kid like him shouldn't have been mixed up in this; he should've been working cows and looking for a wife.

But there weren't very many cows in Antelope Valley. Maybe things couldn't be that simple.

"Then here's where he panned and where he dug. Wasn't he lettered?" Yates complained. "Or is this a cipher?"

"No," Carpenter told him, halfheartedly waving at bugs buzzing around his head. "Don't judge the man, Yates. He ain't the one marching prisoners."

"You ever think, Bill, that if we could find some damn gold we wouldn't need prisoners?"

"Oh, for God's sake."

"No, look. This is interesting." Yates snorted and tapped the paper. "You see? He made a triangle, and he figured there was a deposit here. Right in here.

That's where he thought the quartz had to be. Were there holes?"

"I don't know," Carpenter told him. "It ain't my business."

"Are we meant to be prospectors now?" Silva asked tiredly.

"Might be foolish not to try while we got the chance." Yates looked up from the map, scowling at the trees. "We ain't meant to treat this as government land yet, but we will one day. Might as well get the gold out before that day comes."

"I suppose it don't matter who owns it," Carpenter noted lightly.

"I can't see that I'd lose sleep for stealing from federals," Yates replied.

"What about from Mr. Silva?"

Yates just snorted. "I don't know how good your prospector was, Bill. This here? This is likely bedrock. A deposit could be where he thought. Or it could be here, on the other side."

If Yates was so knowledgeable, where was *his* gold? But it wouldn't have been wise to ask.

"You think there's something there, Mr. Yates?" Rene asked, eyeing Silva suspiciously. Silva wasn't doing anything to put the boy at ease; he challenged him with his eyes every time he looked at him. If Rene had been Hale's son, William, he'd have shot Silva miles back.

But there wasn't any point telling him not to provoke the boy. Silva wasn't listening to anyone right now, and why should he with what was waiting for him? He didn't have much to lose, but he hadn't given up. He was still hoping for a chance.

With Yates, he probably wouldn't get one. Carpenter had met better men than Yates, if that was a fair thing to judge, but he'd met relatively few who were more competent.

He still wasn't convinced that Yates had missed him accidentally. Maybe that had been his chance to get away, and he hadn't delivered on it. Maybe Yates had followed them from the stream, hoping to lose the trail, hoping not to succeed. It was difficult to tell; Yates wasn't an easy read, except for when he was talking about gold. There was no subterfuge there, and no question about how he felt. Gold didn't make men crazy like everyone said; it just made them stupid.

"It ain't *so* far out of our way," Yates said hesitantly, looking at Rene. He was weighing it in his mind, or pretending to. He was thinking about their provisions and how long it would take to go back to the place along the river where he'd missed that shot. He was wondering if that prospector hadn't died before confirming his suspicions.

He was wondering if there wasn't gold there for the taking. It wasn't *really* a deliberation; Yates had already made up his mind.

"It'd be a shame not to look," Carpenter admitted after a moment. He'd have been the last one to discourage the man; anything that could buy time before returning to Hale was worth trying. And there was a part of him that wanted to believe that if there *was* gold near enough to Antelope Valley to bring the prospectors, maybe there was a path forward where Captain Hale didn't have to go through with all this.

There *might* be another way, but getting that notion pushed all the way up the hill and into the bright light of belief would be a big job, and Carpenter was too old. Maybe a younger man could do it, but not him.

All the same . . .

"Aw, hell," Yates grumbled, giving the paper one last look. "Why not? A little extra walking won't kill us. We ain't that old yet." He clapped Carpenter on the shoulder.

T HE SUN ROLLED across the sky as they slogged through the trees, and it was astounding the way every step always seemed to be uphill. The day moved along, but Carpenter's spirit was stuck in place, unsure if revealing the paper to Yates had been the right play. He wasn't much of a chess player at the best of times. Silva was pretty good, but he wasn't thinking at his clearest right now. His dislike of Yates was justified, and Yates hadn't made it any better by bringing up the dog. He had better be wary, because given the chance, Silva would kill him in a heartbeat.

CHAPTER NINETEEN

THE WOODS WERE nice enough to look at, but it wasn't easy to appreciate beauty when one was roasting in the heat and constantly pestered by insects. It was better by the water, where the breeze was always strong and the damp air felt almost cool. It was also flatter, and the smooth stones on the riverbank were less treacherous than the loam and the pine needles.

But it was hard to hear the bubbling of the water without remembering how Yates' shot had shattered the day and sent them running for their lives. It was a good walk back, and it took a full hour of searching to find the grave of the prospector. When they did, Yates seemed struck by it.

"What's the matter?" Carpenter asked, wincing at the pain in his wrists, which were now thoroughly raw. "Did you think I was leading you on?"

"No. I was just thinking it was mighty decent of you to do this for a stranger."

"You'd have done the same," Carpenter told him.

"If I'd been feeling spiritual," Yates replied after a moment, "I suppose I *might* have had the boy do it. But no, Bill, I don't think I would have. Would I have to dig him up to get his dust?"

"You wouldn't do that."

Something twitched in Yates' jaw. "No," he said after several long minutes. "No, I wouldn't."

It was another chore to orient themselves to the makeshift map, which was appallingly bad. The locations of the markers left Yates scratching his head, and even Carpenter felt a touch of irritation. An organized and methodical approach was supposed to be at the core of prospecting. Without that, what did you have? But that wasn't the most pressing concern for a man with his hands tied and a less-than-certain future.

It turned out that the prospector had done some digging before he passed, and the holes weren't too far from where they'd found his body. Rene stayed near Carpenter and Silva as Yates poked around. There wasn't much light for travel left in the day, but this hollow wasn't a bad place to camp. It was near the water at least.

"Could you put that away and make some coffee?" Silva said to Rene, and the words came out sounding surprisingly friendly, considering.

"I'd like to, Mr. Silva." The boy's fingers opened and closed on the handle of his pistol. "But I think I hadn't ought to."

Yates was going through the dead prospector's tools. That was a blessing; if there really was anything worth finding here, they would have everything they needed to extract it.

"Did you see that rock?" Carpenter said to Silva.

"Back in the water, twice your height. Did you see the shape of it?"

"I couldn't say I took note," Silva admitted, puzzled.

"Had a sort of cleft in it, by the look of it."

"What's that mean?" Rene asked.

Carpenter yawned. "Well, the water's flowing right into it. And it just flows on. But the gold's the heaviest thing in that water. Might be some collected there if it's the right shape under the surface."

"Ah," Silva said, giving him a funny look. "I believe I see."

"Say, Mr. Yates," Rene called out, keeping his eyes on Carpenter. "Mr. Carpenter says there's gold in the river."

"Keep trying, Bill," Yates called back without even looking. "You watch them close, Rene. Don't let them pull one over on you."

"Are you making things up?" the boy asked suspiciously, raising the pistol a bit.

Carpenter shrugged. "Couldn't tell you, son. First time I ever went looking for gold, the two of you shot at me. How do I know if there's gold in the river or not?"

"I could've made that shot," Rene muttered bitterly.

"If you think you can shoot better than Yates, then being young ain't an excuse. You're just a fool," Carpenter told him, and sighed. "But you make a good pot of coffee. Why don't you do that?"

"No, Mr. Carpenter," the boy said, turning the gun on him. "I don't think I ought to right now."

"Suit yourself."

Yates was returning from his inspection of the prospector's work.

"Did he find anything?" Silva asked curiously, and Yates scowled at him out of habit.

"It don't look good with these," he replied, pointing at the holes. "The rocks he dug ain't right, and it's just . . ." He trailed off, shaking his head. For a moment he appeared to deliberate; then he looked up and squinted. "I reckon we have enough time to go over the top and have a look at the other side."

With that, he shouldered the bag of tools and glanced at Rene.

"Lighten up, son. You'll have a different look on your face if we see a hint of that color—I'll tell you that," he said.

"It's all right, Mr. Yates."

"Hell no, it ain't, but it will be if we could find *one* half-decent pocket in all this. You never saw a place so barren. There's probably more gold under my old farm than in this whole valley." He glared at Carpenter. "If I hadn't lost my hat trying to chase you, I'd be stomping on it, Bill."

"Your hat has all the luck."

"Don't I know it? Keep on back from him, Rene," he said to the boy. "Old Silva ain't got much left to lose."

"He don't look like much."

"It don't matter."

"Yes, Mr. Yates."

The climb wasn't so bad, and neither was the way down. Even though Carpenter and Silva had their hands tied, exhaustion alone was better than exhaustion and hunger. Yates didn't mind sharing his store with his prisoners, though in Carpenter's reckoning that still wasn't enough to square them up for that shot he'd taken.

Rene made them sit at the foot of an enormous tree while he set up camp, and Yates hurried off. Reaching this place and seeing the prospector's work had energized him, and he was as brisk as if he hadn't just spent the better part of the day hiking. Carpenter had never seen the other man want anything so badly. There had been times in the war when they'd gone five days or more without food, and even then Yates hadn't seemed this hungry.

There was still enough light, though the sun was down behind the trees. It was a strange thing, and a little sad, to see a man work so hard without his heart in in. Yates didn't want to be here, doing this. He'd said himself that he didn't know how he'd spend the gold, yet he was still chasing it as though it meant something to him. He didn't want it, and his wife was dead; that meant he was doing it for Hale and the others.

Carpenter watched as the other man dropped the bag of tools and took a shovel, hurrying off down the hillside.

Rene looked worried, and Silva looked for an opening, but he didn't get one. Rene noticed the way he was watching him and forced both prisoners down into the shade of a tree before taking his bearings.

"For land with nothing on it and nobody rightly owning it, sure do seem to be a fair few fellas about," he remarked after a while. "Did you see him too?" Rene asked. "That raggedy one missing fingers?"

"We did," Carpenter said tiredly.

"That's funny. He didn't say he'd run across you," Rene replied. "Of course, Mr. Yates didn't believe him."

"Oh, I'm sure. He used to be an excellent judge of character," Carpenter replied to the boy, but he wasn't listening to him. He was watching Yates, who had found something that interested him about thirty feet down the slope.

Something changed in Silva, and Carpenter looked over sharply and caught the other man's eye.

Rene *had* given them a chance. He had sure footing, but that would change if anything startled him, and the slope was just steep enough that one good push would stand a reasonable chance of leaving him dead or maimed.

That wasn't lost on Silva, who was steeling himself to do just that. He would launch himself up and throw his shoulder into the boy, heedless of the gun. Rene wasn't fast or cool enough to shoot him, but Yates wouldn't miss. They wouldn't get far with their hands tied, and Silva would spend the rest of the journey being dragged by Carpenter with a bullet in his leg.

And things would go even worse for him when they returned to Hale.

"Don't," Carpenter warned under his breath.

"Why in God's name not?" Silva muttered back.

Because this wasn't the boy's fault any more than it was Silva's.

"You wouldn't get a hundred paces," Carpenter hissed.

The other man glared at him but didn't argue. It wasn't a lie.

Yates was trudging back up toward them, and they all looked at him expectantly. Rene wasn't going to say it himself, but he was of the same mind as the prisoners: that the day had been long enough already, and it was time to make camp and have something to eat.

It was clear that wasn't what Yates had in mind. He drew up a few paces below them, wiping his brow and wearing a funny look.

"Well?" Carpenter said, when it was clear no one else would.

"I reckon I found something," Yates replied, looking a little surprised by the words himself. He drew his knife and cut Carpenter free, offering his hand.

"Mr. Yates, is this smart?"

"Hell, Rene, ain't nothing I do is smart no more. Come on, Bill."

Sighing, Carpenter allowed the other man to pull him to his feet, shaking his wrists and working his shoulders. They hurt even more now.

"But why?" Rene asked, lost.

Yates snorted and shrugged at him. "Because old Bill's stronger than me and you together, son."

Carpenter followed him down to a rock that protruded from the hillside. Yates had already done a little work, shifting some earth to expose more of the stone.

"What do you make of that?" He leaned in and pointed.

Squinting, Carpenter moved closer to look. There was something rough and white there. He brushed away a bit more of the dirt, peering at it closely.

"I see it," he confirmed, straightening up and rubbing his wrists.

"Is it quartz?"

"Hell, Yates. I'm the wrong one to ask," he snapped, running his hand through his hair and looking back up the hill. "Ask Silva. He knows more than I do. I worked a factory in Richmond. What do I know about prospecting?"

"I saw you pan that river," Yates shot back.

"You can't have been too impressed if you decided to shoot me."

"Maybe I was jealous of how proficient you were with a pan."

Carpenter smiled despite himself. "And maybe I'll grow wings."

"Oh, I imagine we'll both have those soon enough."

Yates patted the boulder. "It's a good rock, Bill." He put his finger in the air and drew a circle with it. "Just about the right place as well."

"Ain't the gold supposed to be under the ground?"

"That's the beauty of it, Bill. It was. You see? Look at them trees"—Yates pointed—"and all that there. See them berries? You see it?"

Now that he was looking, Carpenter did. He couldn't help it; his annoyance was melting away. Yates was right; it *was* a good rock, and there was a half-decent chance that rough patch was the very edge of a nice sheet of quartz. And more, there had been a landslide down below. This rock might well have been covered up for a long time, maybe even fairly deep. The mountain had unearthed it, doing the work for them.

It was just a boulder in the woods, but . . . it was a boulder in the woods not far from a spot that a real prospector had a good feeling about. And another would-be prospector did as well. The only trouble was that Carpenter couldn't be sure how much of Yates' confidence was coming from sense and how much was being wishful.

Who could know?

Finding a little gold would change things, likely for the better. Finding a lot of gold would go a *long* way in making these troubles disappear. Hale had no grievance with Silva; he only needed money. And while he wouldn't show Silva any semblance of fairness, Carpenter might still be able to expect some.

"Hell," Carpenter grumbled. "Ain't as though I have pressing business elsewhere. Could we eat first?"

"Once I sit down to eat, I ain't getting back up."

"Have yours later, then."

Yates grinned. "Attaboy, Bill. What do you say?

There?" He indicated a crack in the rock. "And there?"

"Oughta do," Carpenter agreed, resigned.

They took the sledges from the bag of tools. Carpenter hefted his and glanced back up the hill.

"Playing with fire if you leave Silva with the boy. He won't think twice."

"That'd be a mistake," Yates replied, unconcerned. "You seen the boy sweat, Bill, but I seen him shoot. He and I rode together up on two months now." He took his place on the other side of the boulder, measuring his swing. He cocked the hammer back. "There was a fella once that swung on him in front of an apple cart, of all places." He was trying not to laugh, though his eyes made it clear he didn't find it all that funny. "Rene just pulled on him right there, fast as you like."

"Did he fire?" Carpenter asked worriedly.

"He did. Didn't hit nothing but the sky because I was there and I put his arm up, but if I hadn't, he'd've shot that man right there in the street." Yates shook his head. "He ain't soft like you."

"I suppose not."

Carpenter set the hammer back and got ready for the pain that was coming. He was sore just to move after today, and this work would make his whole body feel like fire. Swinging a hammer wasn't exactly easy, but at least it didn't take much thinking. Soon the clanging of the blows echoed up and down the hillside as he and Yates struck the stone in turn.

It wasn't long before Carpenter was dripping sweat, and his fingers ached even more than the rest of him. Although his hands were generously callused, they would be blistered after work like this.

Yates wasn't troubled, though. He banged away with a perfect motion of his arms and shoulders, like a ticking clock that wouldn't need to be wound again for a long while.

When the pain changed from discomfort to a true message that something was wrong, Carpenter halted to get his breath.

Yates paused as well, leaning on his sledge. Together they looked up at the sky, streaked with the red and pink of a sunset hidden by the pines.

"Penelope, wasn't it?" he said after a moment, and Carpenter just wiped his brow.

"That's right."

"The captain told me. Told all of us, I mean." He sighed. "I'm sorry I didn't write you a letter, Bill. I should have, like you done for me when my wife passed."

"It's all right."

"I'm sorry."

"Thank you." Carpenter gazed down at the boulder. "It's a funny thing, you know. Where she went when it was time. She wasn't worried about me at the end, Yates. Or even her brother, and her little nieces and nephews, only kin she had."

"She weren't?" He raised an eyebrow.

"No. No, she lay there, and all she asked about was herself." Carpenter rubbed his shoulder, staring at the trees. "Not in a selfish way, mind. She was just so afraid she hadn't done enough. I think if she hadn't been dying anyway, that would've killed her." He shook his head.

"Done enough?"

Carpenter snorted. "I did all right, you know. I don't know if the captain mentioned it to you. But we did all right in Richmond."

"Did you, really?"

"Oh, we did." He looked down at his filthy clothes, and he'd long ago stopped noticing the smell of his own sweat. The memories seemed especially distant when he was in this state, yet also especially immediate. Like a strange dream. "With a house and a maid and a cook and all. See, Penelope had nothing on her hands but time."

"That's really something, Bill," Yates said, a funny look on his face.

"Don't be like that. She went and spent it all at the church with her sleeves rolled up, ladling soup and so on while I was at the factory. She worked as long as I did, and I'll wager at least twice as hard. And she lay there," he said, squinting as he peered into the memory, "worrying that it weren't enough."

"I reckon it would be," Yates said.

"That ain't the point."

Yates knew that; Carpenter didn't have to tell him. For a moment he just stood there, gazing over the boulder at him.

"You ever worry about that?" Yates asked finally. "The Almighty?"

Carpenter just picked up his hammer. "Can't say I ever had much use for Him."

"You stay there!" Rene warned loudly, and they both turned in surprise. The boy took several steps back, pistol in hand. Silva was still seated, but he must've said or done something.

For a moment Carpenter's heart stopped, but Rene didn't pull the trigger. Only Silva's eyes moved, settling on Carpenter, an urgency there that couldn't be mistaken.

Silva was a chess player, and he'd made his move.

Yates had his back to Carpenter and was gazing up the slope at Rene. His rifle was close at hand, but still leaning against the boulder.

Carpenter considered the sledgehammer in his hands. This was the moment.

He let it pass.

Yates realized what had happened and turned on him, taking a step toward the rifle, head cocked to one side.

"Well," he said, the look on his face a calculating one. Carpenter didn't much care to look at it, but he did; the alternative was the look of disappointment on Silva.

Yates wanted to say something, but he couldn't decide what, so he just stood in the twilight. Maybe it was suddenly dawning on him where they were and what they were really doing. Carpenter didn't even want to know what Yates had been telling himself to bring them here.

Yates' features hardened, and he lifted his hammer, pointing it at Carpenter.

"You know, Bill, if you'd been a little more like Silva, Byron'd still be alive."

"No doubt," Carpenter replied.

"Rene, he says one more goddamn word, you shoot him in his knee. Old Bill won't mind carrying him the rest of the way." Yates sighed. "Will you, Bill?"

Carpenter just went back to the boulder. As the last of the sunset faded and the dark gathered around them, it happened. Yates struck, and the report of the blow was different. He grabbed the lamp from the ground and held it up to the stone, revealing the new crack.

"This is it, then," he said.

"About time." Carpenter didn't have many swings left in him. They repositioned, then pounded in turn, aiming for the same spot. The crack grew on the third blow, and on the seventh the rock split apart. They both dodged out of the way as pieces that would easily weigh eighty pounds or more crashed to the ground. The boulder hadn't split fully, but they'd taken a nice piece out of it.

Yates snatched up the lantern and held it high.

Carpenter wiped the sweat from his stinging eyes to be sure. They weren't what they'd once been, but his eyes still wouldn't lie to him.

The quartz inside the stone was easier to identify: cloudy but standing out clearly from the rock. And no one would ever mistake the gleam of gold.

CHAPTER TWENTY

YATES KNEW HE couldn't possibly do much before morning, but that didn't stop him from going to work with his pickax, then his hammer and chisel as the night grew darker. Carpenter and Silva were tied up again, and the chill was enough that they were content to be near the fire, listening to Yates working in the dark.

Silva looked down at the cup of stale water they were sharing.

"Your friend doesn't carry any whiskey?" he asked finally, his first words since Carpenter's return.

"He don't drink."

"One more reason not to like him."

Carpenter grunted in agreement. There was no hope of comfort, tied and sitting with his back to a tree, but he was tired enough that he didn't particularly mind.

"Stop talking," Rene said bluntly, pointing a warning finger.

"Choose your battles, son," Carpenter told him tiredly.

The boy's eyes flashed, but he didn't shoot anyone, and he wouldn't. Silva was finished, at least for today. He wouldn't try anything else.

"Why didn't you just hit him?" Silva asked quietly after a few minutes. It wasn't an accusation, and he didn't even sound upset. "Because he's your friend?"

Carpenter didn't hurry to answer. The question had a lot of answers, many of which would've been true. Finally, he looked over. "You ever seen a man hurt?"

"I've been beaten into the dirt," Silva replied at once, indignant.

In fact, Silva's beating hadn't been particularly severe. If it had been, he wouldn't have made it this far.

"I don't mean like that. That ain't the same. You ain't been to war."

"Mr. Carpenter, I am *at* war." He snorted. "I'm losing. But would you deny it?"

Carpenter sighed. "They took it all from you, and they done that to your dog." He nodded. "I know you're ready to kill. And if you had that pistol, you'd do it. But it ain't the same, friend or enemy. Up close. It ain't as easy as it is with a gun."

"Sounds like an excuse to me."

"Ears as big as yours, I'd think you could hear better."

"Head as big as yours, I'd think you had a brain," Silva snapped. "You think this'll end any better for you than it will for me?"

Carpenter shrugged, unperturbed. "Gold might change it."

"You really believe that?"

He hesitated. "Ain't much choice in it."

Silva might have argued further, but Yates' pickax

had fallen silent. They couldn't see him at all in the black beyond the firelight, but presently his lantern came over the hill and he appeared, hauling a sack over his shoulder.

Rene looked relieved to have him back; he might have been a cooler hand than Carpenter had initially given him credit for, but being alone with two prisoners was no small chore.

Yates dropped the sack and sat beside it, mopping at his face with his bandanna.

"Well?" Carpenter asked before Rene could.

"I got a fair amount up, though there's a good bit of rock in there as well." He nudged the sack with his boot. "I'll wager there's more."

Rene looked puzzled, staring at Yates' thoughtful face. "Ain't that cause to celebrate?" he asked, spreading his hands.

"Think about it, son," Carpenter told him. "You could celebrate if this was your claim, but it ain't. Even if there is a deposit, you won't build a mine here. Not in secret. About the best you can do is try to get as much as you can out quietly. That means no blasting."

Yates nodded, scowling. "And secrecy means there can't be much help. Hard enough to find a man who ain't afraid of hard work, but to find them that'll work *and* keep their mouths shut?" He snorted. "My luck was never good to begin with."

"Then we found gold, but we can't keep it," Rene said. "Is that your meaning, Mr. Yates?"

"It can still do us good," Yates told him. "It ain't enough to change the world, but it *is* enough to show there's gold in these mountains worth looking for."

"You want to use it to swindle more gullible people into coming to Antelope Valley?" Silva asked bitterly.

"And why not? I won't be around to tell them the gold's really on government land they can't touch."

"The gold is in the valley," Yates said firmly. "It just ain't been found yet. Rene, we can finally carry some good news back with us. It's about time."

Rene shot to his feet, dropping his cup and pulling his pistol. Yates didn't startle, but his brows rose.

"My word, boy. What is it?"

"You ain't heard it?" Rene scanned the trees in the dark, and an uneasiness started to bubble in Carpenter's stomach.

"Hear what?" Silva snapped.

"Wolves," Carpenter said, and Rene looked over at him sharply.

Yates frowned, then put up a hand for quiet. The moments went by, and there it was, carried by the lazy wind: a distant howling. Yates let his breath out and left his rifle where it was.

"They're miles away," he said to Rene. "Sit down."

"I don't know," the young man replied, backing away from the trees. "I don't know, Mr. Yates. I don't like wolves."

Silva snickered, and Carpenter nudged him with his elbow. Rene was on edge, and his pistol was cocked. This was the wrong time to provoke him.

"You only got to fire a shot to frighten them," Yates told him, yawning. "Though there are a number of them in these parts. I ain't seen one yet, though."

He flinched as Rene fired his pistol in the air. Then again.

Yates leapt to his feet, truly shocked.

"For God's sake," he snarled. "They're miles away! *That* ain't gonna scare them!" He got himself under control and let out something like a laugh. "You scared *me*. Put me in an early grave, you fool."

"I ain't no fool. Them wolves is killers."

"Rene, they probably ain't, but you give me that pistol." He put his hand out. "Now you told everyone for five miles where we are."

"Ain't nobody out here," the boy said huffily.

"We *know* that ain't true," Yates told him patiently. "We already met the one fella. Could be man-eatin' savages in these hills for all I know."

"You shot your rifle," Rene accused him, pointing.

"There was a reason for that," the older man hissed.

"Yeah, to scare them off! You didn't even really want to catch them, did you? Then make me the nurse-maid, Mr. Yates. Don't you lecture me."

Yates drew himself up, but halted there and took a deep breath. Carpenter remembered him doing just that during the war, praying for patience when dealing with the duller of the soldiers. Rene wasn't dull, though. He was scared and frustrated but not stupid. Not blind, either.

"Besides," Rene muttered, deflating a little, "any savages out there, I'll kill 'em. I ain't afraid of them."

Just wolves, then.

"And I'll keep my pistol," he added waspishly, cutting Yates off as he opened his mouth.

Yates waved a hand and went back to his seat. "Fine."

Rene scowled at him a moment longer, then rammed the gun into his holster. He turned his back, but then turned right back around. "Don't nobody want to get ate by wolves," he added, and that was true enough.

"All right, Rene. Please don't fire that pistol again unless you got something to aim for," Yates said patiently, giving Carpenter a look, though he hadn't said a word.

The boy just turned and stalked away.

For a moment, Carpenter could only wonder at the grace Yates had shown. Of course, Yates *had* been a father. It was a pity it hadn't been for longer; it seemed, at least to Carpenter, that the man had a talent for it.

Rene was barely out of the firelight before he slipped and fell, branches crunching and rustling in the loam. A moment later, he was cursing; then he cried out in pain.

A shot rang out.

That got Yates' attention. He looked up frowning, but before he could say anything, a second shot crashed down on their ears.

Yates leapt up with his rifle, putting it to his shoulder and taking aim at the darkness where Rene had vanished.

"Rene?" he called out. "You all right, son?"

The reply was a strangled groan. It was the stupidest imaginable thing to do, but that didn't stop Yates from charging into the dark.

"I got him," Rene coughed, and the words didn't come out well. Carpenter's heart had been set off by the *first* shot, and it had never gotten around to slowing down. More noises came from the dark, and Silva was openly bewildered.

"Come on. Come on, now," Yates said.

"I didn't hear no rattle," Rene was saying.

They returned to the firelight, Yates more dragging the boy than supporting him. Rene collapsed in the light, chest heaving.

"I got him, though."

"I saw," Yates was saying, pushing up Rene's shirt.

"Is he bit?" Carpenter asked.

"He is," Yates replied tightly. "Stay still, now, son. No, stay." He pushed Rene back down. "Keep taking them breaths, and don't move a muscle."

It looked like he'd been bitten on the side after he fell. The chill was starting to cut through their clothes, but Rene was shiny with sweat and starting to shake.

"It's all right," Yates was telling him, covering him with a blanket.

Silva was stunned; he stared without blinking. Carpenter kept his eyes on the fire, but he couldn't close his ears to Rene's pitiful sounds and Yates' attempts to comfort him. Even with his hands free, there wasn't a thing Carpenter could do.

He noticed Yates looking over at Silva as though he wanted to say something.

"I design firearms," Silva told him frankly. "I'm not a physician."

There was no faulting Yates' desperation. He scrambled over to Carpenter.

"We can carry him," he said. "You and me. If we hurry, we can reach the horses by midmorning. If we really hurry."

Carpenter tried to look sympathetic, but this was just the panic talking. They couldn't go rushing off at night, even without the deadweight of a snake-bitten man to carry. He hadn't forgotten the prospector; Rene was likely the *second* one struck by a rattler on this hill, which made it a poor place to travel even in daylight. Rene might last the night, or he might not, but he certainly wouldn't have help if someone in a hurry broke a leg trying to carry him.

He didn't have to say any of that; Yates was in a bad way, but he still had his senses.

"All right," Carpenter replied calmly. "If you think it's best."

Yates' eyes flashed. He knew perfectly well it wasn't best, but he'd rather be bitten himself or break his neck than stay here, helpless and doing nothing.

Rene was shivering badly. He sat up abruptly, and Yates hurried back to help him lean over and vomit. The silence was heavy enough that even that seemed loud.

Until the wolves started howling, and they were closer now.

CHAPTER TWENTY-ONE

IT WASN'T OFTEN that the world Carpenter woke up to was even less appetizing than the one he had left behind in his dreams. Morning was supposed to be a relief, and the sun was supposed to rescue him, because no one else was going to do it. Of course, at times like this, he might've been willing to say that a man could be forgiven for not putting his whole heart into finding a way to stop living in the past.

Carpenter came awake when Yates did, before sunrise. Without a sound they peered around in the grainy light, and it wasn't the deep chill of morning that had Carpenter's blood running cold.

Something wasn't right.

Yates caught his eye and took up his rifle, staying low and inching over to Rene. He gave him a light shake, looking worriedly at the trees around them. Rene didn't respond, and Yates shook him more firmly.

Some sad noises emerged from the blankets, and Carpenter set his jaw. What did it say about him that it would've been a relief if the boy hadn't lasted? Now Silva was awake as well but quiet.

But Yates didn't say anything; he only crouched there, listening.

A twig snapped, and he twisted and brought up the rifle but didn't fire. Carpenter couldn't see more than a few feet in this light, and Yates couldn't have been much better off. He waited, rigid, for a long time before lowering the barrel.

"Is he gone?" Carpenter asked; he couldn't even look if he wanted to, tied to the tree.

"I don't know." Yates was hiding his feelings well. His urgency was there, but so was his sense. He wanted a little more light, but it didn't matter now. Someone had been out there, and he hadn't announced himself or approached.

Yates stowed the camp as quickly as possible, leaving behind everything he could. It looked as though he planned to carry the gold, and Carpenter didn't know if there was enough metal in that bag to be a serious burden, but there was also a good deal of rock.

Yates sliced Carpenter free and jerked Silva to his feet.

"You can run if you want," he warned. "But I ain't shooting to wound. We can't carry the both of you. There's wolves that way," he said, indicating with his eyes; they had listened to them through the night. "And someone there. Maybe they're friendly. If I do wish, then I wish you luck."

That was all he had to say. Carpenter helped Yates get Rene onto a makeshift stretcher of a blanket. The boy's color was terrible, and the way he shook and jerked was even worse. They tried to make him drink a little water, but he threw it back up right away. The spot on his side where he'd been bitten was turning brown.

It still wasn't light enough to make it wise, but that didn't matter. They set off down the hill, Silva out in front, choosing his steps carefully with his hands still tied behind his back.

"Don't fall behind, Silva," Yates said, keeping his voice low. "Stay where I can see you."

"Could it be that drifter?" Carpenter asked.

"I don't know what he'd be doing back this way," Yates replied distractedly as he glanced worriedly over his shoulder. "I thought he had the look of a man running from something."

"I had the same notion." The man himself had admitted it, though apparently not to Yates.

It wasn't lost on Carpenter that if a day of walking was enough to put him in a bad state, a day of walking while carrying Rene would likely kill him. They weren't even to the bottom of this hill, not even a quarter of the way into the first mile, and his shoulders burned. He wasn't as practiced as Yates at swinging a sledge. Maybe he hadn't been doing it right.

Chips of bark and wood stung his face as a bullet crashed into the tree to his right. He drew up short and nearly dropped Rene, but kept his hold on him as Yates did the same.

Silva should've run, but he did what anyone would've done and turned to look back. What he saw was enough to stop him, and there was no faulting him for that.

There were three of them: dark figures in the gloom making their way down the hillside. Then the scout who'd been watching them had gone back to his friends, who must have been close.

"Hold up there," one of them shouted down.

"Let us go," Carpenter shouted back at once. "The man's bit, and he ain't got long."

"You're the one who ain't got long if you don't shut

your mouth," the man shouted back. "Don't you move," he warned, making his way down, pistol in hand. "Keep on holding him up. I like where your hands is now. Just hold that boy there."

"You got no grievance with us," Yates bit out. "And we got nothing worth taking."

"That goes for you as well," the man replied, pointing the pistol at him for a moment, then swinging it back to Silva. "You come on over here, boy." He was as tall as Carpenter, but a good deal thinner, and by the look of things in no better condition. His clothes were worn and dirty, and there was a raggedness in the way he moved that betrayed that it had been a while since he'd had a night in a real bed. The hat on his head was one of the funny round ones that Englishmen liked, but he was no Englishman.

"Is it him?" the second asked, catching up. He was only Silva's size, but even more ragged than the first. The third was the roughest of them all, and he wasn't even wearing a coat. His teeth were black, and his hair was the same color, long and tangled.

All three were armed, and the one with the long hair had three sets of saddlebags over his shoulder, so it was likely that, just like Yates and Rene, they had left their horses behind to brave these thick woods on foot.

"Oh, it's him all right," the leader replied, peering at Silva.

Something wasn't right, and they all knew it. Hale's men wanted Silva sure enough, but these weren't Hale's men. Carpenter didn't even have a *guess* for who they were. What could they want with Silva?

"Something to be said here about fair play, Murphy," the shorter one said, shaking his head. "Bad luck, y'all. You almost had him. But this is *our* bounty.

We came too far to let you poach it," he added to Yates and Carpenter.

Silva stared at them, uncomprehending. "Bounty?"

Murphy was still looking him over. "No mistake." He snorted. "Pretty and arrogant. Under all that dirt. Didn't say nothing about him being Mexican, though."

"It don't matter. What about them two?" the shorter one asked as the third one finally caught up; he didn't move as fast as the other two.

"One thing first," Murphy said, facing them. "What were y'all shooting at last night? The snake that done for him?" he asked, glancing at Rene. "You go on and put him down now." He gestured with his gun, and they complied. Yates might've drawn right there, but the shorter one had gotten behind him so quietly that he hadn't noticed. He took the gun from his holster and the rifle off his back and stepped away.

"Where's your shooter?" he asked Carpenter.

"Ain't got one."

"I believe you," the man replied, looking him up and down and making a face. "What about a knife?"

"None."

"Well, what *do* you have?"

Carpenter opened his mouth, then shut it. "Some tobacco, but it belonged to a dead man."

"He don't need it no more. You go on and keep that." He stepped forward and patted him down.

"Al," Murphy said.

"Yeah?"

"Do you see this fellow in front of me? Am I dreaming?" he asked, staring at Yates.

"I don't believe so, Murph."

"I mean it. Come here and look."

Frowning, Al nodded to the third man to take over watching and joined Murphy. Together they confronted Yates, whose face was stony.

"Look at him," Murphy said.

"I'm looking," Al replied.

Murphy pulled Yates out of the shade and and pointed at his face. "That's Stanford Yates, you blind animal."

Al squinted. "I'll be damned," he said. "You know, they done a better job on your picture than his," he added, jerking his thumb at Silva. "His don't look like him at all."

"Would you look at that? There's another five hundred dollars, and aren't you a stupid son of a gun?" Murphy folded his arms, looking genuinely puzzled. "Yates, how were you going to collect his bounty without being hung yourself?"

Yates didn't say a word, and Carpenter didn't know that he'd ever seen a man more miserable. These men thought Silva was someone he wasn't, and they thought Yates and Carpenter were bounty hunters hoping to cash him in. They were wrong about all of it, but they were the ones holding the guns.

Rene lay in his blankets on the ground, shivering. A foam had appeared at the corners of his mouth, and there was no color left in him. None of the three bounty hunters had even spared him a glance.

"What about him, then?" Al asked, turning on Carpenter.

"I don't know him," Murphy replied, using the muzzle of his pistol to scratch his cheek. "What's your name?"

"Bill Carpenter."

"I ain't heard of him," Al said.

"Probably ain't his real name. But he's a keeping company with Stanford Yates, so he might yet be worth something. Is there a bounty on you, mister?"

"I reckon so," Carpenter replied. If there wasn't, what reason did these men have not to shoot him? Reasoning with them would have been a waste of time, and there was no sense bargaining. In a minute they were going to wonder what was in the sack, and they'd take the gold too.

The past few days had made Carpenter more accustomed to change than he had been, but it was always hardest when there was no warning. It was the same for Yates. Last night, his good fortunes had taken a sudden turn. This morning they'd turned worse, and it wasn't easy for him to keep up. Life hadn't treated him kindly, but he still wasn't a man accustomed to being on the wrong end of the gun.

"Purely for my edification," Silva asked calmly, standing with tied hands, "who is it you *believe* I am?"

The third man just grinned at him, showing all his black teeth. Carpenter couldn't be sure, but chances seemed good they thought he was that very man they'd met in the woods. He'd told them there were bounty hunters behind him. He'd said it clearly.

"Well, now we're all acquainted, I suppose daylight's wasting," Murphy announced, making a show of consulting an imaginary pocket watch.

"Well, we sure as hell ain't taking this one with us," Al said, and it happened too quickly for anyone to do anything. He pulled his knife, bent over Rene, and sawed his throat wide open.

CHAPTER TWENTY-TWO

I T WASN'T THE same.

When Penelope had gone and died on him, Carpenter had been none too pleased about it. In fact the dying might've been the easy part. It was the waiting with her for it to come for those long weeks that had brought him so low. Of course it hadn't been right; of course she shouldn't have gone. Of course she should've had a few more years in her, but at least she'd been grown, and in fact nearly five years older than Carpenter himself.

It was different when it was a boy, though it wasn't new. Carpenter had been full-grown when the war came, and he'd quickly lost track of the boys he'd seen killed before their time. What he'd found, and was today reminded of, was that it didn't much matter how many he saw.

It never got easier.

He didn't let Yates have his way; Carpenter knocked him flat with a punch before he could lunge for Al, and planted his boot right on top of his chest, putting his full weight on the other man. Yates couldn't hope to overcome that, and Carpenter held him down as Murphy and Al looked on in surprise.

"Damn you, Bill," Yates snarled, trying and failing to get free.

"What are you looking like that for?" Carpenter asked Murphy coldly. "You just kilt his friend. And he couldn't have been but fifteen."

"He was already did for by my reckoning," Al replied, wiping his knife off. He peered down at Yates, who was no longer struggling, but still seething, face bright red. "Is he worth half dead?"

"I can't recall," Murphy replied, twirling his rifle idly and trying not to yawn. "Tie him up good."

"I will. Just as soon as you throw that knife away, Stanford Yates."

He wouldn't, though. Carpenter just snatched it off his belt, sheath and all, and tossed it away.

"You should be thanking your friend," Murphy said to Yates as Al turned him over and started to tie his hands. Yates was still glaring murder at Carpenter. "All he done is save your life. I ain't heard you was the type to get yourself shot for nothing."

The third man had picked up the cloth sack, and now he brought it over to Murphy.

"What you got there, Two-Eye?"

That was an odd name for a man, though it was honest enough. He had two eyes, same as everyone else. Murphy took the sack and had a look inside. Scowling, he pulled out one of the rocks inside, and it took him a moment to spot the gold in it. His brows rose.

"I'll be," he said. "Our luck's getting better every day, boys."

"What was your name?" Al asked, standing in front of Carpenter with his rope.

"Carpenter."

"Well, Carpenter, I weren't born yesterday."

Carpenter sighed and put his hands together correctly to let him tie them. It had been worth a try; it was always worth a try. Of course, he wasn't sure what he'd do if he *could* get loose. There were three of them, and it seemed as though none of them was particularly squeamish. They were hunting bounties, but they struck Carpenter as the folks who might be wanted themselves.

It had been nice to have his hands free, if only for a moment. It was funny how he'd gotten to taking that for granted all these years, not being tied up. He'd only been tied up once before, and that had been to take his lashes.

He did not care for it.

Silva stayed quiet through all of it, and that was just as well. He didn't know what to say, and there was nothing he *could* say that would improve their circumstances. His anger had broken like a fever, and Carpenter wasn't sure what that left the other man with. Maybe he was thinking about what lay ahead. There *was* no bounty on Silva, nor on Carpenter. If they reached a lawman, that could be their safe road away from Antelope Valley and all that went with it.

Yates was another matter. The bounty hunters had known his name, but had they really gotten it from a wanted poster? Wasn't Yates just Hale's man in the field? The one he sent around to search for gold to lure more prospectors to Antelope Valley? What else had the bearded man been getting up to?

If he really was in trouble, that would explain his attachment to Antelope Valley, where the sheriff was his old friend and the man who owned the sheriff was his employer.

Yates an outlaw?

This journey held a grain of hope for Carpenter and for Silva, though it wouldn't be easy. It sounded as though these three had come a fair distance on foot and that there was an even longer trail waiting once they were mounted. Carpenter would have liked to know exactly where they were bound, but it seemed wisest not to ask. Something wasn't right with the one named Al. Even before he'd so abruptly murdered Rene, Carpenter had known it.

There was something in his eyes, the way he didn't really look at you. His head was somewhere else, somewhere bad. He was one of those men who was capable of anything, and you'd never know what was coming or when. Murphy seemed a little steadier, and it was hard to know what to make of Two-Eye, who didn't speak; he just ambled along behind them all, watching.

Murphy and Al could only talk about how they were going to spend the money from the gold and from the bounties for so long, and when that conversation ran out, they turned to taunting their prisoners, mainly Yates.

He just took it, wearing the same face as Silva, but for a different reason. Silva didn't want these men knowing he was relieved to have changed captors, but Yates had gone through outrage and come out somewhere on the other side. Carpenter didn't know what wounded the other man more: his pride or his circumstances. Either way, if these bounty hunters let their guard down for even a second, they'd pay for it. Yates hadn't wanted to be there, wearing the uniform or doing any of it. But when the time came to pull the trigger, he hadn't thought twice about it.

In fact, Carpenter hadn't ever known Yates to think twice about anything. The fact that he was walking along now and biding his time without complaint meant that somewhere along the way Carpenter had misjudged him.

That was all right. Carpenter had been wrong before, and he had no doubt he would be again before this was over.

They reached a clear place where the air wasn't so choked with the scent of pine and they could see the sky. Clouds crowded in mercifully to give a little respite from the sun, but that turned to a light rain that made the world hazy, forcing them to walk closer together. It wasn't enough not to cause trouble; it was best not to even risk *appearing* to cause trouble.

The rain was initially refreshing, but once they were all properly wet, it became chilly and irksome. The clouds cleared and the sun returned, turning the air into a moist, choking soup. Every step through that was a struggle, and it was a relief to be back under the cover of the trees.

Carpenter didn't care to be a prisoner at all, but if there was no helping it, it was better to be the prisoner of a friend. These bounty hunters weren't inclined to share their stores with their bounties, and they gave only enough water to keep them on their feet. Carpenter had taken Yates' relative decency as a captor for granted, and that had been a mistake.

Sometimes through the trees, he would see the snowcapped peaks of the mountains, and visions and notions would come to him of how cool and refreshing it would be up there, safe and free. Only it wouldn't be. Carpenter had never climbed a mountain, but he'd climbed a hill in the snow more than once. It wouldn't be crisp and lovely up there; it would be cold and lonely. The thought of climbing

anything steeper than a step stool was nearly enough
to make him give up then and there, though the day's
march was barely half over, but as he had for better
than half a century, he kept putting one foot in front
of the other.

"Bill," Yates said, squinting in the glare, "someone has to write to Rene's ma and pa."

"Where are they?"

"In Kansas City."

So Yates still wasn't lettered. "I'll take care of it,"
Carpenter told him.

"Will you, big boy?" Murphy looked over his shoulder. "All three of you going to hang or be locked up."

"I can write a letter when I'm locked up," Carpenter replied.

"Not if you got no fingers," Al told him, and he had
his knife out again, tossing it in the air and catching it.

"True enough."

Al looked disappointed, as though he'd hoped for
a different reply. But he just put a little tobacco in his
cheek. Murphy swore as he walked into a spiderweb
and pawed it away from his face, and Yates made his
play. He drove his boot into Al's side as the knife
spun in the air, sending him headlong into a tree and
knocking him senseless.

Murphy whirled, and Yates was there, dealing him
a headbutt that sent him crashing to the ground.

But there were three of them, and Yates couldn't
take them all alone. Silva had been caught sleeping;
his mind must have wandered as they slogged up and
down the canyons, but Carpenter had known this was
coming. There had been as much chance of gold rain-
ing from the sky as there had of Yates going quietly.

Carpenter turned and rushed at Two-Eye as Yates
kicked away Murphy's rifle, then kicked him hard in
the ribs.

The butt of Two-Eye's rifle, brass plate flashing in the sun, swung so fast that Carpenter could hardly believe it. He saw the stars before he felt the blow and thudded to the ground like a sack of bricks, black and yellow exploding across his vision. Two-Eye didn't speak or look too smart, but he was awake, and he was quick.

He cocked the rifle and fired; blood flew, and Yates fell into the pine needles.

Two-Eye swiveled the barrel over to Silva, who immediately put aside whatever he'd been planning to do. He was close enough that no one could ever miss him, but not nearly close enough to try something.

For a moment there was something like quiet; the shot was echoing away through the mountains, and the pine needles were floating in the air like dust in a sunbeam.

Al groaned and picked himself up, shaking his head. He blinked and set his gaze on Two-Eye and Silva, then drew himself upright.

"Aw, don't shoot him," he said, a touch of regret in his voice. "*He* ain't done nothing." With that, he went to Murphy and rolled him over. "You all right, Murph?"

The fallen man just swore and spat out of a mouthful of blood. And swore some more.

The pine needles were settling, and Al turned on Yates, who was hissing in pain. He leaned over and picked up his knife from the ground, and Yates saw him. He rolled onto his back to look up at him defiantly. His trousers were stained crimson, and the stain was still spreading. He couldn't fight with his hands tied, let alone with a leg shot.

But Al didn't use his knife; he just put it back in its sheath.

"Stanford Yates," he said, shaking his head. He pointed at his own face. "You see this bump you give me? Is it worth three hundred dollars?" He didn't wait for an answer that wasn't coming; he just stepped on the wounded man's leg.

Yates set his jaw and didn't make a sound.

Coughing, Murphy dragged himself to his feet.

"You're a quiet one," Al went on, but he could say anything. Yates wouldn't give him any satisfaction.

"Is it mortal?" Scowling, Murphy bent gingerly to pick up his hat.

"Can't say how long he'll keep. The bleeding don't look likely to kill him." Al put more weight onto his boot, earning a grunt from Yates.

Murphy brushed off his hat and set it on his head. He looked at Silva, whose expression had taken on a hollow character. Then at Two-Eye, who still had his rifle at the ready. His gaze came to rest on Carpenter, who lay in the pine needles as though he'd been struck by shot from a cannon.

He pushed away from the tree he'd been leaning on and stumbled over, glancing at Yates, whose teeth were grinding so loudly that they could all hear it over the rustling of the trees.

Carpenter had heard it said that you would always lose a game you didn't play, but he wasn't certain that he agreed with the saying, at least not at times like this. Two-Eye didn't seem bothered by what had happened, but he wasn't the one in charge.

Murphy looked over his shoulder at Yates, bleeding on the ground under Al's boot. "He can't hardly walk now, Al," he said, annoyed.

"Well, I feel as though I have a second head," Al shot back, feeling at his forehead, where indeed he did have a considerable bump. "And I'm still seeing stars, so you will forgive me for being irate," he added in a snarl, then spit on Yates. "You impatient son of a bitch. What's it to you to hang in a week or two that you want to die so badly here?"

Murphy hid his feeling better, but he was no less angry.

"I don't want him to walk," Al said, indignant. "I think I'll see to him what he wanted to see to me, stubborn old man. Let's see how hard that head of yours really is. See how many times it hits that tree." He pointed meaningfully. "How many times it takes till it ain't so hard no more."

"No," Murphy said tiredly. "His fool head's still worth money."

"He can't walk, Murphy."

"I know that." He stared down at Carpenter. "You're a big enough boy, though. Seeing as our mule's with the horses, you'll have to do. Help me, Al."

Together, they hauled Carpenter upright.

"Just shoot me," Yates bit out.

"Oh, don't talk like that," Murphy said, helping Al lift him up. "We're gonna *save* you. Help keep you alive, even after what you done to us. That's what friends do, Stanford Yates. It's the Christian thing. Ain't you never had friends before?"

They draped him over Carpenter's shoulder and tied his hands in such a way that he couldn't let go of Yates, even if he wanted to.

"There you are," Murphy said, spitting again. "You have a ride, and the rest of us still have to walk. Imagine that."

Yates was too furious to speak. Carpenter opened his mouth only to feel a rope around his neck and a sudden jerk that nearly took him to the ground. Al had just hung the sack of rocks and gold around his neck.

"You carry that for us too," he said, clapping Carpenter on the shoulder. "What was your name? Bill? That's our mule's name too. Seems Old Bill don't never get tired. I'll wager you're just like him, big fella."

Carpenter couldn't reply; he couldn't get enough air to speak, and it was all he could do to stay upright.

"I can take that," Silva said.

"Bill don't mind it. Besides, a fella that behaves shouldn't have to carry anything," Al told him. "That's just common sense."

CHAPTER TWENTY-THREE

N O ONE HAD come out unscathed, and that was the only reason Carpenter made it as far as he did. Yates was lean enough, and not of much stature, but the sack of gold made up the difference. He could barely manage what might be called a shamble, but the others, hurting as well, weren't inclined to hurry.

It never ceased to surprise Carpenter how sure he felt that each step would be his last, only for another to follow as the day wore on. Going down the slope was the worst, but more than once Murphy caught his elbow and helped him. Everything that came out of Murphy's mouth was mean-spirited and meant to be taken as the jests of a man without care, but what he *did* was practical. He wasn't the leader so much as he was a sort of shepherd, finding ways to keep Al and Two-Eye doing more or less what he wanted them to do.

Carpenter recalled having to do that very thing during the war with the younger men, and then again in the factory. It was the most exhausting work of all, a hundred times worse than swinging a hammer, and there was no part of him that missed it.

And he didn't miss a word that was said. It sounded as though Twin Falls was the intended destination, and that was a good fifteen days away, provided they could get on horseback fairly soon. Worse, the bounty hunters intended to stop only once to resupply at a place in Nevada that couldn't be closer than three days.

He started to try to muster the air and will to make his voice heard, to tell these men that wouldn't work. Yates would never last. They had to go to the nearest possible doctor for him to have a chance, but that was where it fell apart.

Carpenter saved his breath. The bounty hunters didn't care if Yates lost his leg. They didn't even care if he died, and in fact they were probably counting on it. The only reason they hadn't killed him themselves was that the longer he lived, the longer it would be before he started to smell.

"Bill," Yates said. It was mostly pain in his voice, not weakness, so that was a comfort. The blood from his wound had seeped into Carpenter's shirt and dried, leaving half of it a rusty brown color.

"Yeah?" Carpenter grunted, choosing his footing carefully. If he took a bad fall, he knew he wouldn't be getting back up.

"You gonna ask me why I'm to hang?"

"No."

Carpenter struggled on, and for several steps, there were just labored breathing and the rustling of the three bounty hunters, all following at a safe distance behind.

"After they died, I wasn't right."

No one ever was, but Carpenter didn't have the

breath to tell Yates that. A fly was crawling on his face, making it itch madly, but his hands were tied. He gritted his teeth and kept walking, his sweat stinging his eyes.

"The captain brought me back and gave me work, and it helped me. Having a place to belong and something to keep me busy. I liked prospecting better than I ever liked trapping." There wasn't much spirit in the words, but it didn't sound as though Yates was fading. He was tough, and the wound could've been worse. If it was real bad, he'd have bled out a good while ago.

"But it weren't enough," Yates said.

"Hold on, now," Al called out, but Carpenter had already seen it. There was a steep drop ahead, and it looked treacherous. He stopped, getting what air he could as the bounty hunters went by. Al and Murphy moved up for a closer look, and Two-Eye stayed where he was, watching them with his rifle cocked.

Carpenter spared a glance for Silva, but there wasn't much change since he'd seen what had happened to Renc. Carpenter didn't know if it was a new thing to him or if it only took him back to seeing Maria with that knife in her chest. Either way, the boy's murder had knocked Silva over the head in a way that no punch ever could.

"Drink?" Carpenter asked, though his throat was dry and his lips were starting to crack. "Or was it the opium?"

"Whatever I could get," Yates said. Under different circumstances, there might have been some shame in the words. "I had to have it, Bill. I couldn't do nothing without it. I was nothing."

Carpenter didn't say anything to that. Even if he could, what was there? He just watched the black birds lining up on the tree limbs above them, looking down in silence.

The bounty hunters were picking their way through the brush, trying to find a way down.

"There was this man in Saint Louis. We was in a house, in his house."

Carpenter didn't ask what he'd been doing for Hale in Saint Louis. All in all, he was probably happier not knowing.

"And he wouldn't sell me no more." Yates cleared his throat, and even that much movement made Carpenter's knees wobble, even leaning against a tree. He could barely feel his feet. "Though I had the money."

Carpenter wished that Yates would stop talking, but he wouldn't.

"I wasn't thinking about it, Bill. I wasn't thinking at all. I didn't mean him no ill. I just followed him out into the street, and I told him I needed help. I told him to help me. But he didn't even look back." A pause. "Reckon he'd seen a lot of fellas like me. I wasn't angry, Bill. But I shot him. In the back."

Silva had his back turned, and it was hard to know if Two-Eye was listening. He was watching, sure enough. A breeze came, and Carpenter closed his eyes as it cooled him.

But then it was gone, and with the stillness came the quiet.

"I do not know," Yates said at last, "how much money the captain spent to get me out of that fix."

A rustling in the underbrush likely meant Al and Murphy were on their way back up. Two-Eye was looking at something, and Carpenter followed his gaze to see a flash of white through the trees. For a moment he wasn't sure what to make of it. Could it have been that same stag?

Yates didn't see it, though.

"And I wonder," he went on, "how much it was. It

must have been a lot. And I wonder if that ain't why it's so tight for him now."

"Could be," Carpenter replied, swallowing with a throat that felt like it was full of rocks.

"I had to get him, Bill. I had to get Silva and round him up. And you. I had to," Yates said. "I had to pay him back. You understand, don't you? Bill?"

"I understand," Carpenter told him.

CHAPTER TWENTY-FOUR

THERE WAS STILL at least an hour of daylight good for travel, but the bounty hunters were finished. It wasn't out of kindness that they unburdened Carpenter; the reality was that he had value to them as a pack mule, and that didn't incline them to mistreat him.

The spot they chose to camp was a pretty one: on the north face of the mountain, where a clearing gave way to an unobstructed view of what looked like the whole range. There were no fewer than four peaks in sight.

Murphy tied a cloth around Yates' leg and made him drink some water.

The bounty hunters were on their guard now, and they kept their prisoners far back from the edge of the cliff, in the shade of the trees. That was all well and good; Carpenter was content to breathe without a sack of gold hanging around his neck, and the notion of doing anything more than that was beyond him. Silva sat in silence, and Yates had nothing more to say. He was in pain, but he still seemed strong enough. His leg was bad, and it would only get worse, but he wasn't yet feverish. He would make it through the night, and at the moment that was the best Carpenter felt he could hope for.

"Pretty stream," Murphy noted, pausing at the edge to look down.

Al was building the fire. "If the big'n don't drag his feet, we might reach Michael by this time tomorrow."

"With luck."

It would take more than luck for Carpenter to last another day. Murphy paused nearby, lighting his smoke with a match. He looked Carpenter over, his eyes lingering on the burning welt across his throat, where the rope had bitten into his flesh.

"You old rebels loved having your slaves to do your work for you," he said tiredly, blowing smoke out through his nose. "Reckon you don't so much love being one."

Carpenter didn't respond to that. It wasn't the present that bothered him; it was the future—that was where the trouble was waiting.

If he collapsed, there wouldn't be anyone to carry him. They might make a sled to drag Yates, dead or alive, but they wouldn't bother with someone as big as Carpenter, not when they didn't know if he was even worth anything. Chances were good that they'd just shoot him, or maybe they'd save themselves a bullet and let Al do it with his knife. Then what? Would Silva have to drag Yates the rest of the way? He'd have to, and he was up to it. He still hadn't quite come back from wherever the sight of Rene's open throat had sent him, but Silva wanted to live. His only chance was for the bounty hunters to take him to the law. They wouldn't be pleased when they found he wasn't their man, but Carpenter had to hope they wouldn't do anything wrong in front of witnesses.

That was the trouble with it out here, all this land and all this quiet. There was no one to see. The law was just a word.

Carpenter was too hot and exhausted to have any appetite, though he hadn't eaten all day. The hunger pains would probably come on suddenly and hatefully when he was about to fall asleep. The only thing worse than a day of hell was a day of hell and fatigue from lack of sleep, and chances seemed reasonable that was exactly what he would get.

"What are you thinking about, Bill?"

"Tomorrow," he replied to Yates.

"You was always thinking ahead."

"Someone had to."

"I suppose."

Something had changed in Yates. His anger was gone, and he almost appeared to be in good spirits. Maybe there was some peace in knowing what was coming, some comfort in no longer having a say. Carpenter knew how it felt; that was why he was telling himself there was only one thing he could do: put one foot in front of the other. If it couldn't be easy, at least it could be simple.

At least, that was what he'd have liked to believe.

"Mr. Silva," he said, summoning all the normalcy he could into his voice.

Silva had been staring off into space, but he looked up. He took a deep breath, and made the same effort, speaking as though they weren't here but rather back at the lodge, sitting over a chessboard with a bottle of whiskey at hand.

"Yes, Mr. Carpenter?"

"You feeling all right?"

"Oh, I think it would be rude of me to complain, under the circumstances. As Mr. Murphy so insightfully brought to our attention, it is not as though no one has ever had it worse," Silva said.

Carpenter twitched.

"Damn Yankees," Yates muttered, but he was smiling.

"Yeah, Silva. Get off that high horse," Carpenter told him.

"Oh, two against one, is it?"

Carpenter's throat hurt too much for him to laugh. "This is my just deserts, then," he said.

"That is correct," Silva replied, leaning back and closing his eyes.

"I believe that makes me feel a little better."

"That was not my intent."

"I know that, Mr. Silva."

"Are y'all enjoying yourselves?" Murphy asked, gazing over the fire at them.

"Are you?" Carpenter replied, keeping his eyes on the sky. He couldn't see the sunset, but from the colors that were coming into the sky in his view from the west, it had to be one to remember. For Yates, if for no one else—he had to be thinking it: it was likely the last he'd see.

Murphy chewed on his cigarette for a moment, then shrugged. "I seen worse days," he said finally. "Bill Carpenter was your name?"

"That's right."

"The Mexican can carry the gold tomorrow," he said, glancing at Silva. Then he put on a face of great politeness. "Provided he don't object, naturally," he added.

"I do not, sir."

"Oh, thank you." Murphy made a gracious gesture and smiled at Carpenter.

"Mighty decent of you," Carpenter told him, clearing his throat.

"Well, when you hang and go up above," Murphy said, flicking the remains of his smoke into the fire, "you put in a good word for me. Al?" He looked over his shoulder. "Al, what are you doing?"

Two-Eye didn't react; he just kept stirring whatever he was cooking over the fire.

Al was on his hands and knees near the edge, peering down. He didn't reply.

"Al," Murphy repeated, louder.

"Mind your business, Murph!"

For a moment, Murphy considered that. He glanced at Two-Eye, then groaned and got to his feet. Brushing himself off, he joined Al at the edge, where the other man motioned for him to get down.

Murphy swore. "Who's down there?" he hissed.

Carpenter and Yates exchanged a look, and Yates moved to sit up a little straighter. Two-Eye still didn't seem interested in anything but the food, but Carpenter had seen his eyes move when Yates did. The man was odd, but he was attentive. Carpenter's jaw still hurt from how attentive he was, and if he had a mirror, he'd likely find half his face black-and-blue.

"You see her?" Al asked.

"Where?"

"There."

"What's she doing?"

"Well, I believe she intends to bathe in that stream," Al drawled.

Murphy snorted, then spoke, sounding taken aback. "You're right. Might be the first time. I guess you're obliged to watch."

"It would be rude not to," Al replied.

They continued to watch, Murphy in mild amusement, but Al a bit more intently. Carpenter didn't like the feel of this, but his hands were behind his back and done up tighter than ever.

Two-Eye spared a glance for Silva, whose face was one of open disgust at the nature of the chatter from the men at the edge of the cliff. Carpenter felt the same way, but he couldn't summon up much outrage, even if there'd been any point to it. There was too much worry.

Al abruptly straightened up.

"I believe I'll pay a call on her."

Murphy looked over at him sharply. "What?"

"I won't be but an hour." Al came back to the fire and picked up his rifle. "Maybe two. She is handsome."

"Al, don't be stupid," Murphy warned, suddenly concerned. "Her husband can't be far off."

"I'll see to him."

"Al, it ain't what we're here for."

"Where's the harm in it, Murph? We're packed in for the day," Al said, jerking his chin toward the fire. "I even got a bump on my head, remember?"

Murphy, making an effort to stay calm, took a breath. "The notion of it all is that we ain't the ones who hang," he explained tightly.

"Aw, hell, Murph. Can't you see I been invited?" He gestured meaningfully at the cliff. "If she's gonna show off right out in front of the whole sky, it can only be her design. I can't be rude. I ain't rude, Murph," he said, grinning as he put his rifle over his shoulder.

"Damn it, Al, I'm telling you no."

"Oh, shoot me in the back, then. Or are you worried?" Al asked, indicating the prisoners. "The big one's half dead, and old Stanford Yates has only got one leg. I reckon you and Two-Eye can handle the Mexican."

With that, he started to pick his way down and was lost to sight. Murphy stood in place, mouth tight, a vein throbbing visibly in his neck.

"Two-Eye, that man'll be the death of us," he muttered, and Two-Eye nodded without looking up. Murphy shambled back to the fire and started to roll another smoke.

Silva hissed in pain, and both men looked over at him.

"Something bit me," he reported, shifting his position and looking over his shoulder. "I may be on an anthill."

"Well, you stay right there," Murphy warned, pointing with his cigarette. "Ants won't kill you, but I will."

"There's men in Antelope Valley that wouldn't take kindly to that," Carpenter suggested. "They would prefer to do it themselves."

"They ain't my concern," Murphy grumbled.

The minutes went by, and the sky darkened.

They didn't have long to wait, though. Carpenter flinched as the shot echoed up from below. Murphy rubbed his face in frustration, and Two-Eye kept eating. Yates looked stony, and Silva appeared to be dozing. Murphy wasn't paying attention to them in any case.

The second shot made him look up in surprise. He frowned and got to his feet, hurrying to the edge to look down, his own rifle in hand.

"Ain't you going to help him?" Carpenter demanded, loudly enough that it startled Two-Eye, who looked up with a frown. "He's your friend, ain't he? He's in trouble," he said.

"Be quiet, Bill," Murphy said, putting his rifle to his shoulder anxiously.

"Al's in trouble," Carpenter pressed.

Two-Eye got uncertainly to his feet, and it was the

last mistake he ever made. Carpenter unfolded his legs and kicked the silent man's feet from under him. People noticed he was tall when he was standing, but they didn't give much thought to how much reach he had when he was on the ground.

Two-Eye fell on his back into the fire, and Yates was ready, rolling himself nearer and dropping his good leg squarely on the man's chest as he struggled and tried to get up. He couldn't properly pin him with just his leg, but he kept him in place long enough for the fire to do some of the work.

Murphy had turned and taken aim, but the scattered sparks and smoke blocked his view. The world was Silva's chessboard, and all the pieces were where he wanted them. He'd kept quiet and to himself, making these men all but forget him. He'd even positioned himself a moment ago so that he could get up quickly, and done so in a way that didn't arouse suspicion.

The moment Carpenter acted, Silva was on his feet, and Murphy never even saw him. He struck the bounty hunter with his shoulder and a good bit of force, even though a light push would probably have been enough.

Murphy went over the edge with a shout, and Carpenter didn't hear him land, as Two-Eye had rolled out of the fire, himself ablaze. Silva hurried back and kicked him to the ground, then gave him a kick to the head that put him to sleep. He dropped to his knees, then his back, fumbling for Two-Eye's knife. He hissed in pain, as the man's clothes were still burning, but got it free and tossed it into the dirt.

Yates reached it first, cutting himself in the process, but he clearly didn't mind. He sawed himself free and sagged on the ground, chest heaving from the exertion.

Silva was on his knees, staring at him. His eyes darted to Two-Eye's rifle, which was still there, leaning against his pack. Yates lunged over and snatched it.

They all flinched as the flames eating Two-Eye's clothes reached the cartridges in his pocket. Bark flew from the tree, and blood spurted as at least one bullet fired through his body. Carpenter threw himself flat, and Silva did the same. Several more shots followed.

"Help her," Carpenter choked out, glaring at Yates. "Someone's wife is down there. She could still be alive. You have to help her."

"Damn it, Bill," Yates snarled. "I know that."

CHAPTER TWENTY-FIVE

Face white, Yates dragged himself to the tree, seized a branch, and hauled himself upright. He kicked the knife toward Bill and limped into the underbrush, cocking the rifle.

For the briefest moment, Carpenter had wondered what to do about Two-Eye, but the bullets he'd been carrying had taken any choice out of it. Two-Eye was lying still with at least two new holes in him, and there wasn't anything anyone could do for him. He wouldn't get up again.

Carpenter sawed himself free and did the same for Silva. Having his hands unbound was enough for him to forget the pain and exhaustion.

"What are you doing?" Silva demanded, rubbing at his wrists as Carpenter started to stagger off.

"I have to help him," Carpenter replied, looking back.

The other man just stared at him in disbelief, but there wasn't time to have a civilized conversation about it. Carpenter plunged into the brush, pushing past the leaves and branches, and searching for a way down in the fading light. Rocks slipped and creepers gave way. He made more noise than a blind steer, but that didn't give him pause.

You'd have to be a fool to come out to a place like this. No people meant no help to be had, though recent events had left Carpenter with a certain understanding of the desire to avoid people. But fools or not, whoever was down there didn't deserve this. Carpenter was no lawman, and neither was Yates, not by a long shot, but they couldn't stand by any more than the sun could stand by at dusk. And it wasn't doing that; the light was going fast.

Carpenter caught up with Yates, who was hobbling determinedly down.

"Murph?" Al's voice came from up ahead, and though there was a hint of uncertainty in it, he didn't sound particularly alarmed. Carpenter hadn't seen him alarmed yet, and maybe he wasn't even capable of it, but they'd find out in a moment.

Yates slowed, moving more gingerly as they came into view of the scene below.

A man lay facedown in the grass of a wide clearing along the creek, and a tidy lean-to was up a few paces back in the trees. Laundry was strung up, and curling trails of blue smoke rose from what had been a modest firepit.

Al was there, knee-deep in the grass with the woman beside him on her knees. He had her by the hair, but whatever he'd had in mind to be doing had clearly been interrupted by the shots from the cliff. He squinted upward, puzzled.

A muffled sound of pain came from somewhere off to Carpenter's left. That had to be Murphy; the fall hadn't killed him, but if he wasn't dead yet, he would be soon.

Al heard it and looked, letting go of the woman's hair to put both hands on the rifle. She hesitated, but only for a second before taking off running. Al looked over in surprise.

"Don't go, sweetheart," he called after her. With a look of regret, he raised his rifle and fired.

Shot through the back, the woman tumbled to the ground without a sound.

Scowling, Al turned back toward the cliff, only to flinch as Yates' bullet sailed past his head. Swearing, Yates got behind a tree, and Carpenter got down low as Al fired back.

It should've been an easy shot, but the pain of trying to stand on his wounded leg had set Yates' hands to shaking. Carpenter hadn't seen that murder coming, and even Yates hadn't been fast enough to stop it. Missing an easy shot would be a blow for a man like Yates, but it was nothing to seeing that unarmed woman killed.

Having his hands free, seizing his moment and striking back, for a second it had given Carpenter a strength that he shouldn't have had in the state he was in. Now it was gone, and he felt as dead as that woman with golden hair.

"Is that you, Stanford Yates?" Al called out in the twilight.

He stood out there with no cover to speak of in the tall grass. His rifle was at his shoulder, and his hands weren't shaking. Al's aim was steady, even if his brain wasn't.

Teeth grinding like thunder, Yates worked the rifle's lever. He looked down at Carpenter, crouched among the ferns.

"You see him?" he asked.

"He's just standing out there," Carpenter reported. "He ain't moving."

Yates closed his eyes and took a deep breath. It was a shot that he should've been able to make in his sleep, but there was sweat beaded on his face, far too much of it. He was feverish.

He glanced down at the rifle. "You do it, Bill."

Carpenter swallowed, recalling the last time he'd held a rifle, standing over Oceana in that barn. He put his hand out, but Yates saw the uncertainty on his face and held on to it.

"Hell," he muttered. "I ain't afraid of him."

He was afraid, though. Just not of Al.

Carpenter opened his mouth, but Yates cut him off. "Throw down that rifle!" he roared.

"What if I am disinclined to do so?" Al called back obstinately. "What'd you do to old Two-Eye, Stanford Yates? You know the man had the mind of a child. You wouldn't hurt a child, would you? That leg ain't giving you no trouble, is it?"

"My bandage needs changing," Yates shouted. "Will you do that for me, Al?"

"Course I will. What are friends for?"

Yates might have retorted, but they all fell silent as new voices rose up. Yates and Carpenter looked to the west. The sun was nearly down, but the howling of wolves rose up over the pines, a grand chorus.

The howls fell away, and Al was the first to recover.

"What do you reckon they're saying?" he asked.

"Telling you to throw down that rifle, I suspect," Yates replied.

"It's a funny thing to hear orders from a man already more or less dead. How long you think you got, Yates?"

"Still longer than you," Yates snarled. He pivoted

into the open, and Al shot him before he could even take aim, let alone squeeze the trigger.

Yates pitched to the ground, and Carpenter tried to catch him, but he wasn't fast enough.

Al's voice came over the air, tinged with laughter. "I suppose it ain't a fair fight if the one's a cripple," he noted, chuckling. "That sits right well with me, though. A fair fight's the last thing you want. I'd never hear the end of it."

Hissing, Yates clutched at his right side where the bullet had come right along his ribs. His mouth was open like he wanted to cry out in pain, but he couldn't get the breath for it. The breaths he took were fast and shallow, and there was a glassy look of shock in his eyes. He clutched the rifle in a death grip, and his eyes found Carpenter.

"I'm sorry, Bill," he said, and the words came out surprisingly conversational, considering. There was something that might have started as a laugh, but just became a fearful grimace of pain. "We ain't as young as we used to be."

"I know," Carpenter said, risking a glance at Al, who lowered his rifle.

"Big fella," Al called out, starting forward through the grass. "I suppose if you were armed you'd have done something. Why don't you come on out with your hands up high?"

Not for the first time, Carpenter hesitated.

"I can think of several reasons," a voice called out, but it wasn't his.

Silva was off to the right, at least fifty paces away, hidden behind a tree trunk. Al reacted as anyone would: he turned and took aim in a flash. Yates lunged to one knee and threw the rifle to his shoulder. His first shot missed, and Al swung back around in time for the second to take him in the belly.

With a look of vague annoyance, he fell into the grass.

That was all Yates had as well. The howling was rising up again as he collapsed into the dirt, letting go of the rifle and clamping his hand to his side. Al had been awfully good, but he hadn't been the brightest. He should've at least taken a knee to present a smaller target, but Carpenter had the luxury of making these observations as the man watching the scene unfold.

Footsteps crunched in the undergrowth as Silva hurried to them. He sank to a crouch beside Carpenter, and one look at his face told a great deal.

The man bleeding in the dirt was the man who would have handed Silva to Hale.

Carpenter had to say something, but he didn't know what it would be.

He would say that he wouldn't leave Yates.

Silva would say that Yates wasn't going to get far regardless.

Neither of them would have been wrong. Carpenter could see and hear it all in his head as though it had already happened, half because it was just that obvious, and half because he'd do anything not to think about that woman lying dead in the grass, or what had happened on the cliff, or any of it.

His thoughts belonged in the future. The future was safer. It probably wouldn't be pleasant, but there was always a chance, a reason to hope. With the past, he didn't have that. He knew exactly what he was in for.

The conversation wasn't needed. Silva knew it front to back, just as Carpenter did.

So Carpenter opened his mouth to thank Silva for what he had done. He might've just taken off; he had no reason to put himself at risk by coming down here to distract Al. He'd likely saved Carpenter's life just now.

The shot came so close to his head that Carpenter

saw a few of his graying hairs float by, caught in the last of the light.

Al was out there, still down, but not finished. Carpenter pushed Silva out of the way and ducked as another shot sailed overhead. There wouldn't be any conversation at all, then. Silva scrambled up, and Carpenter hauled Yates to his feet.

He felt like he'd been running for a while now, but it turned out there were still a few miles left to go. Or less, depending on how good Al's aim was.

CHAPTER TWENTY-SIX

W HOEVER THAT MAN was, the one with the missing fingers, he was in luck.

Two-Eye was certainly dead, Murphy as well by now from that fall, and it seemed unlikely that Al would make it out of the mountains. He'd been able to shoot, but could he give chase? Carpenter doubted it.

That made three fewer bounty hunters that fellow would have to worry about. He might have been the one intended to hang, but Carpenter had liked him a good deal more than the men who'd intended to bring him to justice.

That was where the luck ended.

There was no moon, though that didn't seem to bother the wolves, who were louder than ever and drawing closer. With no light to see by, it just seemed to be a matter of time before Carpenter lost an eye to an errant tree branch as they crashed through the woods. Yates clung to him, doing his best impression of limping with the rifle as his walking stick.

Silva had already fallen once, thankfully without injury, but the night was still young.

Carpenter stopped to look back at the sound of a particularly loud howl, as though he could possibly see anything.

"Was it ever enough, Bill?"

"What?" Carpenter asked, pushing through a tangle of branches, barely keeping Silva in view.

"Your wife," Yates gasped, clutching at Carpenter's shirt. "When she wasn't sure it was enough. What she'd done."

"I don't know," Carpenter replied, wincing as his foot came down on earth that was lower than he had expected. Twinges and pain shot through his leg, but he stumbled on. "She couldn't much talk," he managed to say, breathing raggedly. "There at the end."

"Was she afraid?"

"I expect she was."

"But you were there," Yates said.

"Yes," Carpenter replied, "I was."

The moon peeked out, but only for a moment. It had gotten cold enough that their breaths were clouds in the dark. Carpenter didn't know how many miles they had gone this way. Al couldn't possibly follow so far so quickly, even if he were so inclined, and Silva knew it, but still the other man wouldn't slow down. He had felt Hale's claws and known his intent. He had been no stranger to the gaze of a predator when the bounty hunters came upon them. All the same, none of it could be taken back, and Silva wouldn't ever be the same. These three would follow him. He and Carpenter could hardly have been more different, but now they had something in common.

"I let him down, Bill," Yates was saying.

"It's all right." Hale would understand.

"I was meant to keep him safe." He was talking

about Rene, not Hale. Carpenter swallowed; he didn't have a reply. "I tried to do it, Bill. I kept him from killing that man."

Carpenter couldn't listen to any more. "Enough," he gasped, then found his voice. "Silva, stop!"

Silva did, his form turning to look back in the gloom.

Carpenter helped Yates to sit against the nearest tree and went straight to Silva. "Enough," he repeated, trying to get his breath. "He ain't coming. He won't catch us."

"It isn't him that concerns me," Silva said tightly, looking at the dark trees to the west. The wolves weren't howling now, but they were still out there. "They aren't far back now. We can't stop."

He wasn't wrong.

"Where are we going?" Carpenter asked. "Where *can* we go?"

Wherever it was, it couldn't be far away. It wasn't just Carpenter; they were both nearly done in. The exhaustion *or* the hunger should have been enough to stop them in their tracks, and they had both.

Carpenter scowled. "Truth is, we haven't covered much ground."

"I know," Silva replied, sitting down and leaning back to take deep breaths.

They had done nothing *but* cover ground, but not in a straight line. They'd fled Antelope Valley going west, then begun to backtrack when Yates and Rene found them. The bounty hunters had been leading them northeast. By now they were probably due north of town, and unless Carpenter had completely lost his sense of direction, Antelope Valley couldn't be more than twenty miles away.

Twenty miles was still a long way on foot, and there was a good-sized mountain in the way. There was also the detail that they weren't exactly welcome there, but it would be at least twice as far to anywhere else they might be able to find supplies and horses.

Silva sighed. "Mr. Karr," he said finally. "His property is outside the settlement."

"Will he help us?"

There was a pause, and Carpenter couldn't even see him, but Silva's voice came out of the dark. "Choosing not to help would be a decision that he would regret," he said.

Carpenter started to reply but stopped as the howling rose up again, much closer. He and Silva leapt to their feet, and Carpenter was back with Yates in a heartbeat.

The other man shook him off with a hiss, falling back against the tree with a gasp of pain. He looked down at his leg, then up at Carpenter and shook his head.

"I can't go no more," he said.

"It's all right. I can carry you," Carpenter told him. He put out his hand, but Yates didn't take it.

"No," he said.

"Yates, they're coming."

"You carried me far enough, Bill." He set his jaw and straightened his back against the tree trunk, settling the rifle on his lap.

Carpenter kept his hand out. Silva stood a short distance off, silent. The howls died away again, but it wouldn't be long. Each time they were closer.

Yates produced a bag of tobacco and offered it. "I ain't got no matches."

There wasn't time. Carpenter knew it. If he hadn't, he might have stood there forever. He took the sack. It was leather, hand sewn with colorful thread. Yates had made it himself twenty years ago from a tattered glove they'd found on the march. It was hideous to look at, appallingly made, but no one had ever told him so because they remembered how earnest he had been, sitting there with his makeshift needle and thimble, one eye shut, concentrating as he worked.

Carpenter hadn't understood it at the time, but he did now.

He took the pouch, and Yates sat back.

"Only thing scares me more than dying," he said as the wolves started to howl again, "is going back to Rene's ma to tell her what's happened to her boy on my watch. I won't do it, Bill." He smiled. "And you're the one called a coward."

PART THREE

---◇---

THE WOLVES
OF SEVEN PINES

CHAPTER TWENTY-SEVEN

BURYING HIS WIFE hadn't been the hardest thing Carpenter had ever done. The hardest thing had been living with the knowledge that one day he would have to. He'd wasted so much time being afraid of things he couldn't change, and letting himself be bested by the things that he might have. He wasn't afraid to go to sleep anymore, and he suspected that if he lived long enough for it to matter, he never would be again.

He and Silva weren't inclined much to sleep in any case. A journey of twenty miles, even as the crow flies, would have been a task. The mountain tripled the weight of the grueling trek, and there was no comfort to be found in the absolute certainty that Carpenter never would have made it half a day with Yates on his back.

There wasn't any respite to be found anywhere, least of all in Antelope Valley. Wolves no longer howled behind them, but neither mistook that for their absence. That wasn't a mistake that either of them would make again.

Mr. Karr's property told a story, though it was nothing Carpenter hadn't been able to guess. The house, built of fresh, pungent pine, was well-made, with details, glass windows, and everything a man settling into a position of prosperity could want. Mr. Karr and Silva had come here with money in their pockets and a good expectation of getting more.

High hopes.

Karr himself was out in front of the house, splitting firewood. A figure moved behind the windows, and that could only have been his wife. Their two young daughters were out in the dusk chasing fireflies, trailed stubbornly by a pup still young enough to trip and tumble with every third step.

There was no sign of anyone else, and Carpenter had been careful to make certain the farm wasn't being watched. The dark was coming on, and it was Silva's play to make, only he wasn't. He just watched, and there was no hiding it: he'd fallen into the very trap that Carpenter had spent his whole life trying to climb out of. Once you started to think about what might have been, it was like a deep pool. It didn't take any effort at all to sink, but when the time came to swim out, suddenly things weren't so easy.

He put his hand on Silva's shoulder to wake him up, and the other man scowled at him. Then he sighed and rose from his crouch to step out of the shadows.

Karr didn't notice them at first. He was intent on his work, the expression of intense concentration on his face at odds with the practiced motion of his swings. He wasn't happy, but who was? The fine home that stood behind him, and the even finer family that lived in it—they weren't what was on his mind.

Or if they were, it was for all the wrong reasons. Was he worried about Hale?

He brought the ax down and looked up. For a moment he was still; then he leaned his weight on the handle and watched them cross the grass, leaving the trees behind to stroll onto the property like any other visitors, however disheveled.

Silva stopped ten paces off, his hand on his pistol, which he'd taken from Murphy's things before rescuing Carpenter from Al. Karr wore no gun, though a rifle leaned against the fence post nearby. He hadn't even glanced at it, and why would he? It wasn't an enemy in front of him. It was his partner, and Silva wasn't a difficult man to get along with.

They must have been friendly, at least before.

One of the girls let out a shriek, and Karr glanced over, but she'd just tripped and fallen onto the grass. Laughter rose up, and he turned back to the two of them.

His Adam's apple bobbed as he swallowed. "I have not gone into town," he said, stepping back from the ax, "for five days. Sheriff Fisher rode out yesterday, asking after you."

"I'm sure."

"What did they do?" Karr asked sadly.

Silva shrugged. "All the things I didn't believe they would."

"We were wrong." They watched Karr take his kerchief and mop his face, then twist it in his hands. "My time in the city went too well, Raf. I was so accustomed to it. Not to this." He gestured at the vast sky, rippling with endless bars of clouds, all streaked red. "This quiet. And I thought that we had laws, and that a bandit would . . ." He stopped there, searching for words. Then he snorted and tossed his bandanna aside. "That a wolf would at least have the decency to look like a wolf, I guess."

"I know exactly what you mean."

"Is it settled?"

Silva shook his head, stepping past Karr and making for the well. "No," he said over his shoulder. "I hid the patent."

Now the girls had noticed them and were watching.

"Hello, Mr. Silva!" one of them called out.

"Hello, Annabelle," he called back, quite pleasantly.

"You must be Bill Carpenter," Karr said quietly. "Mr. Fisher mentioned you."

"I'm sure he did." Carpenter picked up Karr's rifle and worked the lever several times to empty it. He put it back down when all the cartridges were out. "I apologize for the imposition, Mr. Karr."

Silva was pulling up a bucket and sipping from the ladle. Carpenter joined him and took a drink. The cool water and the cooler breeze felt about as good as anything could.

"Might think of building a fence," Carpenter warned Karr as he approached. "Wolves in these mountains." He glanced at the girls. "More than you'd expect."

Karr's expression told them that wasn't lost on him.

"I'm going to buy two horses from you," Silva told him bluntly. "On credit."

Karr grimaced, but he looked neither surprised nor inclined to argue.

"All right," he said, with all the strength and vigor of a wilted brown weed. He wasn't alone in his misery, but it still stood in stark contrast to the evening.

The sun was down, the clouds weren't going to let the stars out, and the air was cooling with every passing minute. Karr just watched his girls stumbling around in the grass, surrounded by fireflies.

"It's about time to eat," he said finally, taking off his hat and running his hand through his thinning hair. "Are you hungry?"

FORTUNE HAD ALWAYS been nimble. One moment Carpenter was riding west with a comfortable if melancholy future stretching out ahead of him. He wasn't a young man, so perhaps not a *long* future. But something worth looking forward to, something to hold on to.

Then he'd been standing over his horse, watching Oceana's flanks heave as she tried to get air, and he tried not to see it, or himself in it, alone in a bed when the end came. There was nothing between; he seemed to close his eyes on one moment and open them to another.

He had sat at Hale's table, surrounded by his friends and their families, fighting tooth and nail with his own mind to just take it for what it appeared to be, as something good. He might even have tried to wrestle it further, to twist it into a shape where he really could see things from Hale's side, where Silva was a scoundrel who deserved to be brought low.

Carpenter was amenable to fantasy, but he drew the line at delusion.

Then Joe had been there, standing in the hallway, a knife on his belt where there hadn't been one before. He could say he hadn't meant to really do it. He could say whatever he pleased, and why not? Hale certainly did. Hale had told Carpenter to his face there was nothing he wouldn't do for his family. There was truth in that; the man really did want to provide.

And Carpenter had trudged through the wilderness with nothing but a handful of berries, wolves creeping along behind, and now he opened his eyes to baked chicken and potatoes, served on good plates at a good table in a warm house.

Silva was charitably spinning the tale to the curious Mrs. Karr, who it appeared was entirely in the dark as to why the factory was not yet built. It sounded as though her husband hadn't exactly lied to her yet, but he hadn't told her the truth, clearly.

"Where will you go?" she asked Silva, pouring him a glass of wine.

"That, I have not decided."

Anyone could see the conversation was causing her some anxiety. The Karr family was like everyone else in that they had come to this place for a reason. In Karr's case, the reason was the factory.

"I want to wait awhile yet and see how the gold shapes up," Karr said, bringing out a show of ease and confidence that he couldn't possibly feel. He spoke as though his proposition carried no risk, a mere whimsy. But a single look at Mrs. Karr was enough to know she wasn't convinced they had the means to linger idly with no source of income.

The girls, at least, were more interested in food than in conversation.

Carpenter still couldn't be sure if Karr had taken money from Hale or if he'd simply acquiesced out of a desire not to make an enemy. Either way, he *had* made an enemy. Silva was being careful not to punish Karr's family because of it, but there was a tension in him that hadn't been there even when they had faced the bounty hunters.

There was nothing Carpenter could say or do that would ease Silva's anger. There was nothing he could tell the other man that he didn't already know.

Like everything else, his memories had faded with time, but he hadn't quite forgotten what it was like to be angry.

So he just ate, keeping quiet. This was Silva's business, not his. Karr and his family were perfectly polite to him, and he was perfectly polite as well, but nothing could change the detail that towered a head over nearly everyone, and there was something menacing about that, whether he intended it or not.

Menacing. The last thing Carpenter had ever wanted to do was menace anyone.

Mrs. Karr generously invited them to stay the night, and Silva generously declined.

"As always, Mrs. Karr, you are very kind. I think it would be best if we went on directly. I will accept this bottle, though. And any provisions you could part with."

It wasn't a robbery, not exactly, even if it felt a bit like one.

Carpenter followed Silva out behind the house, where he eyed the stable.

"I don't blame him," Silva confided, offering Carpenter the bottle.

"Hale must have threatened him." Carpenter took it and drank. "Look how miserable they are."

"We both used more or less every dime we had to make this real." Silva rubbed his face. "How could it fail? The Army requested it of us. If the federal government isn't a dependable patron, who is? Surely no one would interfere."

"I suppose if you spend all your time behaving like a civilized man, you fall in danger of starting to think like one."

"A mistake I will never make again." Silva took the bottle back, finished it, and tossed it away. "I'll ride directly to the lodge."

"He'll have a man there. A man," Carpenter added. "Not his boy this time. Someone with a rifle, and likely enough wits left to remember what it's like to be a soldier. You'd best hope it isn't Fred."

"Why is that? Is he an unseemly sort of fellow?"

"He's about the most loyal man to walk this earth. The best friend anyone could ask for." Carpenter shrugged. "But if Hale asks him to, he'll gut you as soon as shake your hand. Or do whatever awful thing they think of to convince you to give up that patent." Silva looked taken aback, but Carpenter went on. "And he'll enjoy doing it. He's not right. But he's the right man. If it were me, in Hale's place."

"Is that something you think about? Being in his place?"

"Not anymore."

"Only by riding from the lodge will I find the place where we camped and where my things are," Silva explained simply. "I don't know that I would recognize the place coming from the other direction."

"And if you're seen at the lodge?" Carpenter pressed impatiently. "His rider will either take you or take word of you, and we won't get away again. I never saw someone get lucky twice."

"His rider will not ride," Silva pointed out, "with my bullet in his brain. I'll see to him before I ever take to the trail."

"There is no *need*," Carpenter hissed, lowering his voice and moving closer to him. He glanced at the house, where the windows were aglow, but the night was still and quiet. "*I* can find our camp without us ever going near the lodge."

"This is not about the camp," Silva said through gritted teeth. "It has come to nothing, Mr. Carpenter. My endeavor *and* that of Mr. Hale. And he will know.

He will *not* run me out of Antelope Valley. *He* is the one who will have to go, and this will be his prompting. He will sit in his fine house, waiting while his men search for me and what belongs to me, and he will sweat and fret and worry every second of every day until word reaches him that his man at the lodge was killed, and he will know that I and my property are already far beyond his reach. I don't know which weighs more in the accounting: my dreams or the life of one of his men. But it is the reckoning that we will have," he growled. "And as he *knows* that his plans have not come to fruition, as he finally knows that though I have lost, so has he, and he has no prospects left to him, he will go. He'll have no choice, because now I am convinced, properly convinced, that he is indebted to men less compassionate even than he, and he will have no recourse but to flee."

His eyes were on the stable, but he was seeing something else entirely. "And I'll return," he added absently.

"Think," Carpenter told him, though it was futile. Silva wasn't thinking. He was feeling, and it was difficult to fault him for it. Difficult but not impossible. "Even if all that *were* to come true, how could you be certain they would all go? Or that any would stay?" he added, because surely Silva's mind was on the girl, O'Doul's daughter. "Would you be able to close your eyes in a town where even one of those men was still living?"

"They are a flock," Silva replied, a hint of smugness in his voice. "When Hale goes, the rest will follow."

"It ain't that simple, though you are if you think that's your course," Carpenter snapped, feeling the stirrings of something like temper. "You don't take a risk just to cause a man suffering, even if he's done you wrong. There's no money in it." Carpenter put his finger in Silva's face. "You haven't been hit in the head. You've been hit in the pride. Use your damn wits before you get yourself killed. And for what?"

"For what?" Silva echoed, swatting his hand away. "For who I am, Mr. Carpenter. Am I not a man like anyone else? May I not pursue my business? Your friends—*your* friends, Mr. Carpenter—say no. To them, I'm not worthy. I don't know what they believe I am. Something less than them, clearly. That's a dangerous misapprehension to linger under, Mr. Carpenter, one that I will relieve them of presently."

Carpenter didn't know what to say. Silva seethed in front of him, the rage that he'd hidden so well these past few days on full display.

"Temper's always easier than sense, I guess," Carpenter said finally.

"You have my gratitude, Mr. Carpenter. You don't require it, but you have it."

"I appreciate it."

"And I appreciate your company." Silva took a step back. "But I don't require it. If my course doesn't suit you, by all means, ride elsewhere."

Carpenter sighed and smiled. He'd been about to ask if Silva would reconsider. Had anyone *ever* asked that to any good result? No. It was a waste of time.

And he wasn't getting any younger.

"I understand," he said, taking a breath. He put his hand out. "So long, then."

Silva opened his mouth, no doubt to say something very gentlemanly, but he did not. As quickly as the lightning could light up the night, his anger left him, replaced by a genuine bafflement, and it suited him better. Anything suited him better than anger, but anger didn't look good on anyone.

Silva's hand stopped short of Carpenter's.

They both looked toward the corner of the house, because that was where the hoofbeats were coming from.

"I'll be damned," Carpenter muttered.

"How?" Silva said, frowning. "*How* did he get word to them?"

It was a good question. But it didn't matter; having the answer wouldn't change anything.

CHAPTER TWENTY-EIGHT

A LINE HAD to be drawn somewhere. A man born blind didn't have a choice in the matter, but Carpenter did. Until now he had chosen not to see the truth, but there was no more time for that. In his mind he'd *tried* to find excuses for what Hale was doing, ones that would hold up. He hadn't stopped hoping, even when Joe Fisher had showed up with that knife at the hotel.

It was time to hang it up.

Karr and his family weren't miserable because their prospects were poor. The truth was that Mr. Karr was the same as Silva. All either of them could do was search for a way to find something like a victory in the midst of everything gone wrong. It seemed no one wanted to leave Antelope Valley: not Karr, not Silva, and not Hale.

But there wasn't room for all of them.

Maybe Hale could get his hands on Silva's patent and plans, and bully his way to a semblance of legitimacy, but that wouldn't suddenly make him competent to make rifles or run a factory. He would still need someone to handle the business, so why not the man who'd been planning to do it all along?

Karr was just trading one partner for another. Whatever he felt for doing wrong by Silva would have been justified as providing for his family, just as Hale was doing. It was no comfort that Karr's conscience was all swelled up and weeping with what he felt he had to do; that might assuage his guilt or do something for whatever stood between him and God, but tears and a conscience wouldn't be any use at all between Silva and a bullet.

It was all just as clear as the sound of someone riding up in front of the house, but Silva didn't so much as begin to inch toward the stable before a twig snapped in the dark trees.

"No," Joe Fisher called out, coming into the moonlight with his rifle trained. "No, Mr. Silva."

Silva's pistol was still empty of course, though no one knew that but him and Carpenter. And no matter how angry he was, Silva wouldn't have touched it, not in front of a house with Karr's two children in it, girls he knew by name.

It was a little worrying that Joe seemed to think he might.

"Joe," Carpenter said.

"Bill. Go on and throw it down," the sheriff said to Silva, who obeyed after only a moment's hesitation. The shiny pistol landed in the mud, and the hooves came clopping around the house. It was Isaiah on the horse.

"I'll be damned," he said. "You shouldn't've stopped, Bill."

"Thank you, Isaiah. I know that now."

"My horse is over the rise," Joe told him absently. "We'll be along."

Isaiah nodded and cantered off, shooting one last look back at Carpenter.

"Did you have a meal at least?" Joe asked, cradling his rifle.

"We did," Carpenter replied.

"Well, that's something, then." He indicated with his eyes that they should start moving.

"Wouldn't it be easier to drag us behind your horses?" Silva asked, though his lighthearted tone wasn't very convincing.

"It's a nice night," Joe told him. "We'll walk."

"We've walked enough," Carpenter said.

"I never took you for lazy, Bill."

"My feet hurt, Joe."

"Worse than your feet if you don't get moving. You can walk, or you can walk with a bullet in your arm." He cocked the rifle.

"That's no way to treat a friend."

"You had your chance to be my friend, Bill."

"Did he?" Carpenter asked, jerking his chin at Silva.

"I don't see that it matters."

"And if I don't want to walk?" Silva asked tiredly.

"Then I'll shoot Bill. He's your friend now. Isn't that right?"

It *was* a pleasant night. There was no howling in the trees, just the hooting of owls. Fortune had made another of her little pivots, and Carpenter was too exhausted to be bothered. And was it really fortune? No. It was greed. They might have come here, taken the horses, and gone in relative peace.

But no, they had been seduced by dinner, seduced by being tired out, and more inclined to argue than to ride. The irony hurt more than the prospect of what was coming. More than once, Carpenter had preached the evils of complacency, evidently without the slightest notion that he'd been up to his neck in it all along.

He looked back at the house and the shapes at the windows, watching them go. Factory work was respectable work for respectable men, men who didn't want any part of this foolishness.

Joe hadn't brought any sort of light, so there was only the glow of his cigarette. They walked in the dark, the feeble lights of Antelope Valley off to the left, passing by an inch at a time. That wasn't where they were going; they were going to Hale's property, taking the straight path down the mountain, then up the next one, through the trees. In the night, the way down was more hazardous than the climb would be.

Joe knew it. He stayed well back from them and chose his footing carefully. Even with his prisoners so thoroughly drained of strength, he was still outnumbered. If he took a tumble, it would not end well for him. Joe had the sense to know that, but not the sense to see beyond it.

They reached the bottom, striking out into a field of grass as high as their waists, less walking than wading.

"Stop there," Joe called out, and they did, turning back curiously.

"What's the matter?" Carpenter asked. "Need a rest already?"

"No. I was just thinking this would be as good a place as any for you to escape, Bill." Joe shrugged, glancing to the east. "You're on your last legs. If I see you go over that ridge, I know I won't have to worry about you coming back." He pointed. "And it's best if you're gone."

"That's mighty decent of you, Joe."

"On account of your service," the other man replied, making an ironic gesture.

"A moving sentiment," Silva noted dryly.

"You want to do me a favor?" Carpenter raised an eyebrow. "For old times' sake?"

"Something like that."

"Well." Carpenter adjusted the straps of his suspenders. "That's considerate. All the same, I think I'll come along."

"You think hard about this," Joe warned, as though Carpenter hadn't already.

"Does Hale pay you by the hour, Joe? Or do you just like to hear yourself talk?"

"Damn it, Bill."

He didn't reply to that; he just turned and started to walk again. After a moment, Silva did as well, his expression hidden by the dark. Carpenter knew what the younger man wanted to say: he would want Carpenter to leave him to what waited for him. Silva didn't understand, though.

His business partner, the man who was supposed to be the law, every living soul in Antelope Valley— not one of them would come through. Even his dog was gone.

Someone *had* to stand with Silva, even if Silva himself couldn't see it.

Carpenter could close his eyes and see the stifling courtroom: a still, foul day in the city—the city that didn't feel anything like normal with the war on. The room packed with men wearing the same uniform, but still enemies, except they weren't.

Because Hale had been there, and Joe, and everyone else. Carpenter hadn't been made to stand alone in front of the men who wanted him hanged, because they had *all* been there.

The only thing worse than facing it would have been facing it alone.

If Joe and Hale wanted to commit murder, they would do it in front of him.

CHAPTER TWENTY-NINE

S ILVA DIDN'T TRY to run or slip away once they
were in the trees. He knew he wouldn't get far.
They were approaching Hale's property from the
rear, and the hush over the woods meant there were
more people nearby than usual. All of Hale's men
would be there, or at least the ones he trusted to be
a part of this business. They wanted to be ready to
ride out to collect the patent right away, once they
knew where to go. A bill of sale was easy to forge,
but the patent itself—that, they weren't prepared to
fake.

Someone was at the firepit at the very back of the
garden, a long way from the house, stoking it. A few
other figures loitered nearby. They all looked up as
they heard Joe and the two prisoners coming.

Hale was the one by the fire. The other two were
Fred and O'Doul. The flames and shadows put hard
lines on their faces, as though they didn't all look old
enough already. Too old for all this in Carpenter's

opinion, but he had a feeling no one was planning to ask him for his thoughts.

The captain was shaking his head.

"I wish you hadn't have come, Bill," he said, snapping the stick in his hands and tossing it on the flames. "I figured old Joe'd let you go."

Isaiah and the others were up at the house, probably making sure Hale's family didn't catch an accidental glimpse of what was about to happen.

"That so?"

"It is." Hale nodded, quite serious. "He gave you a chance at least, I hope."

"He did. But when you stand with a man, that's what you do. You don't run away when the bad times come." Carpenter squinted at Hale on the other side of the firepit. "Your words, as I recall."

"Oh, I know," Hale said, groaning. "I only thought you had more sense about who you stood with, that's all." He got to his feet and caught O'Doul's eye. "Best tie him. He can't be trusted."

"Can't I?" Carpenter was taken aback, but he put his hands out and let O'Doul wrap the rope around his wrists. Silva was bound in the same way, though a little more roughly.

"I know we don't see eye to eye," Carpenter told Hale, looking down at the ropes. "But at the very least, you were never one for bloodshed that could be avoided."

"This can't be avoided."

"Of course it can," Carpenter snapped. "Call it all off. Become a partner. Mend what you broke. You won't be rich overnight, but factory income will keep your creditors at bay. The factory will buy the town time, maybe enough for some fool to find some gold. It can all come together without doing anyone wrong. There's no call for this. For any of it."

"That's a real sweet thought, Bill." Hale perched on the edge of the firepit again, folding his arms. "But it's too late for me to welcome Mr. Silva to my bosom. And I don't need charity from a Mexican."

"What about from me, then?"

"Bill, you aren't in a position to offer charity."

"Why not?" Carpenter shrugged. "Money's all I got left."

"Where?"

"In the bank. Where else?"

Hale seemed to come to his senses. "I don't want your money, Bill. No need for it when I have my own and the means to make more." He started to roll a cigarette.

"Waste of time," Silva said, now sounding more tired than angry. He snorted and looked over at Carpenter. "Supposing someone really did find gold. How long do you think it would be before their claim was quickly and mysteriously transferred in ownership to Mr. Hale? Or one of his men?"

That wasn't lost on Carpenter. Hale already considered Silva's property his own. If he would do that, why *would* it end there? Why would he be any less a bandit to anyone else?

Carpenter turned to look at the grounds, blanketed in flowers and plants that were pretty but served no other purpose. He looked at the pillars flanking the path up to the house, the excess of it all. It wasn't enough for Hale, and nothing would be.

Hale had told stories in his letters of savvy deals, the stories of a man with a head for business. But Hale had no head for business. The stories in the letters weren't true, and Carpenter hoped he would die without learning how Hale *had* come into possession of whatever it was he owned that didn't already belong to the debt collectors.

It was all upside down. The men hadn't stayed together after the war because they were a family; they had been pulled along, or dragged, by Hale. They had been made a part of this. Some must have known from the beginning. Others might have been blinded by their faith in a man who had been, by all accounts, a good and just leader.

"Bill, you're old enough that you don't need to be surprised when things aren't like you remember," Hale said over the crackling of the fire. "Change is what it is."

"That don't bother me," Carpenter told him truthfully. "What I'm afraid of is that one day I'll realize that you haven't changed, and neither have I. That this is what we all were all along."

"Odd thing to be afraid of," O'Doul said, leaning against one of the pillars.

Joe was walking past him, back up toward the house. He paused and handed O'Doul his cigarette. "For you—I mean, Bill."

"He's always been odd," Hale replied dismissively, turning to Silva. "Will you see sense?"

"I wouldn't expect to recognize it even if I did." Silva's mouth was smiling, but the rest of him wasn't. "Is that what you want to use to change my mind?" He was looking at the barbed whip coiled on the ground beside the firepit.

"I expect so."

"He won't tell you no matter how badly you hurt him," Carpenter warned. "He's brighter than the men you're used to, you'll find. He knows you're lying. He knows you don't plan to let either of us leave."

Momentarily, Hale looked offended, as though it surprised him that someone had the audacity not to take him at his word. Then he found himself.

"Bill." He smiled, though it was a melancholy smile. "I wasn't planning to ask him anything."

It was Carpenter's turn to stand speechless. He cocked his head.

"Why would I ask him when I can ask you?" Hale nodded to Fred, who kicked Silva behind the knee, sending him into the dirt. He hauled him to his knees and drew a knife, sawing through Silva's ragged shirt and tearing it off.

O'Doul stayed where he was, leaning but keeping his eyes on Carpenter and his hand on his pistol. Joe finished climbing the path up to the distant house and crossed the grass to go inside.

Hale leaned down and picked up the whip, shaking it at Carpenter.

"You taught me a lesson, Bill. I ain't never taken a lash, but I know it ain't the worst thing that can happen to you. The worst thing is having to watch it happen to your good friend. Like I did. Like we all did." He swept the coiled whip in a circular motion, then brought it back to point at him. "With you. And I don't want that for you, Bill. I don't like your high horse, but I still like you." He hefted the whip, and his eyes flicked to Silva. "Him, though? I don't much like him."

"What if I don't know?"

"Bill," Hale said, very quietly, "you listen to me now. We ain't negotiating. You tell me where my property is right now, before anyone has cause to use this." He shook the whip, then pointed with it. "Look, Bill. Your things are right there." They were, bundled neatly. Hale must've had someone take them from the hotel. "You tell me, and then you go. You go *west*, and you go tonight. And Mr. Silva will stay, safe and sound. Every inch of him. I will not, and my men will not, lay a finger on him. He will remain safe and healthy until my men return with my property, because *you*, Bill, will have told me the truth. Because I trust you. And when I have what is mine, and Mr. Silva has graced me with a few signatures, he will leave here with a horse, money in his pocket, and not a scratch on him. Because we are not animals."

O'Doul puffed on his cigarette, and Fred kept an iron grip on Silva's shoulder, his knuckles white.

"Even from way up there," Hale said, glancing at the whip with distaste, "on that high horse, you can still see I got no desire to use this."

That was true, for all the good that would do anyone. There was a *lot* of truth in what Hale said. Unfortunately, not in the part that mattered.

Carpenter opened his mouth, but the other man cut him off.

"Not a negotiation," he warned.

"Well, it's late," Carpenter replied, speaking up over him. "So if you don't want to negotiate, I guess you best get to whipping."

It was gratifying, the way Hale stared at him. O'Doul nearly dropped his cigarette, and even Fred looked over, frowning. There were so many things these men really were good at, but dealing with the unexpected—it seemed that was still a struggle for them. It had been their weakness when they'd come under attack on the road all those years ago, and it hadn't changed in the years since.

Hale's mouth went tight. Then he got to his feet and threw the whip to Fred.

"Gag his mouth," he said. "I don't want nobody to hear this."

Fred nodded.

"Bill," O'Doul hissed, a bit frantically.

"If you ain't got the stomach for it, look away," Carpenter told him disdainfully. "Like your boss will."

Hale was already starting up toward the house, but he didn't take the bait. He just kept climbing.

Fred watched him go uncertainly, and O'Doul glared at Carpenter, then shook his head.

"You're a fool," he said. "Same as you ever were."

"Roll me a smoke, and I'll reconsider."

"Like hell you will," O'Doul muttered, but he got out his pouch and papers. He rolled one and put it in Carpenter's mouth, striking a match.

"Fred," Carpenter said, taking a puff, "sure you don't want to try prospecting instead? We tried it. It wasn't so bad."

Fred snorted, then shook out the whip and stepped back from Silva.

"Suit yourself. Better tie his feet, then. So he don't run." Carpenter tossed him the ropes that had been binding his wrists.

Fred caught them, startled, and O'Doul didn't even realize what had happened. Carpenter struck him down with a single punch, and perhaps when he woke up, he would realize that Carpenter had held out his fists to be tied horizontally, leaving himself more than enough room to slip out. O'Doul wasn't incompetent, or at least he hadn't been during the war.

But time had made him lazy and inattentive.

Fred went for his gun, and he was faster than expected, but Silva struck from his knees, hitting him in the side with his shoulder so his shot went wild. Fred cocked the pistol, but not before Carpenter knocked him into the dirt.

Shaking his aching hand, he took Fred's knife and cut Silva free.

"You missed your calling," Silva gasped, struggling to his feet, rubbing his wrists, and shivering without his shirt. "Did pugilism never take your fancy, Mr. Carpenter?"

"I'd just as soon make furniture," Carpenter replied, tossing the knife aside. "You're lucky Hale didn't have the stomach to watch."

"I'd argue that it's been a long time since luck and I were on speaking terms."

"Is arguing the best use of your time?"

There was a shout from up at the house, and a bullet struck the firepit, throwing up a swirl of sparks and ash. Silva snatched up O'Doul's pistol and put his back to a pillar. Carpenter took cover at the opposite one.

"You want to run away again?" Silva called out, turning the revolver's cylinder to check that it was loaded.

And it was there, even more than before, burning much hotter than the fire in the pit. Silva's anger hadn't gone away, and it wouldn't. Nothing had changed. If anything, it was worse now.

Carpenter sighed. Nothing good would come of Silva's anger, but nothing could stop it, either.

At least he'd come by it honestly.

CHAPTER THIRTY

"ALREADY TRIED RUNNING," Carpenter replied, leaning out to pull over his belongings. He drew out his shotgun from its sheath and took a fistful of shot from the pouch. "And now my feet hurt."

That appeared to suit Silva. "I'm going to pay a call on Mr. Hale," he said.

"I don't know how many men he's got. Two or three at least." Carpenter broke the shotgun open and loaded both barrels.

"All the same, I think it's imperative he hear my counterproposal."

"And if he don't like it?"

Silva pulled back the pistol's hammer. "I'll have five more."

"I'm sure the first will suit him."

"That won't offend your delicate sensibilities?" Silva asked lightly.

"He's made his bed," Carpenter grumbled, snapping the shotgun shut.

A bullet from a rifle struck the column, sending stinging shards of stone flying. Carpenter cocked both hammers and stepped out, firing twice at John, who dove out of the way, landing among the flowers in the dark, then scrambling back up the hill.

Silva ran into the dark, and Carpenter advanced up the path, opening the shotgun and tipping out the smoking cartridges before putting his back to the next column up. John and his pistol would be up there somewhere and all but impossible to see. Lights were going out in the house, and there was no moonlight to help.

There was no telling where Joe was. And Hale?

Well, the best way to find out would be to go see, and Carpenter couldn't drag his feet, because Silva certainly wouldn't be dragging his. He leaned out for a peek in the dark. Something moved, and he fired, sending dirt and stone flying. Carpenter twisted and went out into the shadows on the other side of the column, hurrying to the next one.

"It's so dark," he called out, replacing the spent shot, "you'd hardly notice if a man decided to just leave and go on his way."

"I was just thinking the same thing," Joe called down from the top of the hill, and he'd opened his mouth knowing perfectly well he was telling Carpenter just where he was.

That could only have meant John was getting into place on the other side.

Carpenter fired both barrels, and there was a cry of pain from behind the brush as at least some of the shot found flesh. He sank to a crouch, reloading the shotgun as John's swearing filled the air.

Joe fired twice, making Carpenter flinch and hunch over in the meager shelter. That was the trouble with being tall and broad. He shook his sore fist, which had a tendency to ache even when he *hadn't* punched anyone, and jumped in surprise as a pistol shot put an abrupt end to John's cursing.

Carpenter saw John, younger, wearing his uniform, offering his tobacco pouch.

Silva slipped into the shadow of the other pillar, now wearing a belt lined with cartridges and thumbing one into his commandeered revolver.

"Mrs. Hale," he shouted, conjuring a powerful voice for a man who wasn't particularly large. "With a military man for a husband, I trust you've taught your children to duck? I will be calling on him presently," he roared.

With that, he fired three shots in the direction of where Carpenter suspected Joe to be, near the corner of the house, then drew back into shelter.

"If he runs, I ain't chasing him," Carpenter warned.

"He won't," Silva replied confidently, tipping the shells out of his pistol and loading it. "He'd rather die hoping he might win than live knowing he won't."

"What if he surrenders?"

"He won't."

"If he does?"

"Would he have let me live if *I* did?" Silva hissed.

"Give it up, Bill," Joe shouted down from above. "You want to live like a fool, that's your business, but don't die like one! I got the numbers and the high ground!"

"Joe," Carpenter snarled, leaning out, "you can wait your turn!" He fired twice, blasting away a window near the corner and showering the garden with wooden splinters. Silva fired several shots as well, and they both pulled back behind the columns.

"You were correct when you said it," Silva said, shaking more shells out. "I won't be able to close my eyes as long as he draws breath. It's that simple."

"I thought you were sentimental."

"Only for dogs."

"Look out," Carpenter warned, pivoting to fire the shotgun back down the path, toward the firepit, where O'Doul was back on his feet. The Irishman got a shot off, but just the one before scrambling out of the way.

Carpenter swore and dropped flat, crawling into the bushes. An uphill battle was bad enough on its own; having someone behind made it untenable. It was odd, though. He'd thought he'd hit O'Doul hard enough to keep him asleep for a good while. There was no telling if it was his notions that age had gotten to or his fist.

It didn't matter; pulling a trigger didn't take much thought, and he'd used his fists enough. This wouldn't be the first hill he'd ever helped take, and the last time he'd wormed his way through the dirt as well. Sometimes it felt as though he'd been worming his way along ever since.

Three shots rang out from Silva's pistol, answered by the crack of a rifle, and a vulgar taunt from a voice too young to belong to anyone who'd been in the war. That was more the pity; Hale even had his hired hands making themselves a part of this business.

Carpenter could hear O'Doul moving up, none too stealthily, and he rolled onto his back and took aim.

The breeze was picking up, but this rustling wasn't just the wind. O'Doul crept into view and froze, realizing his mistake. He was still, kneeling in the dark, not making a sound, pistol in hand. He let go of it, and it fell to the dark, soft soil of the garden. Still looking straight ahead, he opened his mouth, but a bullet from up above took him through the throat. He looked down in surprise, touched the fountain of blood, and fell over.

The first time Carpenter and O'Doul met, O'Doul had been complaining of another artillery unit, one that in its haste had fired on O'Doul's former company by mistake.

Throat tight, Carpenter slowly inched away on his back, keeping the shotgun at the ready. There was a shout of triumph.

"I got the one on the right," someone called out.

Someone would be along to check the body, and Silva opened fire again. Even the way he was shooting sounded angry. Where Silva had found the vigor to do all this after their days in the wilderness, Carpenter couldn't fathom. He didn't even feel up to getting off the ground.

Though he supposed he'd have to. They'd move up now, confident that there was only a lone enemy, and that confidence would not be to Silva's advantage.

"The hell you've killed me! All you done is killed Bear O'Doul, you dumb son of a bitch," Carpenter bellowed, rolling over and crawling swiftly. Giving away his position was worth it if he could sow a little chaos on the other side, and knowing they'd shot one of their own would hurt almost as much as a bullet would.

He rose to a crouch and hurried to the next bit of brush, only for several bullets to come punching through. He got down flat, wondering if he'd even know if he was shot; he'd never been so sore in his life.

There was one on the porch, up there behind the pillar with a revolver in his hand. With a rifle and eyes that were twenty years younger, or even ten, Carpenter could've gotten him. As it was, there was nothing he could do about him, though the fellow wasn't even entirely concealed. As soon as Silva noticed him, he was done for.

There was another on the balcony, and that would be Isaiah with his Henry rifle and enough patience not to fire at anything he wasn't certain he could kill. He was the real problem; Carpenter knew perfectly well he was up there, but Silva likely didn't.

Flowers waved against the wind on the far side of the garden; someone was trying to circle around Silva, who was somewhere in there, probably among the rippling tiers of blue petals, which would have looked very nice indeed if the garden weren't a battlefield.

And Joe—where was Joe?

Carpenter squinted through a gap in the leaves and took careful aim. He fired, blowing away a modest chunk of the handrail and giving Isaiah something to think about. With that, he rolled over and hurried off over the garden soil and into the trees, putting his back to the bark and taking a look at the east side of the house.

Glass shattered; some idiot had just announced which window he was watching, and Silva took the bait and fired. There was a shout of alarm from inside the house, and Carpenter didn't have a choice. He pivoted into the open and fired just as Isaiah did, making the dark figure on the balcony duck.

He didn't hear Silva yell, so Isaiah had probably missed. Carpenter broke open the shotgun to load it, squinting at the shadows in frustration.

A window on the east side opened, and Carpenter hoped to see small or female forms emerging; it would be best if Hale's family took this opportunity for what it was and got out.

But it was a man who climbed out, though there was no telling which one in the dark.

Carpenter had to move, but he had to choose his steps carefully; there was no doubt that Isaiah and his rifle were now searching for him, not Silva. He considered his options. What he *really* needed to take this hill was some artillery.

He snorted and crept into the dark.

"Hang it up, you damn fool!" William was shouting. "Bill Carpenter had you right, Silva! You don't know when you're beat!"

That was a pity; it would've been better if the boy hadn't shown up for this. He was too young to do what was smart, but that wouldn't save him from Silva. And he couldn't hold his tongue, but Silva could. Carpenter had seen enough to know that Silva hadn't carried that fancy gun entirely for show. He was better than most men would be inclined to credit him for, seeing his clothes and manner. If he got close enough, Hale's men would learn a painful lesson.

But to reach the house, he'd have to leave the protection of the flowers and cross ten paces of open ground, covered not only by Isaiah but by this fellow who'd come out of the house around the side, one of Hale's younger hired hands. He was likely the one who'd shot O'Doul, and he was eyeing the rows of flowers intently, holding something in his hand and rubbing it with his thumb.

"That's dangerous," Carpenter murmured. The man looked back in surprise, and Carpenter struck him with the butt of his shotgun, throwing him against the side of the house. He slid to the ground without a word, and Carpenter bent to pick up the unlit stick of dynamite. Well, it was one way to try to flush someone out, though Mrs. Hale might not take kindly to having her garden blown to bits.

Carpenter took the man's place at the corner of the house, but there was movement from inside the broken window. He froze, but he'd already been heard. An Army revolver appeared, firing wildly. Carpenter grabbed the wrist and jerked the man through, sending him tumbling to the ground. It was another young fellow.

Carpenter cracked him on the temple with the shotgun as he reached for his gun, and that put him to sleep without fanfare. All the same, it didn't matter how quiet he was: he was standing in the open, and Isaiah was there on the balcony, drawing a bead on him.

Silva rose from the flowers and fired from a distance of at least thirty yards. The bullet went through Isaiah's shoulder, twisting his body and sending the barrel of his rifle wide. Silva advanced, cocking the pistol and lifting it to fire a second time, this time landing his shot square in the middle of Isaiah's chest.

In the gloom, Isaiah looked more surprised than anything. He fell against the side of the house, then slumped onto the railing. His rifle slipped from his fingers and fell, clattering on the porch below.

Carpenter might have stood and stared a moment longer, his memories crowding behind his eyes, but a man at the far corner was taking aim. He snapped up the shotgun and fired, making him think twice, and Silva fired as well from the hip, all three shots as quickly as he could.

The noise of pain that came next meant that one of them had hit the man.

Carpenter dumped the empty shells out of the shotgun. Silva did the same with his pistol as he strode out of the flowers, his gaze fixed on the house.

Drops of black blood dripped from above, where Isaiah was draped over the railing. It seemed as though there wasn't enough light to tell which way was up, but somehow there was enough to see that Isaiah's eyes were still open.

The blood fell on the rifle, the same rifle that Isa-

iah had held out by the barrel when they'd crossed
the Appomattox, and Carpenter had grabbed on and
let Isaiah help haul him up onto the bank.

Silva was going to the door, and he took his place
on the right, slipping the last cartridge into his pistol
and cocking it. Without a word, Carpenter took his
place on the left.

O'Doul. John. Isaiah. And Silva had done for one
or two more by the sounds of things.

It should have been enough.

"Women and children in there," Carpenter warned
him, reaching into his shirt pocket for more shot. "You
made your point. No need to walk through this door."

"My eyes aren't as tired as yours," Silva replied,
the sweat shining on his bare chest. "I won't shoot
anything I don't mean to kill."

"You mean to kill my past?"

"Better your past than your future."

"Do I look like I worry about my future?"

"Well, I still have one," Silva said, "even if you don't."

"Then walk away," Carpenter told him frankly.
"Let him go."

"I do not think we will agree on this."

Carpenter made tables. Silva made rifles. There had
never been any danger of them agreeing on anything.
It wasn't worth arguing over, and the past couldn't be
killed in any case; it could only be buried.

Silva kicked the door open and stepped aside as a
bullet sailed past.

"Mrs. Hale," he called out, "identify yourself so
that my associate and I might know where not to
shoot!"

The silence from the house was deafening. Silva
had been right, though Carpenter hadn't doubted
him. There hadn't been even the single sound of a
horse. No one was fleeing. A part of Carpenter hoped

that Hale had at the very least sent his children out of the house on the other side, quietly. It was the same part of him that kept hoping to wake up in his bed in Richmond.

He peered cautiously around the doorframe; the house was dark, though light danced on the wall. He could just see the fire in the parlor's hearth, still crackling merrily. If they had any sense, they'd be on either side, and such that they wouldn't hit each other in the cross fire. Carpenter indicated that with his eyes.

"We'd warn you," he called out. "But we'd be wasting our breath. Dead men don't take a hint." Carpenter slung the stick of dynamite through the doorway and into the fireplace. The resulting blast would have been modest on a mountainside, but inside it was overwhelming. A fog of angry black dust and soot exploded through the house, whose tortured groaning was barely audible behind the ringing in Carpenter's ears.

He went through the doorway, firing both barrels at the men in the kitchen, who were trying to pick themselves up from the floor. Silva advanced boldly, firing repeatedly at someone in the hallway.

One of the hired hands actually stumbled out into the open, bleeding from his ears, no weapon in his hand. Carpenter just knocked him down and stepped over him, coughing.

Silva turned like lightning and fired from the hip. Carpenter looked back in surprise to see Fred in the doorway, now with a hole in his belly. He fell to his knees, then onto his face.

"You should've hit him harder," Silva said, but went to the right without waiting for a reply, vanishing into the smoke.

Carpenter stared at Fred's body a moment longer, then coughed again and lifted his shotgun, pressing forward. The room to his right shrieked, and the ceiling fell in, blowing a storm of embers into the corridor. He shielded his face and pushed through, only to see the lamplight flicker, or appear to. It was a passing shadow.

He turned and fired through the wall. There was no scream or cry, just a groan. Carpenter stepped forward and leaned into the doorway to look, seeing Joe standing there in the smoke, his gun in hand.

Carpenter brought up the shotgun and moved in. "Put it down," he warned, squinting with burning eyes and trying to breathe with a throat full of soot.

But Joe wasn't waiting for him. He might've been a moment ago, but now he was looking down at his bloody hand and the stain spreading from his belly. He looked up and focused on Carpenter, then took a step back and collapsed.

He made a noise of pain, gazing at the ceiling.

Carpenter stood over him, watching him try to breathe.

"Bill," he said thickly, peering up at him. His Navy revolver was still in his hand, slick with blood, but he made no effort to use it. Maybe he wouldn't have tried to use it to begin with.

"Yeah, Joe?"

"Is it true, what Will said? That you couldn't put down your own horse?"

Carpenter sighed. After a moment, he shook his head.

"No. It ain't true," he told him, lifting the shotgun and cocking the hammer for the remaining barrel. "I did. In the end."

CHAPTER THIRTY-ONE

HALE WAS IN the dining room, and his wife and children were with him.

A bad day could always get worse.

Seeing that no one lurked just inside the door, Silva entered the room with his pistol ready, trained on Hale, though he was just behind his wife. Carpenter was relieved to see William with empty hands; at least Hale had had enough sense to know his eldest would surely do something foolish if armed.

Carpenter listened, but there was nothing to hear but the creaking of the house, and it sounded as though the ceiling of the parlor might not be the last to fall in. The killing out back hadn't been enough to drive off Hale's help, but the dynamite had done the job. Several had run.

It was a pity he hadn't taken his family and fled with the rest of them.

"I surrender," Hale said clearly, an earnest look on his face and a gleam of sweat on his brow.

"Mighty wise of you," Carpenter told him.

"I can't understand it, Bill. You won't shoot a Yank, but you'll shoot us? We were together, Bill. We were all together at Seven Pines. Why can't we be together now? What happened to you, Bill?"

"Same thing that happened to you." He shrugged. "I got older. And a little tired," he added.

"I misjudged you."

"That makes two of us."

"Mr. Hale, I'd like you to send your family outside," Silva said politely.

"Mr. Silva, I don't expect you to feel anything but what you do," Hale told him directly. "I wouldn't try to change your mind. But don't let it come between us making an arrangement. Anyone would be upset."

"Upset," Silva echoed.

"But don't let it stand before business."

"You defy belief, Mr. Hale. Even now, with a gun on you, you still believe it's your right to issue me a directive." Something twitched in Silva's cheek. "Even if things were different, who *are* you that you believe that?"

"I'm a businessman." Hale had tried to conjure up a little false confidence, but it was bleeding out of him fast. One of his smaller daughters grabbed her mother's skirts, but he shooed her back behind him.

"You might have been once," Carpenter said dryly. "Now I'd call you a highwayman, only you aren't. You just sent your men to do the work." He turned to Silva. "It's done. He can still do some good."

Silva ignored him.

"I am extending you a courtesy," he said to Hale. "Something you never did for me. Have them step away. I would prefer they not see. Spare me," he said to Carpenter, before he could object. "I won't spend the rest of my life looking over my shoulder. It's gone on enough. It needs to be settled."

It was a testament to the look on Silva's face that Hale didn't so much as open his mouth.

"Planning to kill the boy too?" Carpenter asked, glancing at William.

Silva twitched. "I beg your pardon, Mr. Carpenter?"

"You'll have to. You think he won't avenge his pa, whether he sees you do it or not? In fact, you might as well just shoot them all." Carpenter shrugged. "Mrs. Hale too. If she's steady enough to raise six little ones, she's more than steady enough to blow you away, and we did just destroy her house."

Carpenter waited, watching Silva's hand, already regretting what he'd said.

Silva took a deep breath. "I will ask once more," he said. "And only once. Mrs. Hale, please take the children outside."

William's face was getting redder by the second, but his mother had a death grip on his hand. He was about ready to shake her off, though.

"Better do as he says," Carpenter warned.

"You can stop him, Bill," Hale said, and his nerves were showing.

"So can you," Carpenter said, hoping he wasn't lying. "Do as he tells you and get on your knees. You seen for yourself that Mr. Silva ain't soft. He'll kill, but you can still hope he won't murder. Either way, it ain't something for your boy to see."

"For God's sake, Bill!"

"I'd appreciate if you didn't use my name in that familiar way," Carpenter said, "as it seems we aren't so well acquainted as we thought."

"Enough," Silva said. "Step out from behind your wife, Hale."

William tore free and lunged. Silva shot him at the same moment Hale fired the pistol he held behind his wife's skirts. The children scattered, blood flew, and Silva fell as Carpenter took aim and pulled his trigger. Hale cried out and reeled back, crashing into the sideboard and scattering the fine silver.

William stumbled into the table, bleeding from his arm. He snatched up a knife, but Carpenter turned the shotgun on him, and he froze.

Silva gasped on the floor, his hand clamped over his chest, blood bubbling between his fingers.

Mrs. Hale was still upright, frozen in horror as her smaller children huddled in her skirts and took shelter under the table.

Eyes burning, William tore his gaze from Carpenter.

Hale had been too close to his wife; Carpenter had aimed wide, so she wouldn't take any of the shot. Only one piece had struck Hale, but it had clipped his neck, and the amount of blood didn't leave much mystery about what would happen. He was only on his knees, but he was already dead. The last of his strength went, and he crashed to the floor.

William's indecision didn't last. The knife clattered to the table, and he rushed to his father. The last gunshot of the night had come and gone, but the room was louder than seemed possible. The terrified, sobbing children and the stony, thunderous silence from Mrs. Hale.

William speaking to his father as though there were even the slightest chance of a reply.

Silva's shuddering breaths and the ringing in Carpenter's ears weren't as bad as artillery and horses; they were worse. Blood pooled on the floor and speckled Mrs. Hale's pale dress.

Carpenter knelt over Silva, placing his bandanna

over the wound. The pressure had to be painful, but Silva didn't make a sound. He simply couldn't, and Carpenter couldn't, either, though he wanted to. Suddenly he knew just how William felt; there were still words for Hale, questions for him. And for Silva.

This wasn't what he'd wanted. Carpenter knew that much. What he didn't know was why they had both seemed so surprised that this was where their violence had brought them. What had they expected?

It didn't matter.

William wasn't talking anymore; he understood what Carpenter had before he'd even pulled the trigger. Silva understood now as well, for all the good it would do him.

EPILOGUE

T HE CHILL HAD never been friendly to him, not even as a young man.

It was worse now, but Carpenter still got his legs out of bed and put his feet on the floor. And there he sat for a while, as was his custom, though it seemed each day he sat a little longer. He could bemoan the cold all he liked, but he knew that if this was what passed for winter here, he was a good deal better off than he would've been in Richmond.

In another life, he might have liked to dress and be on his way quickly, so as to avoid the noise and bustle of the camp as the day began. As it was, there wasn't much bustle to be had, though it was still more than it had been when he first arrived.

On his porch he pulled on his coat, looking out over Antelope Valley. Even if other things changed, the view wouldn't. At least, not in his lifetime. That was a comfort on mornings like this one.

Hopper hadn't made a sound as he approached.

The hound just sat in the sun, tongue out, watching him expectantly.

In the stable, Francine seemed particularly bad-tempered today, and he was tempted to saddle her up and spare himself the walk. As usual, he didn't. He made sure she had enough feed, then put on his hat and started on the path down, tossing a stick for Hopper.

There were enough people in the street that it seemed like a settlement, if not exactly a town. It went against his humor, but he found it in himself to bid a few of them good morning, at least after they did so to him. Hopper growled at the man pushing the cart laden with caged chickens, but fell silent when he noticed the man outside the charred remains of the sheriff's office.

The Reverend Brown had been speaking to several women who were clustered around him with their bonnets and baskets, but he'd stopped on noticing Carpenter. Well, God's word wasn't going to spread itself, though it would've been nice if the reverend had taken notice of Doug Hill lying in the gutter not ten feet away.

The bottle in Doug's hand was still half full. Carpenter nudged it out of reach with his boot, then kicked it under a trough. He bent to haul Doug to his feet, brushing him off a little. It wasn't as though the man didn't have a bed to sleep in; he did. Carpenter was paying for it. And it wasn't as though Carpenter didn't know perfectly well himself that didn't always matter.

Doug looked around blearily for a moment, squinting painfully. Then he cleared his throat, or tried to, and shambled off without a word, patting himself down for tobacco.

In the hotel, Carpenter took his place at the bar and gave the barman no sympathy at all. He'd made

Carpenter's breakfast as usual, only he'd made it too early and it had gotten cold, so he was making it again. It wasn't the worst problem to have. The girls were all idle, sitting on the steps, sharing a newspaper.

He took his time with his bacon and eggs, which were exceptionally good.

The walk out of town was warmer and more pleasant. He caught up with Doug, who had made it all the way to the creek, where he was now vomiting. At least he'd had the courtesy to do it to the side of the trail and not in the middle of it.

"You're half my age, Doug," Carpenter told him as he supported him. "You're supposed to be the one helping me."

Hopper gave a single bark of agreement, and Doug just winced from the pain in his head.

"Mr. Carpenter," a voice called out as they came into view of the factory.

"Morning," Carpenter replied without much warmth. There was no faulting Ramon for his cheerful bearing, but day after day, it had a way of wearing you down.

He gave Doug a push, and the foreman caught him, steering him inside to get to work.

Carpenter followed them in, taking off his hat and sneezing from the sawdust. Shaking his head and groaning, he creakily mounted the steps and dragged himself up to the office.

Silva looked up from his papers, but frowned as Esmerelda shot from behind the desk, and Hopper leapt forward to greet her, and with all the same feverish energy they had the first day they met, they chased each other around the office, as they did every morning.

"You'd think they'd get tired of that," Carpenter muttered, hanging up his coat and going to his desk.

"I wouldn't," Silva replied.

Carpenter sank into his chair with a groan, and Silva got up, grabbed his crutch, and poured coffee. He brought it over, along with a letter, which he threw down on Carpenter's blotter.

Carpenter scowled at it. "What the hell is this?"

"It has your name on it. I do not open your mail, Mr. Carpenter."

He tore it open and considered the contents.

"Well, I can't read the damn thing. It's wrote too small." Carpenter pushed it back toward Silva, who patiently leaned the crutch against the desk and picked it up.

"Do you know a Quincy Elliot of Richmond?"

"Oh, just send him whatever he wants," Carpenter said, taking a sip of coffee.

"You are certain it's him and not someone else trying to get your money?"

"Does it look as though it was written by a cross-eyed . . ." He trailed off, searching for the right words. "Deer carcass?"

Silva raised an eyebrow, then considered the letter. "That's apt," he said after a moment.

"It's him, all right. Send him fifty dollars. He needs it more than we do."

"All right."

Silva returned to his desk with the letter. The dogs were settling down; Hopper would lie down somewhere one of them would be sure to trip over him, and Esmerelda would go to sleep on Carpenter's feet.

He took another sip of coffee. "Are we out of sugar?"

"I don't know where it's gone."

"There's a safe full of gold and money, and someone's taken the sugar?" Carpenter asked, puzzled.

Silva just shrugged. "You could tell the sheriff if we had one."

In fact, they were getting along reasonably well without one, though that would change if anyone ever found any gold.

Carpenter put his cup down. "There was no more of the jam I like for my biscuit at the hotel today. For just a second, I thought I might get annoyed and say something." He shook his head. "Can you believe that?"

Silva glanced out the window. "When we were out there, I think we would have been pleased just to have the biscuit."

"And there were times when I've been a good deal hungrier than that," Carpenter said, rubbing his face. "What it does to you, things going well."

They both winced at a crash from below. For a moment they held their breath, but there were no cries of pain, and the muffled swearing from the factory floor was only the normal amount. Silva let out his breath, relieved.

"Phillip told me in passing this morning that Flora had her litter. Thirteen pups, he said."

"Thirteen," Carpenter echoed, impressed.

"I told him we might ride out and have a look this afternoon." Silva glanced at the floor. "Barring any difficulty. If you would care to."

Carpenter put his cup aside and opened his ledger, then dipped his pen. "Might as well," he said.

Ready to find
your next great read?

Let us help.

Visit prh.com/nextread

Penguin
Random
House